COLBY CONTROL

BY
DEBRA WEBB

AND

COLBY VELOCITY

BY
DEBRA WEBB

MILLS
BOON

Debra Webb was born in Scottsboro, Alabama, to parents who taught her that anything is possible if you want it badly enough. She began writing at the age of nine. Eventually, she met and married the man of her dreams, and tried some other occupations, including selling vacuum cleaners, working in a factory, a day-care center, a hospital and a department store. When her husband joined the military, they moved to Berlin and Debra became a secretary in the commanding general's office.

By 1985 they were back in the States, and finally moved to Tennessee, to a small town where everyone knows everyone else. With the support of her husband and two beautiful daughters, Debra took up writing again. In 1998, her dream of writing for Mills & Boon came true. You can write to Debra with your comments at PO Box 64, Huntland, Tennessee 37345, USA or visit her website at www.debrawebb.com to find out exciting news about her next book.

COLBY CONTROL

BY
DEBRA WEBB

This book is dedicated to my lovely niece, Tanya. Her many visits
to Las Vegas inspired me to set this story in that unique city.
Tanya is very much like my character Nora Friedman—she is
determined to succeed no matter the trials that befall her.

First published in Great Britain 2011
Harlequin Mills & Boon Limited,
Eton House, 18-24 Paradise Road, Richmond, Surrey TW9 1SR

© Debra Webb 2010

ISBN: 978 0 263 88512 5

46-0311

Harlequin Mills & Boon policy is to use papers that are natural, renewable
and recyclable products and made from wood grown in sustainable forests.
The logging and manufacturing processes conform to the legal environmental
regulations of the country of origin.

Printed and bound in Spain
by Litografia Rosés S.A., Barcelona

Chapter One

Ted Tallant waited in Victoria Colby-Camp's office as requested. This morning's briefing had been a little wild and a lot freaky. The merger talks between the agency and the Equalizers had been going on for months. Contracts and benefits and legal technicalities had been resolved. A number of orientation and training sessions had been conducted between those in charge here at the Colby Agency and the staff members of the former Equalizers.

The deal was done and all involved would have to get used to the changes. Today the four from the Equalizers shop who had opted to make the transition had been officially introduced as new agency staff members. Ben Steele, Leland Rockford, Evonne Cassidy and the infamous Nora Friedman.

Irritation tightened Ted's jaw even as her name filtered through his brain. *Nora.* The woman was a looker; he couldn't deny that. Tall and willowy, with sleek black hair and dark, dark eyes. Her presence in a room set him on edge.

She specialized in deception.

Ted rolled his eyes. Yeah. *Deception.* The whole idea rankled the hell out of him. But it was an Equalizer thing. Jim Colby, Victoria's son, had started the Equalizers five years ago, and he'd made it a point to hire the very best at going around and through the law.

Five months had passed since Victoria and her son had made the decision to move forward with the merger. Tension had been running high since. Nothing about the plan had been easy. Jim had acquiesced to Victoria's operating rules and code of conduct for the most part, but keeping the members of his former staff in line had proven a pain in the butt.

Not that a single one of his former Equalizer team was anything other than highly skilled and admittedly brilliant. But they had their way of doing things and change wasn't coming easy.

What ticked Ted off the most about Nora was the fact that she not only understood she was brilliant, but she also reveled in the idea.

Ted was just a regular guy. Born and raised in the

heartland of Idaho. He'd spent a few years working as a skip tracer back home. After earning a criminal justice degree at Boise State University, he'd quickly learned that law enforcement—at least as a cop—wasn't for him. Too much red tape, too often the victims were the victims on both sides of the law. So he'd committed to freelancing for a couple of P.I. firms.

Six years of experience had landed him an opportunity with the Colby Agency—the very best in the business of private investigations.

And Nora Friedman wasn't going to make him miserable no matter if she questioned or challenged every word he said. She had, apparently, selected him to be her verbal punching bag. Maybe she was still frustrated with the change in rules dictated by the merger. After all, following rules, period, didn't appear to be her preferred professional model.

The door behind him opened and Ted kicked Nora Friedman right out of his head. He stood and turned to greet his boss as she strode into the room. "Morning, Victoria."

"Good morning, Ted." She beamed a smile that only Victoria Colby-Camp could produce. The woman was amazing. Nothing stopped her. And the bad guys tried. Oh, did they try. January's siege was a prime example of just how unstoppable the lady had proved time and time again. One of the aspects of working at this agency that pleased Ted the most was a boss who never expected anything out of her investigators she wasn't prepared to do herself.

When she'd rounded her desk, her gaze locked with his. "I'm sorry to keep you waiting, Ted." Victoria gestured to the chair he'd vacated. "Let's sit. This may take some time."

"Yes, ma'am." Ted dropped back into his seat while Victoria settled into the big, lush leather one behind her desk. Sounded like he had a new assignment. He would be only too happy to get away from the office while the dust settled on the merger. Nora Know-It-All Friedman was making him crazy.

The boss took a moment to organize what appeared to be notes she'd made. When she turned her attention back to him, he didn't miss the worry in her eyes. "I had a very disturbing call this morning, immediately following the weekly briefing."

Ted wasn't really surprised to hear that. Since the siege back in January and the subsequent steps the agency had been forced to take, there had been a series of disturbing events. The powers that be at the Colby Agency, Victoria, Jim, Ian Michaels and Simon Ruhl, had been working overtime to sort out legal details and to smooth ruffled feathers. With the help of Victoria's husband, Lucas Camp, most of the trouble, legally speaking, was behind them at this point. But there remained a considerable ways to go in getting all phases of the numerous changes reconciled.

Thankfully the media frenzy had calmed. The trials against former district attorney Timothy Gordon and crime lord Reginald Clark were under way. Leonard Thorp, the stepfather of one of Clark's victims, was extremely ill and very near death. He'd already outlived the few months he'd been given when diagnosed with terminal cancer. His devoted wife, who kept the agency posted on his condition, claimed the oncologist treating her husband insisted the man simply didn't want to die. Most of the folks here at the Colby Agency figured he had no intention of dying until he saw that Reginald Clark was sentenced to a proper punishment for his vicious crimes.

Thorp, due to his illness, had been sentenced to house arrest for orchestrating the siege against the Colby Agency. No one, including the new Cook County D.A., wanted to see the man go to prison when he would certainly be dead before his three attorneys finished their stall tactics. An acceptable plea bargain had settled the issue. Particularly since Thorp's hired gun, Pederson, had been the one behind the two fatalities. Pederson had taken it upon himself to cross that line. For all his extreme measures, Thorp hadn't actually wanted anyone to die—except Reginald Clark.

Then the merger between the Equalizers and the Colby Agency had commenced. To Ted's way of thinking, the presence of Nora and her colleagues was almost another siege in and of itself. But Ted kept his mouth shut and hoped it would all work out… eventually.

"A call?" Ted repeated when Victoria remained seemingly lost in thought.

She gave her head a visible shake. "I'm sorry. I…" Victoria drew in a deep breath. "I was so surprised when I received the call. I'm still a little stunned."

After all Victoria had been through the past year, Ted had to wonder what could shock her as much as this call clearly had.

"I have a distant cousin—by marriage—in Los Angeles." She paused, her expression reflecting the faraway path her thoughts had taken. "I haven't heard from her in years…decades actually."

"There's a problem," said Ted, guessing. Whatever the situation, Victoria was genuinely shaken.

"Yes." She nodded, the movement hesitant, thought-ful. "She's only thirty-eight. My mother's younger sister was her stepmother. But my entire family died out years ago. Heather…" Victoria looked directly at Ted. "Her name is Heather. She never clicked with her stepmother, my aunt. In fact, it's safe to say Heather wanted nothing to do with any of our family…until now."

That was relatives for you. Win the lottery or let someone you haven't heard from in decades have a problem and suddenly you're *family* again.

"Her husband is a cosmetic surgeon and she believes he is cheating on her."

Ted wanted to feel sorry for the woman but the only person he really felt sorry for at the moment was Victoria. Her pained expression told just how deeply the situation had affected her. "Does she have reason to believe he's done this before?"

Victoria considered the question a moment. "Heather is certain this is nothing new. She says she can prove a pattern over the past several years. But this time is different." Again Victoria's gaze met his. And this time the pain had turned to worry. "Heather believes her husband wants her out of the way… *permanently.*"

"And California is a community property state," Ted observed. He got the whole picture now. A divorce would mean the husband would have to share. A sudden, accidental death would leave him everything—including any death benefits from life insurance policies.

"Her brakes went out in her car," Victoria went on. "*Her one-hundred-ten-thousand-dollar car.* The crash was minor only because of her quick thinking and sheer luck. She's terrified to leave the house now."

"Did a certified mechanic find evidence of foul play?" Brakes occasionally went out...even on the high-end vehicles. Usually a faulty part or system. It wasn't unheard-of and happened to the best of automobiles. But he didn't have to tell his boss that.

Victoria shrugged. "Her husband insisted on seeing to the repairs, so Heather can't say for an absolute certainty."

"Could be paranoia," Ted suggested simply because it was a plausible possibility. He didn't know this Heather but he did know Victoria. If she thought the situation merited looking into, there had to be more than the brake failure incident.

"She awakened to a gas leak just last week. Her husband had already left for work." Victoria sent Ted a pointed look. "I suppose it's possible their five-star gas range had some defective part, as well."

He agreed. A second *accident* in such a short time frame was a little too neat for a mere coincidence. "I see your point."

"Her husband also has a practice in Vegas," Victoria explained. "He spends one week each month there. The woman he is allegedly seeing on the side lives there. She's a manager at one of the casinos.

According to Heather, her husband is in Vegas this week. She wants to find out what he and his mistress are planning, particularly if it involves her continued well-being—or lack thereof."

"What about protection for your cousin?" Ted didn't have to point out to Victoria that being out of town when his wife got murdered during a robbery attempt at the house was a useful alibi. Ted felt confident she had already considered that scenario.

"I'm sending Leland Rockford to L.A. to keep an eye on Heather," she said, confirming his speculation, "but I'd very much like you to look into the husband's activities. Your background in finding people and information will be immensely useful."

Ted had never been to Vegas. It would be hotter than blazes this time of year, but the assignment sounded intriguing personally as well as professionally. This was his specialty. "Absolutely. I can leave immediately."

"Good. Mildred is working on travel arrangements now." Victoria cleared her throat, glanced around her desktop, avoiding eye contact. "As you know, we're working to integrate Jim's team with ours, and the best way to do that is to share assignments. Let those folks see how we do things firsthand."

Ted had known that was coming. Victoria didn't need to be worried about his cooperation. "Not a problem. I'll work in conjunction with Rocky. Keep him up to speed so that the wife knows what's going on at all times." Leland Rockford, Rocky, was a cool guy. A team player. Ted was immensely grateful that he would be working with Rocky and not that uptight, snobby…

"I'm glad you feel that way," Victoria replied, cutting into his assessment. "Jim is briefing Nora now. I'm certain the two of you will make a great team."

"Nora?" He couldn't have heard that right. "I thought you were talking about Rocky." About forty pounds of concrete settled in Ted's gut.

"I'm aware," said Victoria, broaching the subject gingerly, "that you and Nora don't see eye to eye on many things. But Nora has experience in the Vegas casino world. She knows her way around that setting. Her knowledge will be an invaluable asset."

Ted felt sick. "As long as *she* is aware that I'm lead in this investigation," he said, hoping like hell that would be the case.

"Of course," Victoria assured him. "You will be lead. No question. Nora's job is to watch and learn. She's a skilled investigator, but it's very important that Jim's staff becomes acquainted with the way we do things here at the Colby Agency. My goal is to see that each of the Equalizers who opted to come on board works with each member of the agency. An acquaintance rotation of sorts. I feel that strategy will create a deeper sense of cohesion more quickly."

He couldn't fault her approach. "I'm certain her knowledge of the casino world will be useful." The words were bitter in his mouth. Ted wanted to bite off his tongue at the reality of what his agreement meant.

He would be spending every minute of every hour for the next few days in a city he'd never visited with Nora the know-it-all, who evidently knew her way around the place. Perfect.

"I'm counting on you, Ted," Victoria said, again interrupting his troubling tirade. "This merger is of the utmost importance to me. I want every aspect of the transition to go as smoothly as possible."

What could he say? Ted loved working at the Colby Agency. He respected and admired Victoria. He couldn't possibly let her down.

"Yes, ma'am," he promised. "You can definitely count on me. I'll get the job done and show Nora the ropes."

If he didn't kill her first.

Chapter Two

"You are kidding?" This couldn't be possible. Nora shuddered at the idea of working with Tallant. No way, no how. His mere presence in a room grated on her nerves like no one else she'd ever met.

He made her…*uneasy.*

"This is the way we'll be doing things for a while," Jim Colby reminded her. "Until the transition is complete, we'll be working in pairs. Tallant will be lead. You'll watch and learn."

"Learn what?" Jim had to be out of his mind. There was no way on earth she could learn one thing from good old boy Ted Tallant. No way!

He was… He was too…*I'm in charge.*

"The Colby Agency has a certain way of doing things. There's more finesse involved. As a Colby investigator you will be playing by the rules." Jim narrowed his gaze for emphasis. "*All* the rules."

This was ludicrous! "I don't need anyone to teach

me that," she snapped. "The guidelines for conducting an investigation have been laid out over and over. Does Victoria think we're stupid?"

Nora instantly regretted the remark. The shadow that passed over Jim's face warned that his patience was thinning. He'd almost lost his mother. He was going above and beyond to ensure he pleased her. Which ultimately made life damned frustrating for Nora and her comrades, the other former Equalizers. *Former* being the operative word here.

"Do we have a problem, Nora?" Jim's face cleared instantly, his expression wholly unreadable now. "Four months ago you were given an option of coming on board with the Colby Agency or six weeks' severance pay going out the door. If you've changed your mind, now's the time to speak up."

Her bad choice of words had left a seriously bad taste. She'd stuck her foot, stiletto included, directly into her mouth this time. "No. I…" She heaved a disgusted breath. "*We* don't have a problem. I just don't like Ted, that's all."

"You don't have to like him," Jim offered. "You just have to follow his orders."

Well, that made all the difference in the world. "I can do whatever I have to do." Working for Jim had given her the credibility she'd been looking for her whole adult life. Joining the Colby Agency crew would add prestige to her position. She wasn't a fool. This was a priceless opportunity.

More than that…it offered her a way to continue helping those who needed it most. Generally when people came to a P.I. group, they were desperate because they hadn't been able to find that help with the police. Maybe here the clientele would be a little less desperate and a lot more inclined to want discretion, but according to Jim, there were still plenty who were truly desperate for the right and fair kind of help Nora liked to provide. What more could she ask for?

She wasn't letting a smart aleck like Ted Tallant screw this opportunity up for her. Working with him this one time wouldn't be the end of the world. All she had to do was look at it for what it was—a bad assignment in an otherwise good job.

"I'm good to go." She produced the expected smile. "You know I'll do whatever I have to in order to facilitate the merger."

"Good." Jim passed a file across his desk. "You'll find the details about the case there. Victoria is briefing Ted. It's imperative that the two of you get on location as quickly as possible. We have reason to believe time is not on our client's side. When we're done here, check with Mildred about the travel arrangements."

Nora couldn't wait. *Not.* She scanned the dossier on a Dr. Brent Vandiver, cosmetic surgeon. Forty-four.

Judging by the photos, he'd been enjoying a number of the procedures he got the big bucks for performing on his patients. Store-bought tan and personal-trainer physique, all nicely packaged in a couture suit. Apparently the man had a penchant for infidelity.

Clearly this was a case that didn't include desperation in a real sense. Yeah.

"This isn't the first extramarital affair," Jim went on as she scanned the pages and photos, "but the wife feels that this time Vandiver wants his freedom with no strings attached."

Nora's gaze met Jim's. "He wants her out of the way, as in dead and gone."

Jim nodded. "She suspects so. I'm sending Rocky to L.A. to check out the wife. See if we're getting the whole story."

"I could do that and let Rocky work with Ted." Why the hell hadn't Jim laid it out that way in the first place? He had to know she couldn't stand Tallant. Why not make this easier for everyone? She'd gone to high school in L.A. Still had a mother there somewhere.

Probably still hawking her body downtown after business hours.

Jim's gaze narrowed once more. "Did you miss the part in the dossier that the mistress is a manager at a Vegas casino and hotel? Or that the husband is in Vegas as we speak?"

Damn. "I gotcha." Five years ago she'd completed an assignment in Vegas for her previous employer. Nora had spent eight weeks under deep cover there. She'd made it her business to know the ins and outs of the city…the life. Of course she was the logical candidate for the assignment.

Just her luck.

"We're square, right?" Jim stared at her with an unyielding gaze that warned he didn't want to hear otherwise. "This goes down just the way it's supposed to. No personal feelings getting in the way."

"Sure." She closed the file. Lifted her chin in defiance of the protests screaming in her head. "I'm a professional. Just because I'm better than Tallant doesn't mean I can't step back and learn—" she lifted one shoulder in a shrug "—*something* from him."

"You might just learn *something,* all right," Jim tossed back, his tone pointed.

Nora frowned at what was clearly a not-so-subtle reprimand. "I'm not sure I understand."

"When you stop learning," Jim explained, "that's when you no longer have a place in this business. No exceptions."

Enough said. "I understand." She stood. "Anything else?"

Jim moved his head from side to side. "Just remember, none of this changes what I expect from you, Nora. You're damned good. Don't let me down."

Nora's smile was real this time. "Now, that's one guarantee I can make without the first reservation. I will get the job done." For an Equalizer, failure was not an option. "I wouldn't dream of letting you down."

"Keep me posted," Jim said as he turned his attention to the mountain of files on his desk.

Jim Colby was in the process of reviewing every case the Colby Agency had worked for the past five years. His team, including Nora, was doing the same. The decision had been made, and he would do whatever it took to fit in…to make this merger work.

Nora would do the same.

All she had to do was get through this one assignment.

She exited his office and headed for Mildred Ballard's desk at the other end of the corridor. Her office was actually the small waiting area outside Victoria's office. Jim had taken an office at the opposite end of the corridor from his mother.

Space had been made for everyone.

As long as Nora had her space, she could deal with anything temporarily.

As she turned into Mildred's area, she came face-to-face with Tallant.

A truckload of frustration laced with a hint of disdain instantly drowned out her determination to play nice.

Maybe she was wrong…but she highly doubted an entire city block—or two—would be enough space between her and this guy.

The idea of spending the next few days with him, forced to submit to his lead… Well, maybe they would both survive.

One thing was certain, Nora would.

She had been equalizing situations long before she'd hired on with Jim Colby.

Tallant was the one who needed to be worried.

Chapter Three

Palomino Hotel and Casino, Las Vegas
4:00 p.m.

At least it wasn't the Copacabana.

Nora kicked aside the nasty memories that accompanied the thought. Five years was a long time. She hadn't heard a peep from the sick bastard in more than four of those years. Chances were she had nothing to worry about on that old score.

Still…she was back in Vegas.

There was always the possibility.

"That's her."

Nora blinked and followed Tallant's gaze. A tall, lithe blonde floated across the gaming floor, then paused to chat with a guest.

"Camille Soto," Tallant went on. "Twenty-eight. MBA from UCLA. She—"

"Yeah, yeah," said Nora, interrupting his narrative. "I read her dossier."

Tallant shot her a look.

Yeah, yeah. He was in charge. She was supposed to listen. Even if she already knew exactly what he was going to say.

"She was hired as an assistant manager for the casino one year ago. Promptly promoted to manager just six months ago."

Soto had grown up in Brentwood, a whole different world from Nora's North Hollywood roots. And Nora had barely finished high school, much less gotten a foot in the door of a fancy university.

"Our client's husband started…" Nora considered the best way to put it "He started interacting with Ms. Soto six months ago. Ironically about the same time she was promoted."

Tallant sipped his club soda as he watched the blonde schmooze with patrons. "That's what the wife says, but we have no documented proof of the allegation."

Nora had a feeling there was more to this than she knew. Jim had gone over the file with her, but something about the client had sounded personal to him on some level. When she'd asked, he had dismissed the question by moving on to the next topic.

A little jaunt on the Internet last night hadn't

provided Nora with any sort of personal connection between the client and the Colbys, but her instincts were buzzing with the idea that there was something beneath the surface. This was more than just another case. A lot more.

Maybe her new partner had a little inside info. At this point she didn't see any reason for him not to share. "Does the Colby Agency generally take cases with such a personal connection?"

Tallant turned from his surveillance of the blonde to stare with no small amount of frustration directly at Nora. "We've gone over the strategy for this assignment." He thrust his half-empty glass at her. "Don't ignore check-in time," he reminded as she took the glass. Then he walked away.

Nora glared at the glass, then at his back. She was to check in with him every hour when they were separated. No exceptions.

This…no, *he* was going to be a major pain in the butt.

Nora caught a passing waiter and placed the tumbler on his tray, then smiled appreciatively.

Time to interject her own strategy into this game. He hadn't specifically said she couldn't.

When Tallant was fully engaged in conversation with the *other woman,* Nora headed for the bank of elevators in the glamorous lobby.

The Colby Agency had their way of doing things. But in Nora's opinion there were far more direct methods. She stepped onto the elevator and selected the twelfth floor. Leaning against the back wall of the empty car, she clutched her satin purse close to her chest. Traveling via commercial airliner these days made it difficult to carry one's tools of the trade. But she had devised methods for getting around the possibility of her checked bag being inspected. Incorporating various listening devices and breaking-and-entering tools into her jewelry, cosmetics and such worked like a charm every time.

On the twelfth floor she exited the elevator car and strolled to room 1221. Dr. Vandiver was having a drink with friends in the lobby bar downstairs. According to the waiter serving his table, the group had ordered an appetizer from the restaurant next door. He wasn't going anywhere.

Nora surveyed the door to his room. He would never know she'd been here. With a quick glance right, then left, she gingerly plucked the access card from her purse and slid it into the electronic lock. A small wireless scanner about the size of a makeup compact flashed red, then yellow and finally green. The light on the door's lock went to green. Nora opened the door, simultaneously removing the access card from the locking mechanism.

And she was in.

When the door had closed with a soft click behind her, she surveyed the suite. Same layout as the one she had two floors below but far larger and grander. Management likely ensured that Vandiver always got a VIP suite. Unlike Nora's small sitting room, this one was immense, with a generous balcony overlooking the famous Strip. The first of three telephones sat on a table next to an elegant sofa. Less than a minute was required to place the bug in the cordless handset.

A dozen steps across the plush carpet and she entered the well-appointed bedroom with its enormous bed piled with lush bedding. Vandiver's luggage stood near the walk-in closet, untouched as of yet. The luxurious bed, flanked by wide tables and proud lamps, and a distinctive highboy-style chest of drawers lined the walls not adorned with exquisite art or imposing windows. Two lush chairs, separated by another gleaming ornate table, stood in front of a floor-to-ceiling, wall-to-wall window framing a gorgeous view of the miles of bold, brash architecture and exotic lights that set Sin City apart from any other.

The second phone, on the table to the left of the bed, was the next target. Her fingers moved deftly as she installed the tiny device. The third phone was in the en suite bathroom. Yards and yards of sleek marble and state-of-the-art fixtures cloaked the room. Thick white towels hung on warming racks.

A few seconds more and her work was done.

Nora made her way back to the sitting room and paused long enough to sync her cell phone with those in the room by putting a call through directly to the room. She slid the phone back into her crowded clutch purse and headed for the door.

Tallant would be wondering where she'd gotten off to. She was supposed to be hanging out in the bar, watching Vandiver.

Her accomplishment here would do a hell of a lot more good than watching the guy sip Scotch and nibble at finger foods.

She had no intention of spending any more time than absolutely necessary on this assignment with Tallant. The sooner she was back in Chicago, the happier she would be. Her rotation with him would be over and her next assignment would be with someone else.

Anyone else would be fine by her.

The shadow of his tall frame flitted across her mind's eye. She shook off the distant yearning that accompanied the image.

No man had ever gotten to her in such an annoying manner. The vague idea that she was deeply entrenched in denial frustrated her all the more.

She didn't like him. End of story.

At the entry door she reached for the handle; the distinct hum of the electronic lock stopped her dead in her tracks.

An even more distinct click warned that someone was about to enter the room.

She flattened against the wall just in time for the door to open. It stopped mere centimeters from her nose. Nora held her breath.

"Yes, I'm aware of the consequences."

Vandiver strode across the room, his cell phone pressed against his ear in one hand, the other working his tie loose from his throat.

Nora remained stone still, her lungs bursting to draw in more air, as he wandered left toward the bedroom, still struggling with the knot in his tie and speaking firmly to the person on the other end of the line.

"That's out of the question," Vandiver snapped as he disappeared into the bedroom.

Nora dared to breathe.

She had to get out of here before he came back into the sitting room.

Tallant would kill her if she got caught.

Holding her breath once more, she reached toward the door handle.

The spray of water in the bathroom stalled her escape once more.

Vandiver was preparing to take a shower.

That could work to her benefit in a very big way. If he'd left his cell phone in the bedroom…she could add a device to it, as well.

What a break that would be.…

Tallant's voice rang in her ears. *Don't make a single move without my approval.*

Okay, so maybe he had warned her not to formulate her own strategy.

Nora blinked. She'd certainly already barged past that line in the sand.

What was one more infraction?

Especially if it served to resolve this case.

The move was a risk, no doubt.

If she was caught, she would simply have to wing it. She'd done it before. Would likely do it again.

Go for it.

She slipped off her stilettos and left them at the door. Her steps silent on the thick carpet, she moved quickly toward the bedroom. As she drew nearer, the water sounds grew louder.

Vandiver started to sing.

Not well and certainly not in tune, but providentially loudly.

Three steps into the room and she hesitated. The door to the bathroom was open.

A couple of her favorite curse words flitted through her mind.

Along with a pair of black trousers, a white shirt and a red power tie, the cell phone lay on the bed, as if he'd tossed it there…as if he had nothing at all to worry about.

Adrenaline moved through her veins. Nothing but Nora Friedman. A smile tilted her lips.

Seven feet stood between her and the phone. She glanced at the bathroom door. The glass-enclosed shower had fogged with the billowing steam.

She could do it.

Piece of cake.

Feet wide apart, she braced for the move.

Her purse vibrated. Her fingers clenched around it as if that would somehow stop the insistent tremor.

Her muscles tightened.

Tallant was checking up on her.

Another glance toward the bathroom.

Just do it.

Three long, soundless strides put her at the foot of the bed. She snatched up the phone and backed up, taking the same number of steps.

The off-key melody wafting from the bathroom assured her that Vandiver remained occupied, allowing

her to focus on removing the back from the phone.
She dug through her clutch for the tiny device required to do the job. With the purse under her arm
once more, she installed the electronic splitter in the
phone.

Oxygen didn't fill her lungs again until the back
was on the phone and she prepared to toss it onto the
bed.

It rang.

Her eyes widened and her heart practically stopped
as the phone's raging tune blasted a second time.

Heated oaths resonated from the bathroom.

Move!

Nora tossed the cell phone onto the bed just as it
erupted into musical notes again. Without a glance
in the direction of the shower, she dashed back to the
entry door and snatched up her waiting shoes.

"Yeah."

Vandiver's voice. He was out of the shower and on
the phone.

If he heard the click of the door latch disengaging…

His voice grew muffled.

He'd walked back into the bathroom.

Her knees wobbled just a little with relief.

She held her breath, wrapped her fingers around
the door handle and pushed downward.

The click of the lock disengaging echoed like an explosion in the air.

Nora slipped into the corridor, slowly let the door close and the lock reengage. With a liberating sigh, she backed up a step.

Clear. She'd accomplished her mission.

Strong fingers wrapped around her forearm.

Her gaze collided with furious gold eyes.

Tallant dragged her several strides down the corridor before leaning his head close to hers and demanding, "What the hell were you doing in Vandiver's room? No." He shook his head. "I don't even want to know."

Busted. "Looking through his briefcase." Sounded good. But from the ruthlessness of his grip and his continued march toward the stairwell exit, he wasn't buying it for a second.

When he'd pushed through the stairwell door, with her in tow, he surveyed the landing as well as the stairs going in both directions. Confident they were alone, he pointed an outraged face at hers. "I don't know what the hell you were thinking, but we had this talk, Friedman."

They had indeed.

"And I clearly remember thinking it was totally ridiculous at the time." Not the right thing to say, judging by the way his jaw clamped hard and his lips thinned into a flat line of fury.

He was totally ticked off.

The cool tile floor beneath her bare feet served as a harsh reminder that she had taken a huge risk.

He would likely report her to his superiors. Who would in turn convey the entire incident to her boss, Jim Colby.

She was dead.

The great idea didn't seem so great at the moment. Except she had accomplished her goal…assuming he gave her the chance to explain.

"I'm lead on this assignment," he said, his voice low and lethal. "You will follow my orders or you will go back to Chicago."

Funny, she'd never noticed how those thick curls of his swept across his forehead. Gave him an almost boyish look. But there was nothing boyish about his grip or his gaze. He was madder than hell.

"You were tied up with the blonde," she offered humbly, innocently. "The opportunity presented itself and I jumped at it. Isn't that what you wanted me to do?" She widened her eyes, tried her best to look sincere. "Did I misunderstand?"

"Yeah, right." He released her arm only to grab the purse dangling from her right hand.

He opened it.

There would be no explaining that away.

"You just happened to be carrying all this—" he opened the clutch as wide as possible to display the contents for her perusal "—when that lucky break occurred?"

Nora leaned to the right and tugged one shoe on, then leaned the opposite way and pulled on the other. "I like to be prepared, Tallant. Don't they teach you that at the Colby Agency?"

She doubted breaking and entering was a part of the orientation at the Colby Agency. The whole staff was a little uptight for Nora's taste.

He shoved the purse back at her. "Let's go," he ordered.

Her gaze narrowed with suspicion. "Where?"

"Time for a conference call."

The man didn't waste any time. She'd give him that.

"Look here, Tallant." She had no idea how she would do it, but she had to convince him to go with the flow on this one.

"What?" he growled.

Her purse vibrated.

Surely it was too soon for... She opened her purse, stared at the screen on her phone.

A call to Vandiver's room phone.

Nora held up a hand for Tallant to wait as she

opened her phone. Two more rings buzzed before Vandiver answered the call.

"Ten p.m. Your contact will meet you at the Parisian Hotel, under the Eiffel Tower. Bring half the cash and a photo."

Male voice. No detectable accent.

"What does this contact look like?" Vandiver wanted to know. His voice sounded strained…nervous.

"Don't worry," the unidentified man said. "The contact will recognize you."

The caller dropped off the open line.

Vandiver swore, then hung up.

Cash and a picture.

Nora closed her phone and lifted her gaze to Tallant's. "Ten o'clock tonight. He's bringing cash and a photo to a contact."

Understanding dawned in her partner's eyes.

It was going down.

And she had gotten the heads-up.

She savored his stunned expression. "That, Mr. Play-by-the-Rules, is how it's done."

Chapter Four

6:50 p.m.

Friedman was out of control.

Ted paced his room.

His so-called partner sat on the sofa, acting as if he was the one who'd done something stupid.

For the last half hour he'd contemplated calling Victoria.

But…Friedman had garnered a major lead.

Less than twenty-four hours on-site and she had a serious lead.

He'd scarcely made any headway with the alleged mistress.

But then he hadn't broken two laws, one being federal, in the process.

"You're overreacting."

When he whipped around, he fully intended to glare at her with all the frustration and impatience

twisting inside him. Didn't happen. Instead his traitorous gaze zeroed straight in on those long, toned
legs, one crossed over the other, where the hem of her
sleek black dress rested provocatively at the tops of
her thighs.

"I am not—" with effort he shifted his focus to
her face, which was every bit as distracting "—overreacting." Ted took a breath, ordered his respiration
to slow to a more reasonable rate.

He was ticked off, that was all. As if to defy his
assessment, his errant gaze wandered back to those
shapely legs. Gritting his teeth, he forced his attention
upward. He blinked when his eyes committed mutiny
once more and stalled on her breasts, encased tightly
beneath that slinky black fabric. "We have a certain
standard and protocol at the Colby Agency." He managed to look her dead in the eye at that point. "It
doesn't include breaking the law unless it's a matter
of life and death."

She crossed her arms over her chest and lifted her
chin in defiance. "Isn't it? Vandiver is planning to off
his wife, right?"

Another deep breath. *Stay calm.* He needed patience here. As much to get his head on straight as
to tolerate her attitude. "But the danger is not imminent," he countered, "and the wife is under our

protection. Those terms set the tone and pacing of our movements."

The Colby Agency had definitely broken laws in the past; just a few months ago breaking some major ones had been unavoidable. But those instances were the exception, not the rule. "As long as the goal can be accomplished the *right* way, that's the way we do it," he added.

He started pacing again, mostly to prevent staring at any part of her. Around the office she wore slacks and blouses. Not once had she worn anything that drew such attention to her...shape. Was it really necessary for her to be decked out like this now? Clearing the thoughts from his head, he said in conclusion, "I don't understand why that concept is so difficult for you to comprehend."

Standard field operating procedures, client relations, all of this had been gone over time and time again since the merger between the Colby Agency and the Equalizers began. Friedman seemed to be the only one who refused to embrace the ultimate objective.

She stood, planted her hands on her hips, accentuating the perfect curve from that narrow waist to gently sloping hips. "Fine," she announced with obvious disdain. "I got it. Are we going to put together a strategy for tonight or not? Time is wasting."

The set of those full lips told him she was only

saying what he wanted to hear. She had no intention of changing her MO, any more than she planned to acquiesce to his lead.

But she was right.

Whether this involved the wife or not, Vandiver had a clandestine rendezvous tonight, and it was his and Friedman's job to determine the nature of the meeting.

"Unless another call is intercepted," he informed her, "we'll attempt to get close enough to eavesdrop on Vandiver's conversation with the contact. We'll snap a few photos and forward those to the agency for analysis and to Rockford, in case the contact shows up at his location."

Friedman strutted across the room to the wet bar. While Ted struggled to evict from his head the way her hips swayed, she poured herself a double shot of bourbon, neat. He opened his mouth to remind her that Colby investigators didn't drink on the job, but she started talking first.

"That could work." She shrugged. "But if we want to ensure success, we intercept Vandiver. I'll act as the contact. Get the story straight from the horse's mouth while you keep an eye out for the real contact. Distract him or her if necessary."

She was unquestionably out of her mind. The flash

of fury in her eyes warned that he'd stated the thought out loud.

"You have a better plan?" she challenged, then took a long swallow of her drink.

He crossed the room to stand in front of her, took the drink from her hand and set it aside before parking his arms over his chest to match her stance. "First of all, we're here unarmed. We don't know who this contact is. If he or she is local, chances are he or she is armed. In view of the fact that we haven't been able to assess just how desperate Vandiver is, maintaining a cautionary distance is the proper step. We will prepare for that strategy."

Though they weren't armed with weapons, Ted was prepared with the usual intelligence-gathering equipment. All he needed was the place and time—those he had thanks to Friedman—and a proper vantage point for watching and listening. Today's technology provided ample means to gather the necessary information without face-to-face contact.

She glared at the drink he'd set aside and then at him. "That's an option, I suppose." She tilted her face up to his, making him all too aware of just how close they were standing. "But I like my plan better."

"That's irrelevant." He turned away, headed for the bed, where his luggage still lay unpacked, other than the black trousers and shirt he'd selected for making contact with Camille Soto. He dug through the bag and picked out the equipment they would need for tonight. Binoculars. Personal parabolic bionic ear. The lighting in the area would be sufficient so as not to require night vision.

"I should change," she called out to him.

That would definitely make life easier for him.

He strode back to the sitting room as she reached the door. "Give me five minutes and I'll go with you." No way was he letting her out of his sight. She would ditch him and do this her way. He had her number already.

She leaned against the still-closed door and studied him a moment. "I had no idea, Tallant."

Suspicion narrowed his gaze. "What's that supposed to mean?"

She lifted a shoulder and let it fall suggestively. "Considering the way you've been staring at my legs and breasts, I suppose seeing me naked would be entertaining for you."

Fury tightened his jaw. Unfortunately, the images sparked by her statement tightened other areas of his anatomy. "We stick together until this is done."

"Whatever." She pushed off the door, executed a catwalk strut to the nearest chair and plopped down in it, stretching those long legs out in front of her.

He'd asked for that one. Shifting his focus back

to business, he gathered the equipment and reached for a summer-weight black sports jacket. The super ear clipped on his belt like a cell phone. He slid the parabolic microphone into his right jacket pocket, the compact binoculars into the left.

Good to go.

He stalked right past her and all the way to the door. When he opened it and paused for her to precede him, she rolled her eyes and pushed out of the chair. He stared at the ceiling as she waltzed past him. This new turn of events was obviously a very bad cosmic joke.

Or maybe it was merely her determination to ensure he stumbled, giving her the lead.

She could forget about it.

He was in charge.

She would learn that lesson one way or another.

Her room was next door to his. She shot him a look as she inserted the key card and shoved the door inward. Something about the look in her dark eyes warned that she wasn't giving up just yet.

Reluctance miring his step, he entered enemy territory—her room.

The whir of a zipper jerked his gaze upward—just in time to see the black dress slide down the gentle curves of her body and puddle around the matching black stilettos, which she promptly kicked off.

"I'll only be a minute," she called over her shoulder.

Wearing only a lacy black bra and perfectly co-ordinated thong, she disappeared into the adjoining bedroom.

Sweat beaded on his upper lip. So she was going to play it that way, was she? His unexpected preoccupation with her feminine assets had given her a whiff of weakness in the competition.

Not going to work. He was only human and certainly not blind. Looking at what she flaunted wasn't a weakness. To the contrary, it was a natural instinct. His being male would not override his professional sense.

He had his orders. She would learn to play by the Colby rules or she would be out the door.

That would make his professional life far less stressful and annoying. Back to normal, to the way things were before the merger.

Then why did he feel as if a rock had just settled in his gut?

No. No. No. He absolutely refused to admit, even to himself, that the woman was growing on him in any capacity whatsoever.

"Ready?"

Ted blinked. The slinky black dress was gone. As

were the pointy stilettos. But the new outfit was every bit as disturbing on a purely primal level.

Black formfitting slacks with a matching black scoop-necked silk blouse that molded to her breasts as if she wore nothing at all. Could a person actually wear anything under something that tight?

"You ready or what?" she demanded when he didn't immediately react.

It took two seconds too long for his tongue to catch up with his brain. "Yes."

He opened the door, wondering where the heck she'd managed to stuff her cell phone.

As she sashayed past him and into the corridor, he got an answer to the question. The sandals she sported weren't stilettos, but the chunky heels were sky-high. Leather straps and silver chains wrapped around her ankles. Clipped to a strap on the inside of her left ankle was the black slimline cell phone.

Chances were anyone—males in particular—who caught sight of her wouldn't be looking at her feet. Not by a long shot. Ted mentally kicked himself for staring at her swaying backside.

This was going to be harder than he'd imagined.

Chapter Five

The location was perfect for privacy, slap in the middle of the Strip. Lots of patrons as well as tourists. Easy to get lost in a crowd this size.

Nora strolled along the sidewalk running parallel to the miniature river Seine re-creation. The Eiffel Tower replica, half the size of the original, provided numerous locations for a clandestine rendezvous. Talking Tallant into splitting up for better coverage had been a major pain. He didn't trust her one iota to stick to his plan.

He was smart.

He shouldn't trust her to follow a strategy she wasn't convinced was the best course of action.

She was smarter. Or at least not as attached to the rules.

"Still no sign of the target," Tallant's voice murmured in her earpiece.

"Affirmative," she responded. Tallant hadn't bothered to thank her for the device she'd installed in Vandiver's phones. At nine o'clock sharp a command had been sent to the software to block all communications directly to his cell phone and his hotel room. The move wouldn't prevent a caller from calling his room from a house phone; it would block only calls from outside. But that was no longer an issue since he'd left his room more than half an hour ago.

Nora scanned the crowd. Glitzy evening dresses, jeans and tees. Young and old. Vegas was the hot spot for those from all walks of life seeking a thrilling vacation. Or simply a wide assortment of casinos at which to gamble away their hard-earned cash.

She gave her head a little shake. *Never play a game unless you know how to hedge your bet.* That was her motto. She'd spent enough time here in the past to know how to win. Observe, analyze, then strike. Any other way that resulted in a win was pure luck.

She had never once depended upon luck.

Her gaze zeroed in on the man with the thinline briefcase making his way through the crowd clustered near the entrance to the Eiffel Tower. For a minimal fee one could take the elevator to the top for the best views in the city.

But the only view Nora cared about was of the man dressed in black trousers and a white shirt. The red power tie was like a beacon. She purposely hadn't mentioned to Tallant the clothes she'd seen arranged on Vandiver's bed. She wanted to spot him first.

Removing the earpiece and stuffing it into her pocket as she hustled in the target's direction, she understood that it would take Tallant mere seconds to spot her and realize what she was up to.

Timing was everything.

If she got to Vandiver first, Tallant would have no choice but to back off, however reluctantly, and allow her move to play out.

But if he intercepted her before she reached the target…she was done. He would have her on a plane back to Chicago first thing in the a.m., and by the p.m. she would be facing a Colby firing squad.

Nora didn't get another good breath until she was right on Vandiver's tail. So close she could smell his exclusive cologne.

She had counted on him being early.

Matching his pace, she moved up beside him and slid her arm around his. "Hello, Doctor." She smiled. His eyes widened with uncertainty. "Let's find a nice, quiet place."

She guided him toward the pool deck and small adjoining café du Parc. The spot came with a phenomenal view of the Eiffel Tower and plenty of distractions to avoid drawing attention.

A waiter cruised by and Nora ordered drinks.

"I thought you would be a—" Vandiver cleared his throat "—a man."

Nora smiled. "Don't be fooled, Dr. Vandiver. I'm very good at what I do."

As in the photo included with his dossier, Vandiver looked young for his age. Not a sign of gray in his full head of hair and not one wrinkle on his tanned face. She imagined that he kept a personal supply of Botox, along with a state-of-the-art tanning bed. No wasted time at a spa for this man.

He glanced around nervously. "I'm not sure how to begin."

Nora waited until he'd made eye contact once more. "I'm certain you explained your needs to my employer. I'll require the photo and the cash, as promised." He reached for the briefcase at his feet as she continued. "We'll review the most relevant details."

He passed the briefcase to her. "It's all there," he said. The line would have been cliché if not for the fact that this was clearly his first time being involved in a deal such as this. He was far too nervous to be anything but a novice. "The photo's there, too."

A quick peek at the photo confirmed that his wife, Heather, was the mark. Confusion lined Nora's brow as she glanced at the envelope containing the cash. Not exactly a beefy bundle.

She set the case at her feet, then scooted it forward, out of sight under the table. "You're sure the money is right?" A guy like him could surely afford the best when it came to hiring a hit man—or woman—for the job of offing his wife.

"Yes." His head moved up and down with enough momentum to make the single word quiver. "Five thousand, just as I was instructed. The rest when… the job is completed."

A ten-thou hit? She wouldn't even take the job for that price and she wasn't exactly a specialist in the field of assassination.

Whatever. "All right then."

The waiter arrived with their drinks. She smiled in dismissal and he hurried away without the usual barrage of questions about appetizers and such.

"Let's go over the details," she suggested.

He reached for his glass but apparently changed his mind and dropped his hand back into his lap. "I'm in love."

Oh, yeah. She really wanted to hear this. Before she could tell him that it wasn't necessary to divulge an account of his infidelity, he continued.

"I know it's wrong." His chest puffed, then deflated

with a long, deep breath. "But my wife is…indifferent to me. She has been for years."

Cry me a river. "There's always divorce," she said before she could recall the words.

Those bedroom blue eyes searched hers. Ironically she couldn't deny the pain she saw in his. "I know. But she refuses to discuss that option." This time he grabbed his glass and downed a hefty portion of the Scotch. She'd ordered what he appeared to prefer based on what she'd observed in the bar earlier.

In an effort to put him at ease, she sipped her wine, then asked, "The property state laws?"

He set his drink aside, those long, perfect fingers still curled around the glass. His hands looked soft and delicate. She doubted he had ever manicured a lawn or even washed his six-figure vehicle.

"I don't know why that would be an issue," he denied with a shake of his head. "She knows I'm more than willing to give her half of everything. It belongs to her as much as it does to me."

Nora was utterly confused now. But whatever. "Would you like any input on how this goes down?"

Even Botox couldn't prevent the line that formed between his eyebrows. "I'm…not sure what you mean." He downed another gulp of Scotch. "I've never done this before. Hired someone…like you, I mean."

Tell me something I don't know. "Are there activities in which your wife regularly participates? Particularly any ones that carry significant risk? Places she goes routinely? Is she prone to accidents? A reckless or careless driver?"

"Oh." The word echoed with mounting confusion. This guy really was nervous. "I think I see what you're getting at."

Nora doubted it.

Three tables behind Vandiver a new guest settled into a chair.

Tallant.

Fury radiated all the way across the expanse separating him from Nora.

She flashed him a triumphant smile and redirected her attention to Vandiver.

"Yoga and Pilates are on Mondays and Thursdays," he recited. "She takes an art class on Wednesdays." He stared at the glass he was turning with those skilled surgeon's fingers. "The spa on Friday. She says it relaxes her." He shrugged. "She's not involved with any groups or even friends. That I know of."

"That may work to our advantage," Nora offered to keep the conversation going.

"Look…" Vandiver studied Nora, his expression

pinched with uncertainty and pain, as if he were about to break down. "I suppose I'm not allowed to know your name. But I've done everything I know to do and nothing makes her happy. She just won't be satisfied. I think she wants me to suffer." He looked away. "At least that's what I thought until a few days ago."

Something was wrong here, besides the obvious that the man intended to hire someone to kill his wife. "What happened a few days ago?"

"She changed." His gaze lit on Nora's once more. "Suddenly I couldn't do anything wrong. I was perfect. She insisted we go out to dinner at a place where the friends we used to have go out. She couldn't keep her hands off me. Bragged to everyone she saw how wonderful I was and how our anniversary was approaching."

"Maybe she's decided that the marriage is worth salvaging?" Nora had never met the woman but his story didn't mesh with someone so certain that her husband intended to kill her.

He sighed. "I wish I could believe that."

"You would be willing to attempt an amicable resolution?" Now that was straight-up bizarre.

Annoyance sent his eyebrows into a collision over the bridge of his nose. "Haven't you been listening? Of course I would be! This is beyond insane! I go to sleep next to her every night terrified that I won't wake up the next morning. Do you have any idea how incredibly difficult that is?"

Though she wouldn't tell him as much, she actually did. Five years ago she'd been in exactly that position. Right here in Vegas in fact.

"I'm certain it's very difficult." Time to cut to the chase. "That's why we're here tonight."

He nodded. "I can't live with the uncertainty anymore." He squared his shoulders. "That's why I decided to take action. My friend, the only one I have left, is an attorney and he suggested I take this route."

Nora blinked. She couldn't have heard that part correctly. "You discussed *this* with your attorney?" Was the man out of his mind?

"Certainly." His expression provided clear evidence that he had no idea why she considered the step so strange. "I don't do anything without consulting my attorney first. I have too much to lose."

"Your attorney advised you to take this step." She needed to make absolutely certain they were talking about the same thing. "To hire someone like me."

"He insisted. She's left me no choice. I can't keep living this way."

Nora resisted the impulse to throw her hands up in surrender and to look for the hidden cameras. This had to be a joke. An episode of some bad reality show.

Vandiver leaned forward, glanced around, then whispered, "This is not only terrifying, but it's humiliating."

She supposed she could see that. What man wouldn't be afraid of getting caught hiring an assassin to murder his wife? Likewise, what man, an elite surgeon at that, would want the world to know that he couldn't control his own wife?

"I understand, Dr. Vandiver." She forced her expression into one of understanding. "Why don't we move on to the final stage of our strategy and put this behind us once and for all."

He straightened, glanced around again at the other patrons, as if he feared everyone around him understood exactly what he was up to. "I want her watched 24/7. As soon as you've confirmed what I believe she's up to, then we'll take the next step."

Nora nodded despite the fact that she didn't understand why he wanted to put off the inevitable. What was the point?

"My friend, the attorney, has a close contact in the D.A.'s office. We'll take your findings to him and he'll take care of the rest."

Nora's hands went up stop-sign fashion before her brain could suppress the action. "The D.A., as in the district attorney?"

"It's the only way to stop her," he argued, his voice

a harsh whisper. "If she's trying to kill me, that's conspiracy to commit murder."

Shock radiated through Nora's bones. Okay. She had to proceed with caution here. This was not at all how she'd expected this conversation to go. "You have evidence that your wife is planning to or attempting to kill you? Is that what you're saying to me?"

Huddling close again, he whispered, "There was a gas leak in our home. The repairman said the valve couldn't have come loose on its own."

The gas leak.

"Were you home?" His wife had insisted he had gone to work, that *she* was the one left at home to perish.

"I was supposed to be at home that day," he explained without another covert look around. "But one of my patients had complications. I had to spend the entire morning at the hospital."

"Anything else?" Nora recognized the disbelief in her voice; she only hoped he didn't.

"The brakes went out in our car," he shared. "The mechanic said the line had been tampered with."

"Is that the car you drive to work?" Nora dared a glance in Tallant's direction. He was not going to believe this.

"Generally," he confirmed, "but that week she needed the car and I drove the SUV."

"So," Nora continued, "any other instances you believe are relevant?"

He shook his head.

"Perhaps your wife is trying to kill herself." Sounded that way to Nora. She had the brakes tampered with in the car, the one he generally drove, and then she needed the *car*. If she had prompted the gas leak, after he'd left for work, she could certainly have taken care of it.

He shook his head again. "No. I'm telling you," he reiterated, "my wife is trying to kill me."

Chapter Six

"Rockford's running a check on all Heather Van-diver's communications the past three months," Ted informed Friedman. "He's checking with a contact on where she's been according to her vehicle's GPS. That probably won't help but it will let us know if she's been going someplace regularly that isn't in her usual routine."

Friedman had stripped off the high heels but still wore the supertight outfit. "Rocky'll find out what she's been up to." She jerked her head toward the wall separating her room from his, where they'd tucked Dr. Vandiver for now. "If she's got plans for her cheating husband, he'll get the truth out of her."

Ted wasn't sure that was a good thing. The Equal-izers were known for tactics, especially during a criti-cal situation, that fell somewhat below Colby Agency standards of interrogation. "Ms. Soto should be here in the next five minutes."

"That should be interesting." Friedman settled on one end of the elegant sofa that served as the focal point for the sitting room.

"That's your cue to go next door," Ted reminded, fully aware that she knew the strategy they had discussed. He'd learned really fast that she liked pushing the limits—his limits in particular.

"You sure you can handle her alone?" Friedman asked as she pushed to her feet once more. "She could be involved in all this beyond being the other woman. There's always the chance she's on the edge. Dangerous maybe."

The only danger Ted could see was the one right in front of him. "You keep Vandiver company. I'll take care of interrogating the lady."

Friedman arrowed him a skeptical look. "Lady?"

Ted opened the door and jerked his head toward the corridor. "I'll be watching," he reminded. "Don't do or say anything you'll regret."

Friedman strolled toward the open door but paused directly in front of him. "Who's going to watch you?" she asked in a throaty voice that made him think of hot sex.

Before he could dredge up a response, she was out the door.

What was up with this sudden fascination he had with looking at her? With inventorying her every asset? Since she'd started showing up at the office, he'd been able to ignore how she looked…for the most part.

Had to be post-traumatic stress syndrome. Spending more than twenty-four hours with her had clearly had an adverse effect.

Ted secured the door and moved to the wet bar, where he'd set up his laptop. While Friedman had persuaded Vandiver to relocate to the room next to hers, Ted's room, he had installed the necessary surveillance devices to keep watch on the allegedly worried doctor.

The sound was muted since Soto was due to arrive any moment. Ted watched as Vandiver opened the door and Friedman glided into the room. The woman's movements were as fluid as fragrant oil slipping over bare skin. Ted shook his head. How had he not noticed that before? Working too hard to avoid her, he supposed.

The woman was good. He had to give her that. Not only had she trumped him by going straight to Vandiver when he'd ordered her not to, but she had somehow persuaded him to buy into her cover one hundred percent. Now that was talent.

That whole deception thing again.

How did a man ever trust a woman like that?

Friedman had convinced Vandiver that her people were looking into his concerns regarding his wife while she would serve as his personal protection—no extra charge. Vandiver had bought the story without a second's hesitation. He appeared genuinely desperate to know the truth. Just as desperate as his wife had when she'd contacted Victoria about her husband. Rockford was, thus far, equally convinced that the wife was legitimately concerned for her own well-being.

Victoria had been brought up to speed on this latest turn of events. She, too, was puzzled and had assured Ted that she would do some follow-up of her own.

His gut instinct was sounding a distant alarm. This looked more and more like a game of bait and switch. Lure the attention in one direction while the real trouble went down in the other.

The only question was, who was playing the game?

A rap on the door drew him in that direction and away from surveillance of the activities next door. Friedman had proven she could take care of herself.

But then…that was precisely why he should be worried.

The blonde at the door wore the same tailored black suit she'd worn earlier on the gaming floor. Her eyes were wide with worry. "Where's Brent?" She cleared her throat. "Dr. Vandiver. I checked his suite. He's not there. I tried calling his cell but it went straight to voice mail. Is he all right?"

"Come in, Ms. Soto."

She checked the corridor on either side of her, then moved quickly into the room. He could understand her anxiety, but did she have reason to fear someone might be watching?

He'd soon find out.

"We talked earlier this evening," she said, turning to face Ted. "I thought you were a guest…just visiting." She made no attempt to disguise the accusation in her voice.

Whatever she knew or thought, her anxiety and concern were genuine.

"That's correct," he said, gesturing to the sofa, "in part."

She perched on the edge of the sofa. "I don't understand. Where is Brent?"

To put her at ease, Ted took a seat in the chair to her left. "He's safe."

Camille Soto blinked. "What does that mean? Was there an accident? He said he had a meeting."

"If there had been an accident," Ted offered evenly, "the police would be speaking to you now."

Her stiff posture relaxed marginally.

"Are you aware that Dr. Vandiver and his wife are in a bit of an awkward situation?" He didn't want to feed her information. He wanted her to spill what she knew or suspected.

"Yes." Her voice trembled. "We…we've been having an affair for several months now. He said his wife refused to give him a divorce."

Ted picked up a document from the table that stood between them. "Did he also tell you—" he pretended to review the page "—that he intended to be rid of her one way or another?" Ted zeroed his scrutiny in on the lady. "That he'd hired *someone*."

Her hands fidgeted in her lap. "Certainly not. He would never even think such a thing. That's something his wife would do. She's unstable."

"The two of you have met?" The wife hadn't said anything about confronting or meeting the other woman. Interesting that she would opt to leave such a significant fact out of the background material she had provided to Victoria.

The blonde nodded. "She came here…once."

"Do you recall the date?" Ted prepared to make a mental note.

"About two weeks ago." Camille Soto wrung her hands now, the enormous rock on her left ring finger an obstacle to her apprehensive movements.

A gift from the doc? he wondered.

"Was there a public confrontation?"

Another concise nod. "I was working. She made quite a scene." She released a heavy breath. "The whole thing's documented if you'd like to watch the security surveillance recording."

Bingo. Documented. That warning that his instincts had been gearing up to screeched into a full wail now. Something was way off here. "That was the first and only time the two of you have met?" Ted watched her eyes closely as she responded.

She blinked. "Yes." Then she looked away.

The lady wasn't a very good liar. "Did security take care of the incident or was it necessary to call the police?" He had a feeling he already knew the answer before he bothered to ask.

"Security escorted her off the property." Direct eye contact now.

"Did you take any legal action? An order of protection?"

She shook her head, the pain in her expression seemingly real. "I didn't want to embarrass Brent.

His reputation is very important to his practice. He could lose clients over that sort of thing."

"Was Dr. Vandiver here when this confrontation occurred?"

"No, thank goodness. He was in New York, at a medical conference."

She'd relaxed substantially since the topic turned to the wife's exploits. "Would you like something to drink?" Now that she had relaxed, he wanted to ensure she stayed that way through a few more key questions. Questions that she might not want to answer.

"No." She looked around the room. "I need to know where he is." She searched Ted's face. "You're sure he's all right?"

He inclined his head and studied her just as intently. "Do you have reason to believe he's in danger?"

Her lips pinched for a time before she answered. "I...told you his wife is unstable."

"You did." He braced for her reaction. "But you are the *other woman*. The chances of hearing a compliment about the wife are slim to none."

She shifted her position on the sofa, reached into her jacket pocket. "I should try his cell phone again. He should have called me back by now."

"You have my word, Ms. Soto." Ted stood. "Dr. Vandiver is safe." He crossed to the laptop. There was no reason not to show her that the doctor was right next door. Ted had gotten all he was likely to at this point.

One point he had gleaned was that all parties involved in this investigation were keeping secrets.

The image on the screen sent adrenaline firing through his veins.

"He's still not answering."

Ted ignored her comment.

He was at the door in three rapid strides.

The blonde called after him as he bounded into the corridor but he didn't look back.

The door to his room stood wide open.

Moving cautiously, he eased into the room, where Friedman was supposed to be babysitting Vandiver.

Deserted.

Ted had been right next door. Separated by one thin wall.

There hadn't been a sound.

No scream.

A tumbler of Scotch sat on the table in front of the sofa. Friedman's purse lay on the bar.

All was exactly as it should be except for one thing.

The overturned chair said all that Ted needed to know.

Friedman and Vandiver had not left of their own free will.

Chapter Seven

Wednesday, 1:05 a.m.

"Get her in the car."

Nora didn't relent in her struggle. She glared at the ape attempting to shove her into the backseat next to Vandiver. Let him see her determination.

"Now!" his buddy roared from across the top of the car.

The jerk crushing her arm rammed the muzzle of his weapon into her rib cage. "Get in."

Like he was going to kill her.

"Make me," she tossed back, showing no fear.

Fear equated to weakness.

Weakness would get her killed even faster.

A furtive glance at the guy waiting at the driver's side door confirmed her assumption.

They weren't going to kill her or Vandiver...yet.

Not that she was a mind reader, but she'd heard the

one who appeared to be in charge say that their orders were to bring her in undamaged. Maybe Vandiver didn't matter.

Just as the guy's attention shifted back to her, she plowed upward with the heel of her left hand, connecting with his Adam's apple.

He stumbled back, gagging and choking.

She tore free of his grip and reached for his weapon.

The very idea that they'd come here unarmed. The Colby rules were nuts!

Her head jerked back from the abrupt, cruel grip in her hair. "Drop the weapon and get in the damned car," the jerk in charge spat against her ear. The muzzle of his weapon jammed into her skull to emphasize his fierce statement.

"All you had to do was ask nicely." She unclenched her fingers and let the weapon bounce on the concrete floor of the parking garage.

The brute purposely bumped her head against the roof of the car as he shoved her into the backseat. She winced. *Bastard.*

The front doors slammed shut and the tires squealed as the car lunged like a rocket out of the parking slot. They'd backed into the spot closest to the elevator for a fast getaway.

Nora rubbed at her head. Any minute now, if not

already, Tallant would realize they were gone and he would give pursuit.

Without a weapon. Dumb. Dumb. Dumb.

She scowled at the creeps in the front seat, dressed like Wall Street execs, driving a European luxury sedan. Weapons kept hidden until there was no choice but to show excessive force.

Not like any P.I.s she'd ever encountered.

Who gave the order to ensure she was unharmed? Who were these guys?

Trouble, she mused, that was for sure.

"What's happening?" Vandiver whispered.

She turned to face him, nose to nose since he was leaning toward her. Not that he'd intended to get so close. The driver had taken the time to blindfold him before shoving him into the car. That they hadn't bothered to do the same to her spoke volumes about intent. Mostly vis-à-vis her.

Another bad sign.

"Hold on," she whispered back, frustrated as hell— mostly at herself for letting these nimrods get them in the car. Seemed it wasn't her night, after all. "Let me get my crystal ball and I'll tell you exactly what's going on."

The doctor's face had paled despite his store-bought tan and the blindfold that covered a good portion of it. The pallor had slid all the way down his throat. "What do they want?"

They'd been abducted. Couldn't be good any way you looked at it. Still, she had an assignment and she wasn't about to let Tallant get a heads-up on her. "You tell me, Doc. Maybe these are the guys your wife hired."

His sharp intake of breath told her he hadn't even thought of that. Maybe she was crazy, but if, as he'd insisted, he was truly worried about his wife's plans for him that would have been the first thought to cross his mind. She stared straight ahead, shook her head. "That's what I thought."

He clammed up like the latest fresh catch on the dinner menu.

"What do you want?" she demanded of their hosts. She had no intention of sitting back here and waiting to see what happened.

"You'll know soon enough," the driver said with a vicious glare in the rearview mirror.

So much for straight talk. She'd keep her eye on the shorter guy—the one in the front passenger seat who'd let her tag-team his weapon. He was the weaker of the two. For sure the least experienced. All she needed was one more opportunity before they got where they were going.

She glanced at Vandiver, who'd caved without so

much as a struggle. He would be on his own if he didn't have the guts to make a run for it.

Yeah, and Jim Colby would have her hide when she got back to Chicago.

Twenty minutes later they had left the Strip behind for the unending road that seemed to disappear into the dark desolation of the desert.

They had patted down both her and Vandiver. Taken his wallet and cell phone. Her purse was in the room. If she hadn't tossed the communications link Tallant had given her that could help. She had nothing. Damn it.

Wait.

Vandiver's cell phone was up front with the two goons.

A smile pushed the corners of her mouth upward. All Tallant had to do was activate the tracking software of the communications interceptor she'd added to Vandiver's cell phone and he could track their movements.

As if the driver had read her mind, he picked up the cell phone in question, removed the battery, then threw both out the window.

Dark or no, when the driver made the next right, recognition flared deep in Nora's brain.

Hope…certainty…bravado…all of them drained as surely out of her as if her throat had been sliced.

She knew this place.

Whether she gasped or stiffened, she couldn't say, but whatever she did, Vandiver was suddenly leaning toward her again. "What?"

"Shut up!" the short guy growled.

Just as well. She didn't need Vandiver freaking out on her and he probably would if she told him they were as good as dead. The guy's hands weren't even tied and he hadn't once reached up to attempt removing his blindfold. No way this guy could be planning to kill his wife. He was way too lightweight for that.

The long drive was lit only by the moon. As they rounded the final curve, the mansion came into view. The barren landscape and soaring mountains around the massive fortress were lit up like a lost piece of the Vegas Strip that had somehow ended up out here in the middle of nowhere.

Sweat dampened her skin as the towering gates opened, beckoning them into the enemy's lair.

Why couldn't this bastard be dead?

Why hadn't someone grown a backbone and put a bullet straight through his arrogant head?

Just her luck.

Karma or something equally annoying.

She'd stepped on too many toes. Used too many people when the need arose.

Now she would pay the price.

The car stopped and she reached for the door. No point waiting for the shortest of the two apes to drag her from the backseat.

The business end of a handgun flew up to her face. "One wrong move and I'll have to disobey orders," her escort warned. He'd jumped out of the front passenger seat and leveled his weapon before she'd had time to open the door and get one foot on the ground.

Evidently he'd dredged up a little courage during the doomed ride.

"Do I look stupid to you?" she demanded, resisting the urge to roll her eyes.

The driver ape had wrenched Vandiver from the car. This time the poor guy resisted.

Too little, too late.

He shouldn't bother.

Barring a flat-out miracle, they were toast.

As they climbed the front steps, memories of the last time she was here flickered like a bad movie reel in her head. Falling down those stone steps. Rolling onto her back and putting a bullet right between the eyes of one bodyguard. A shot to a kneecap of another. Then she'd scrambled to her feet and run like hell, barely making it through the gate as it closed behind the property owner as he drove away.

He'd thought she was dead by the time he cleared

the gate. Imagine his surprise when she'd put a bullet into one of the tires of his limo. She'd aimed for the driver and for him, but in the condition she'd been in, she'd missed them both.

She'd eaten the dust left in the wake of the vehicle's frantic departure.

Then she'd grown a brain and run like hell. Luckily a passing car had picked her up before the rest of his security could rally and come after her.

The door opened and a third well-dressed goon stepped back for them to enter.

"Take him downstairs," the guy closing the door announced. "He's waiting in the study for *her*."

He.

Yeah, *him*.

Vandiver called out to her in desperation as the short guy dragged him away.

So much for this case.

Tallant was going to be seriously ticked.

The driver jerk manacled her arm and hauled her farther down the long entry hall. Second door on the left. She knew the way. She hadn't needed any directions.

He shoved her through the door, then closed it behind her.

He sat in a leather wingback, a His Majesty's Reserve cigar in his hand. Only the best for the reigning emperor of Sin City.

"It's been a long time, Nora." He puffed the hand-rolled cigar, which cost more than most people earned in a week.

She walked to the closest chair and dropped into it. "Not long enough."

"You look well."

Who else would be wearing a two-thousand-dollar silk suit at two in the morning? Imported leather shoes. Not a hair out of place, though there was more gray at the temples than before.

Only Ivan Romero, the man who owned the largest piece of every casino on the Strip. Sadistic scumbag.

"I thought you'd be dead by now." She relaxed into the chair.

Those evil brown eyes flickered with scarcely contained fury even as a smile split his deceptively handsome face. "You left me quite a mess the last time you visited my fair city."

His city. Right. She presented him with an equally insincere smile. "I try."

"Why are you here?"

The smile was gone and so was his patience. Time to get down to the nitty-gritty.

"I'm here on business." She folded her arms over

her chest and stared back at him with matching
frigidity.

"Whose business?"

"Not yours." That would be his foremost concern.

"Shall I ask the question again, *querida?*"

She arched an eyebrow at the disingenuous endear-
ment. "Checking out a cheating spouse," she said,
knowing exactly what nerve that would hit.

Fury blazed in his expression just as surely as if
he'd spontaneously combusted. "Still making a living
prying into the private affairs of others, I see."

Affairs being the key word there. "Why don't we
cut to the chase, Ivan? You cheated on, abused and
almost killed your wife. I helped her leave you and
start a new life with a brand-new identity, which you
still can't crack. We've been down this road before.
I don't know where she is or what her new name
is. That was the deal. I can't divulge what I don't
know."

Even the woman's own father didn't know the final
details. The two had said their goodbyes ahead of
Nora's setting the operation into motion.

Chalk one up for her. Nora resisted the impulse to
lick her finger and hold it up in the air.

"I'm well aware that you did your job thoroughly,"
Romero admitted. "If it was possible to find her, I

would have done so by now. I've come to terms with that reality."

"Then why am I here?" This little tête-à-tête seemed like a colossal waste of time to her. Vandiver was likely hysterical. Nora had an investigation to conduct.

"I didn't arrive at this understanding overnight," Romero reminded. "It was slow in coming. When I admitted defeat, I shifted my energies to a different avenue of satisfaction."

Revenge. Yeah, she got it. That was why she was here after all these years.

"Imagine my surprise when you showed up here." He laughed softly. "You always did have perfect timing."

Yeah, yeah. Give her a gold star.

"I've waited five long years for this moment." He chuckled. "To have you here in my home. Under my dominion."

Did he really believe she would ever be completely under his control? She would die first. Almost had the last time. She'd escaped with a fractured jaw, two cracked ribs and a mild concussion to prove it.

"I'm certain you've known my whereabouts the entire time. All you had to do was call and we could've had lunch." Why was he beating around the bush? This wasn't his usual style.

"True." He nodded. "I've kept up with your activities to some degree. Not that I had a precise plan for revenge. Not really." He tamped out the cigar, left it in the crystal ashtray. "More a fantasy of sorts."

Oh, now, that was what she'd really wanted to hear, that she was this creep's fantasy on any level. "Wow, I'm flattered."

"Actually." He rested his elbows on the intricately detailed chair arms and steepled his fingers. "I've considered at length the varied and painstaking ways I might teach you a lesson about the choices you've made in life."

"What? You're my father now?" Her pulse rate had adjusted to the threat of the unknown. She was resigned to her fate to some degree, but that didn't mean she was looking forward to it.

"Brace yourself, Nora." He stood, adjusted his elegant jacket. "You're going to experience extraordinary pain. You will wish for death, but it will not come. Then perhaps you'll know how I suffered after you raped my life."

"You know, Ivan—" she pushed out of her chair, not about to give him that position of authority "—you really should get over it. You're just ticked off because someone got away before you were through with them."

"Ah, I see. You thought you were so smart back

then. Still do, it seems." He made that annoying, condescending tsking sound. "You're wrong, dear Nora. It wasn't simply a matter of her getting away."

"So she took a small portion of your vast fortune." She made a scoffing sound of her own. "I'm certain you don't even miss it. In fact, it's rather petty of you to whine over a few hundred thou."

Romero moved a step toward her. As if on cue the door opened and two of his goons moved up behind Nora.

"What she took, dear naive Nora, was by far more precious than money." He sneered at her, sheer hatred glittering in his eyes.

Her senses moved to a higher level of alert. He couldn't possibly know.

"She took my child."

Chapter Eight

2:00 a.m.

"Run that back on visual search." Ted's gut clenched as the tech did as he requested.

The hotel's security system was top-notch. The video footage of the two men entering the room where Friedman and Vandiver had been was clear and crisp. The intruders had used what looked like a hotel key card for access. But Ted was well aware the card could have been acquired elsewhere. Technology could never outrun those determined to breach or otherwise dissect it. Friedman had used a similar technology earlier tonight.

Less than three minutes after entering the room the two intruders had escorted Friedman and Vandiver to the elevator. Ted was surprised by that. The likelihood that other guests would be on the elevators was great, whereas the stairwells were more often deserted.

The bastards were either damned cocky or felt confident that they had nothing to worry about. That was the most disturbing part.

Ted glanced at the security surveillance booth's open door, where Camille Soto stood just beyond hearing range, deep in conversation on her cell phone. She looked tired and frustrated. Maybe a little scared.

But she hadn't once brought up the subject of reporting the incident to the police. Instead, she'd insisted on seeing what she could learn off the record.

"You want to watch it again?"

Ted pulled his attention back to the screen where the tech had played the same seven minutes over and over. "Once more."

As the four on the surveillance video reached the basement-level parking garage, Friedman had given the guy attempting to force her into the car one hell of a hard time. A smile nudged at Ted's lips. If it hadn't been two against one—two armed men at that—she likely would have gotten away clean.

While Vandiver hadn't resisted in the least. Ted rolled the idea around in his head even as he watched those final moments a fifth time. Maybe the guy was afraid of injuring his hands. Or just afraid.

Soto stepped into the small, gadget-packed room. "The license plate gave us nothing."

The plate had been captured on the video. For the good it had done, apparently. "Thanks for nudging your Las Vegas PD contacts at this hour."

"What do we do now?" Her worried gaze locked on the final frame of the surveillance video and she pressed the back of her hand to her mouth as if to hold back a desperate sound.

Ted gave the tech a pat on the shoulder. "Thanks, man." He gestured to the door. "Why don't we go to your office," he said to Soto.

She nodded, then led the way. They'd been there once already this morning. Ted had more questions. He wanted her in that office, surrounded by all the photos—particularly the two of her and Vandiver to-gether—where her reactions would be less guarded.

Her well-appointed office had a perfect view of the main gaming floor. The glass wall behind her desk was a two-way mirror. She could see those below but all they saw, if and when they peered upward, was reflective glass.

Framed photos and certificates lined another wall. Comfort and luxury were the themes surrounding Ms. Soto's position of authority. A position that not only encouraged but also required that she know her clients as well as her competition. Vegas was a large city, no question, but the world of casino management was small. The players knew each other. Made it a point to become familiar with the each other's associates.

The moment the surveillance video had been played the first time, Ted had noted the recognition in Camille Soto's eyes. She did know the men who'd taken Friedman and Vandiver. The question was, why wasn't she cooperating with Ted? If she wanted her lover back safely, why delay his reaction to the overt move?

Unless there was an agenda she preferred not to share.

He settled into the chair in front of her desk. "I've spoken at length with my colleagues in Chicago," he began. "At this point I believe it would be in Dr. Vandiver's best interest to contact the authorities."

Her eyes widened with fear but she quickly schooled her expression. "But we haven't received a ransom demand. If this is another escapade of his wife's, contacting the police may only end up news fodder."

Dig that hole a little deeper, lady. "But," Ted challenged, "you said that Ms. Vandiver's confrontation with you was the only incident of that nature. That being the case, I'm having trouble making the leap to this abduction being her doing."

An unnecessary survey of her office delayed Soto's response. Scrambling for a logical one, he would wager. The idea that she had information that could help Ted propelled his frustration and anger to the next level. But he wasn't ready to play bad cop just yet. If he gave her enough rope, she would hang herself.

"It was the only time she confronted me," Soto insisted. "But there have been a couple of times when she hired some bully to threaten him…Brent. No physical altercations, just threats."

"These threats were carried out face-to-face or by phone?" Pushing her to be specific was the quickest way to detect deception.

"Face-to-face…I believe." She checked her cell phone to avoid continued eye contact.

Hard to conceive that she wouldn't know with certainty, considering her relationship with Vandiver. "These confrontations occurred in public settings? At his practice here in Vegas?"

Her gaze met his briefly. "I think so."

"I ask since there might very well be surveillance footage of the incidents—if they occurred in a public place. Perhaps one of the two men who took Dr. Vandiver and my associate was responsible for one or both of the previous confrontations."

"I'm just not sure," she lied. "Brent didn't give me all the details." She moistened her lips and looked Ted straight in the eye. "He wanted to spare me the ugliness his wife initiated."

How thoughtful and convenient. Ted pulled his cell phone from his pocket. "We shouldn't put off contacting the authorities. The first forty-eight hours in an investigation of this nature are crucial."

The pause as he slid open his phone was accompanied by complete silence. His thumb poised over the first digit even as the air in the room thickened with the weight of tension.

"One of the men," she said, drawing his attention away from the keypad and across her desk, "looked kind of familiar...maybe."

Ted closed his phone and probed her gaze with his own. The telltale signs of being cornered were written clearly on her face. "You recognized him?" He prepared to reopen his phone. "All the more reason to make the call."

Outright fear seized her face. "No." She shook her head. "You don't understand." She hesitated, blinked. "If the person behind this is the man I suspect, calling the police will only make things worse."

Ted felt his eyes narrow with mounting doubt. "I'll need his name."

She moistened her lips. "Ivan." A big, shaky breath. "Ivan Romero."

Ted waited for her to continue.

"He owns the Copacabana." Her lips pinched with

that mounting uncertainty. "Among others. He's a very powerful man."

"You're certain these men work for him?" Ted understood there was a lot more she wasn't telling just yet.

Soto nodded. "Ivan called me a few minutes ago."

So that was the call she'd gotten while he was reviewing the surveillance video. "And?" Ted prompted, his patience history.

"He said he had an old score to settle with your associate. That if I didn't call the police, Brent…Dr. Vandiver…would be released unharmed." Another of those quaking breaths. "This has nothing to do with him."

Ted opened his phone and entered Simon Ruhl's number.

"You can't call the police," Soto urged, leaning forward. "Ivan is not a man you want to cross."

Simon answered on the second ring. "I need anything you can find on Ivan Romero," Ted explained. "We have a situation."

Soto's eyes widened as he related recent circumstances to his colleague at the Colby Agency. When Ted ended the conversation and closed his phone, she shook her head slowly from side to side.

"What've you done?" Her hands shook as she

clasped them atop her desk. "You don't understand...."

"I understand perfectly. Simon Ruhl is my colleague at the Colby Agency. Not informing them of this situation was out of the question."

The relief that claimed her expression was palpable. "He won't contact the police?"

"Not as long as I assure him I have the situation under control." There was no time to placate her anxiety. All he needed was her cooperation. "Tell me about Romero." Simon would get back to him with all he could find, but Ted needed whatever the lady had. "Where can I find him?" She'd mentioned the Copacabana. A classy, well-established casino hotel. But before Ted went barging into the place and encountered what would likely be top-notch security, he needed inside information. A way to get to the man outside that setting.

"He doesn't spend much time at the casinos anymore. He prefers his private residence."

"Give me the details of his private residence," Ted prompted.

"His personal security is primo," she said, not exactly answering his question. "There's a lot I don't know about Ivan. A lot no one knows. But what I am certain of is that he isn't someone you want to go up against. Certainly not alone. I've heard rumors."

"Rumors?" The phone in his hand vibrated. A report from Simon had downloaded.

"The kind," she warned, "that lets me know that I don't want trouble with him."

"What details do you know about the security at his residence?" Ted wasn't beating around the bush anymore. He needed facts. Now.

"Well-trained. They're pros." She shrugged. "Ivan is a very wealthy man. He's not taking any chances. It's a ten-acre compound. He uses cameras and dogs."

Not good news. "You've been there?"

She nodded. "To a Christmas party once. A birthday celebration earlier this year."

Sounded like she knew the guy better than she wanted to let on. "Whose birthday?"

"His."

Oh, yes. There was the guilt. It clouded her expression, as if she'd been caught with the smoking gun in her hand. "Then you must know him quite well."

"As well as anyone in the business, I suppose," she confessed.

"Good." Ted locked his gaze with hers. "Then you won't mind getting me inside."

Soto held up both hands. "That would be impossible."

"No problem." Ted prepared to open his cell phone.

"I'm sure I can find a cop or a fed who isn't afraid of him."

"I'd like to keep my job," she offered, her voice too quiet. "But I want to stay alive a whole lot more."

2:45 a.m.

SIMON'S RETURN CALL SURPRISED Ted. Not simply because he'd already sent a thorough report on Romero, but because the call was actually a teleconference that included Jim Colby. But then, Friedman was a member of Colby's team. Ted shouldn't have been surprised.

"Ivan Romero is bad news all the way around," Colby informed Ted. "He's on several federal watch lists. Drugs. Gunrunning. Human trafficking. Just to name a few. But no one has ever been able to finger him for any of the suspected crime activity."

A volatile mixture of fury and fear trickled into Ted's veins. "Have you been able to establish a connection between him and Vandiver?" If not, there was every reason to go with Soto's claims. That Friedman had been the target. Vandiver just happened to be in the way. Or perhaps he was collateral to ensure Soto's cooperation, as she'd alleged.

"None. Camille Soto," Simon explained, "worked for Romero prior to taking the position at the

Palomino. She knows him better than she's admitted. As far as we can determine, Vandiver doesn't even know the man."

Ted had wandered into the corridor outside Soto's office to take this call. He leaned his head to the right and verified that she remained behind her desk, shuffling through papers. Her landline as well as her cell lay in plain sight on the desktop.

"This isn't about Vandiver or Soto," said Jim, speaking up next. "This is about Nora."

That fury simmering in Ted's blood ignited into a full blaze. "I presume this has something to do with her previous time in Vegas." Victoria had explained that Friedman had been assigned to this case because of her experience in the Vegas casino world.

"Five years ago Nora worked for Romero," replied Jim.

A frown nagged at Ted's brow. "In what capacity?" he asked Jim.

"It was an undercover operation bankrolled by Romero's former father-in-law."

Ted absorbed the information, worry rising inside him, as Jim Colby laid out the details of Friedman's interaction with Romero five years prior. His wife of three years had finally confirmed what her father had suspected all along: Ivan Romero was a monster. The wife had learned she was pregnant and decided that to protect the child she had to get away from Romero before he learned her secret. The wife's father had looked until he found the best, Nora Friedman, to make it happen.

Friedman had taken it upon herself, after achieving a deep cover status with Romero, to ensure the wife got a little something for her pain and misery. One point five million dollars disappeared with the wife.

Friedman had barely escaped from Romero with her life. A mock federal investigation had kept him from retaliating immediately after her escape. But like all the other times before, he had been cleared of suspicion.

"I can only assume," Jim went on, "that Nora believed Romero had decided to let it go. I was aware she'd worked an investigation in Vegas, but since Romero hadn't attempted to track her down in the past five years, there was no call for concern. This was supposed to be a low-profile assignment."

Intelligence gathering. Ted got that. All involved agreed that going to the authorities was a risk at this point since there was reason to believe loyalty to Romero went deep in the local law enforcement scene. But to go in alone, Ted would need certain assets. "Do you have a contact for me?"

"Yes," Simon confirmed. "He's waiting for you in

the lobby bar now. I've sent a photo and background info to your phone. He'll supply you with whatever you need. He carries an entire store in his trunk."

"Use extreme caution, Tallant," Jim advised. "The man who hired Nora to help his daughter escape from Romero died within days of her disappearance."

"Romero killed him?" Didn't bode well for Friedman.

"The death was ruled an accident," Jim clarified. "The man was seventy-five and wheelchair bound. A fire in the middle of the night burned his home to the ground with him inside. A power failure was blamed for the home security system's malfunction. But Nora believes Romero was behind it. Maybe attempted to learn his wife's location."

"We're sending Trinity Barrett as backup," Simon put in. "He'll arrive via the agency's private jet at four-thirty. You must realize that the strategy you outlined is too dangerous to attempt alone, Ted. The chances of success are minimal."

Ted braced for battle. "I can't wait that long. From what we know about Romero, it may be too late already. Waiting is out of the question."

He had advised Simon of his recovery strategy in their first phone conversation an hour ago. Soto had reluctantly agreed to take Ted there under the pretense of picking up Vandiver. But she had refused to go to the police. If Ted did so, she would deny all that she had told him. She'd already had the surveillance video destroyed.

There was no other option.

An extended pause on the other end had Ted's teeth grinding. He had to get moving. There was no time for debate.

"The decision is yours," Simon said, capitulating with audible reluctance. "We'll do all we can from here. I have a call in to a friend of mine assigned to the Bureau field office in the area."

Ted ended the call. His gaze locked with Soto's. She was watching him, the same defeat on her face that had lodged itself deep in his gut.

If Friedman was still alive, it would be an outright miracle.

Chapter Nine

2:50 a.m.

The walls were concrete. Cold and gray.

Nora turned around slowly, sizing up her predicament.

The cell was about nine by nine with no chair or bed or anything. Just a concrete box. The door had a small window built into it. There were metal bars over the small opening. Not even a knob or handle on the inside of the door.

Romero was a freak.

Nora had known about the tunnels. The wife had told her.

Wife. Brenda. Her name was Brenda. Or it used to be when she was married to the psycho upstairs. Romero had so many enemies and so many black-market activities going on that when he'd purchased the mansion on his stately ten acres, his first order of business had been to have an escape route excavated beneath the house.

To guests of his home, it appeared to provide passage from the private basement game room to the pool and the expansive entertaining area behind the house. But there was a secret passage that led into a trio of tunnels, one of which led to a hidden helipad nearly a mile from the property. Along with the helicopter was an all-terrain vehicle. And weapons.

All the amenities a wealthy, overachieving criminal would want.

Nora hadn't seen Vandiver since he'd been dragged away from her. He could be down here somewhere, but if he was, he was damned quiet. The slightest sound echoed in the endless sea of concrete.

Could be dead, for all she knew. Victoria Colby-Camp would be less than happy, but Nora wouldn't have to worry about that. She would be dead, too. Whatever Ivan said, he would kill her. He would never let her leave here alive. Tallant would have to deal with the fallout.

She set her hands on her hips and walked around the perimeter of her cell.

Wasn't the worst place she'd been held. The idea that it might be the last ticked her off.

Five years! Romero couldn't have come after her way before now?

No. She shook her head. He'd exhausted every avenue possible to find his wife on his own; then he'd sat back and waited for Nora to grow complacent. And then show up in his city, disarmed.

She hadn't given him a thought in years.

Big mistake.

He'd been lying in wait…like the snake he was. Protecting his territory and waiting for her to wander back into his dominion.

She'd completely dropped her guard where he was concerned.

Seriously big mistake.

Tallant didn't like her at all. She wondered how much trouble he would go to in a rescue attempt. Knowing him and his Colby rules, he'd just call the cops and hasten her demise.

Romero owned the law in Vegas.

No one was going to bust in here and demand to know what he'd been up to. No way.

She executed an about-face and traced her steps in the opposite direction. Then there was the Vandiver case. The wife had insisted her husband was trying to kill her, but now Nora wasn't so sure.

Vandiver appeared convinced that his wife, their client, was trying to kill him.

Tallant could deal with that. Besides, Rocky was in Los Angeles with the missus. He would get the truth out of her. The Equalizers and the Colbys were vastly different when it came to getting to the bottom line.

If Rocky were here in Vegas, he would find a way to reach Nora before it was too late. No one or nothing would stand in his way. Not even the law.

Just her luck to be stuck with Tallant.

Her feet stalled. He'd given her credit for her strategy to get to Vandiver. Maybe he wasn't that bad. And she'd caught him looking at her in a way that had surprised her. It was possible, she supposed, that he liked her more than he wanted her to know.

But did he respect her investigation skills?

Truth was she'd been denying a physical attraction to him since day one. No use denying it now. It wasn't like she would live to regret allowing the thought.

Maybe that was why she'd been so determined to make sure he respected her ability as an investigator.

She looked around the box again. Okay, there was a slight chance she'd overrated her skills.

After all, she was in here and Tallant was out there.

Could be he had a point about strategy.

"Nah." This was just bad timing. Bad timing and ancient history.

Nora crossed to the door and tried to see past the

bars of the small eye-level opening. Sounded deserted out there. Dimly lit.

Ancient history or not. Bad timing or not.

She was in deep trouble here.

Wait.

She'd surveyed the cell three or four times and hadn't noticed any holes for hidden cameras.

But they would be here. That was one absolute certainty. Romero would be watching every move she made. He would take no chances whatsoever.

"If the mountain won't come to Mohammed," she mumbled as she reached for the hem of her blouse and then pulled it over her head and tossed it to the floor. "We'll just bring Mohammed to the mountain." She reached for the waist of her slacks next.

"WHAT IS SHE DOING?" ROMERO leaned forward and stared at the screen. Nora had stripped down to her bra and panties. "You searched her?" He stared up at the bodyguard towering next to his desk.

"Thoroughly, sir," his most trusted employee, Quinton Lott, insisted. "She has nothing on her except the clothes."

That now lay on the floor.

Uneasiness slid through Romero. He knew this woman too well. Far too well. She could not be trusted on any level. Not for a single second.

"Check her again," Romero ordered.

"Yes, sir."

The door closed behind his head of security.

Romero studied the woman on the monitor. Slender, toned. He had wanted her so badly five years ago. Still wanted her now. Nora had not changed. If anything, her body was even more appealing.

But he would not have her now any more than he had five years ago. For wholly different reasons this time, of course. This time it was because his relentless desire to watch her suffer far outweighed his lingering wish to ravage her sexually.

This time she would not escape his wrath.

Even as he determined not to be distracted by her antics, she bent at the waist and removed one shoe, then the other. That she held on to the last shoe and inspected the sole sent an alarm shrieking in his brain.

On the monitor, the cell door opened and Lott entered.

Now Romero would see what she was up to.

GREAT.

Nora sized up Lott, Romero's head of security, as he entered her cell.

Big. Mean as hell. Nearly a decade of service to his master.

Would've been nice if the less experienced dope from the car ride here had made an appearance.

"What're you doing?" Lott demanded as he strode toward her, leaving the door open behind him.

Nora shrugged. "It's hot in here. So I took my clothes off."

"Give me the shoe."

She tightened her grip on her right shoe. "It's only a shoe." Too bad it wasn't one of her stilettos. She'd aim for an eye...or maybe a jugular.

He held out his hand as he came closer. "Give it to me."

She had one shot.

She had to be fast.

Faster than a big, muscled-up guy wearing a tailored suit.

"Fine." She reached the shoe toward him.

He wrapped a cruel, indignant grip around it.

She released the shoe.

He made the mistake of inspecting it.

She darted around him. Out the door.

The scrub of his shoes on the concrete echoed right behind her.

She ran harder, had no idea where she was going. She'd only been down here once and that was five years ago.

Faster.

If he caught up with her…

He roared curses behind her…so close she could practically feel his hot breath on her bare back.

Run!

Faster!

She couldn't slow for the fork up ahead.

Right.

She propelled herself to the right. Pushing with all her might.

Go!

The tunnel twisted right again, almost causing her to lose purchase on the cool, damp floor.

Lott was close.

She leaned forward, barely escaping his grappling fingers.

Steps.

Damn!

She lunged up the broad steps. Her chest tightened. Just breathe.

He stumbled. His fingers raked her back.

She propelled herself forward. The palms of her hands hit the step in front of her. She kept scrambling…moving…up. Up! Faster!

"You're dead when I catch you!"

She burst up onto the final step.

Outside. Pool.

She zigzagged around the pool.

Voices shouted in the distance.

Security.

Dogs barked.

Oh, hell. Don't stop! She had to escape the land-scape lighting.

A ping echoed around her.

Gunshot.

Wall. Straight ahead. ·

Oh, God.

Something latched onto her ankle. Teeth buried into her skin. She felt the pain before she heard the growling.

Dog.

She glanced down. Tripped, landed face-first on the ground.

Her jaw clamped down hard to prevent screaming as the feral teeth ground into her flesh.

"Down!"

The dog abruptly released her.

Only then did she become aware of the salty taste of tears on her lips or the thundering beneath her sternum and the jerky spasms of her chest.

Cruel fingers manacled her arms and jerked her upward. Her ankle was on fire.

The men on either side of her twisted her around to face the head honcho.

Lott's palm connected with her jaw. Her head twisted to the right from the force.

"Take her inside," Lott ordered, his face contorted with fury.

The men hauled her forward. She resisted, earning a spree of harsh curses.

By the time they reached the entrance to the kitchen, the adrenaline had receded enough for her brain to fully inventory her injuries.

Chewed-up ankle. The soles of her feet were skinned and raw. Her arms, where the jerks continued to grip her, were bruised. And her face stung from the slap. Too low on the jaw to give her a black eye, but her lip was definitely swelling.

She'd tried. She couldn't just sit back and wait for Ivan to have his way.

"Put her there."

Speak of the devil. She smiled at Romero as he directed that she be placed into a kitchen chair.

He folded his arms over his chest and pointed a stare at her that would have ignited a rain-dampened forest. "You're not escaping me this time," he guaranteed. He nodded to her chest, where her lacy bra showed off her cleavage. "This time I will watch you pay."

"You sure know how to sweet-talk a girl."

Lott reared back his hand to slap her again.

Romero shook his head. "No. When the time comes, I'll have the honor."

"Mr. Romero."

Romero shifted his attention to yet another well-dressed creep who entered the room. This one had shoulder-length blond hair. He whispered something in his boss's ear. Nora watched Romero's face for some indication of the news his associate passed along.

"I'll be right there."

Evidently nothing troubling, since his expression remained calm and unmoved.

To Lott, Romero instructed, "She's tested my patience. If she makes a sound or a move, go ahead and break her neck."

He glared at her once more before exiting the room.

Bastard.

"You heard him," Lott reiterated. "Don't feel as if you're putting me out if you choose to disobey." He rubbed his palms together. "I would love to twist that slender neck of yours until it snaps like a twig."

She ignored the big jerk when she wanted to tell him where to go. Maybe what to do when he got there. But Romero had said she wasn't to make a sound. She'd already pushed his patience to the limit. Having

Lott perform a move even a good orthopedic surgeon couldn't undo wasn't exactly her plan A.

A woman's voice filtering in from somewhere in the house silenced Nora's thoughts.

Romero had company?

She strained to listen beyond the goofballs muttering behind her. Romero was railing at someone but she couldn't make out more than a word here and there. Judging by his tone, he was not a happy man.

Lott leaned against the kitchen island, his ugly glower resting fully on her. Nora worked at keeping her face clean of anticipation.

More shouting.

Something was *unacceptable*. Definitely a female. A mad one at that.

Lott moved to the door that led into the main entry hall. Obviously to listen to whatever was going on with his boss.

Nora checked the position of the other two in the room. Still hanging out by the French doors directly behind her.

Just her luck.

The rise of voices, male and female, shattered the low buzz of conversation around Nora. The male voice she recognized as Romero.

The female…Camille Soto!

Did that mean Tallant was here?

Hope swelled in Nora's chest.

She considered Lott's back. If she screamed, would he have time to turn around and shoot her before Tallant got in here?

Definitely.

Break her neck?

Maybe not.

She dared to glance over her shoulder at the two behind her.

No making it outside or into the hall…

Lott abruptly turned, as if he'd heard the thought. Nora's pulse skittered.

Lott motioned for one of the men by the French doors to come to him. Nora watched as the two huddled, Lott passing along instructions she couldn't hope to hear. The other man nodded, then disappeared into the hall.

Was Soto in danger? Were they going to drag her in here, too?

Nora couldn't just sit there and do nothing.

Still, there was one man stationed at the French doors behind her.

Lott crossed to where she sat and manacled her arm. "One word," he reminded with a lethal glare, "and you're dead."

She nodded her understanding. He hauled her to her feet. She winced. More at how sore her arm was from all the manhandling than from the scrapes on her feet or the injury to her ankle.

He forced her out of the kitchen through the French doors. His pal followed. Since she hadn't noticed Lott ordering him to do so, she imagined that the guy followed only to watch her hips sway in the skimpy panties as she walked.

Why not give him a show he wouldn't soon forget?

"Come on," Lott muttered as he dragged her toward the entrance to the underground tunnel beyond the lavish pool and patio.

Back down the cool concrete steps. Along the dimly lit gray corridor.

To the cell where she'd been held before.

Back at square one.

He shoved her into the cell. "Put your clothes on. You wouldn't want your corpse to be discovered naked, would you?"

She made a face at the big, ugly thug.

Taking her time, she dragged on her slacks and blouse. Then the shoes. Hurt like hell with no socks but nothing she could do about that.

After a quick inspection of her ankle, she crossed to the back wall, leaned against it and slid down to the floor.

She needed a new plan. Not that it would stop the

outcome of this situation. Even if Tallant had arrived with Soto, the chances of him finding her were about nil. Ivan wanted to torture and to murder.

Odds were that would happen.

But she didn't have to make it easy.

Chapter Ten

"You did exactly as I instructed?" Romero had never known Camille Soto to double-cross him—if he had, she would be dead now—but he had an uneasy feeling about this negotiation.

She nodded firmly. "Yes." She inclined her head and eyed him circumspectly. "Haven't I always followed your instructions to the letter?"

"Of course, but…" He folded his arms over his chest and tapped his chin with his forefinger. "This is a very delicate matter. A personal matter. You're certain this associate of Nora's has no idea where she is?"

"None." She shook her head for emphasis. "He called his employer and they're going to the police." Soto smiled—the smile that had first drawn his attention when she'd been a mere waitress. "And we both know how that will go."

"Bear in mind, Camille," Romero warned, "that

if you do not hold up your end of this bargain where the investigator from Chicago is concerned, I will see that your precious doctor ends up every bit as dead as his vengeful wife wishes him."

"Then neither of us has any reason to be concerned," she insisted.

"You will handle this with Vandiver?"

"Just another attempt on his life by his crazy wife," Soto assured him. "He was very fortunate that you intervened. Sadly, the woman was not so lucky."

"Sadly," Romero echoed. He gestured to the front door. "I'll walk you out."

Camille Soto appeared puzzled.

"He's in the trunk of your car," Romero explained as he ushered her forward. "Blindfolded and secured. When you arrive back at the Palomino, you explain how you and I acquired his release."

Soto's smile was brittle, nervous. "Thank you, Ivan."

He gave her a nod.

She hesitated before leaving. "I almost forgot." She turned back to him.

Perhaps now he would have an answer to this nagging doubt.

"Tallant, her associate, mentioned that another investigator from his agency is coming here. Aboard a private jet, I believe."

"Interesting." Romero would see to that matter. "If you recall anything else, you'll let me know."

"Of course."

He watched as she hurried down the cobblestone drive to her car.

Strange, he considered as she circled the fountain and drove away. She'd parked on the far side of the magnificent fountain he'd had imported from Spain. Generally she drove right up to the front steps.

That heavy feeling revisited him.

To the man who had attended to Vandiver's transport accommodations, Romero said, "Watch her. See that she makes no misstep."

Romero considered Soto's taillights as they faded into the darkness. The past twenty-four hours had been quite peculiar.

"She's secured," Lott informed Romero as he approached the door where Romero still stood.

"Excellent." Romero closed the door and inhaled a deep, satisfying breath. "I have a few preparations." His gaze settled on that of his most trusted employee. "Then I'll be ready to proceed. Her associate is expecting support to arrive via a private jet. Take care of that for me, please."

"Yes, sir."

Romero surveyed the luxurious foyer that greeted his visitors. Two decades of hard work had gone into his life here in Vegas. This was his world—his empire. Nothing transpired within his domain without his knowledge and his approval. Maintaining power had not been easy. Others came and went in hopes of tipping the balance, but each one proved unsuccessful. For one reason and one reason only. Romero understood the importance of patience and timing.

His watcher in Chicago had informed him of Nora's departure and intended destination. By the time she'd gotten settled into the Palomino, Romero had already prepared for a move. Still, he'd waited for the right opportunity. Timing was everything, after all.

For five years he'd had various sources keeping watch on Nora. Recording her comings and goings. Keeping tabs on who she called and why. Not once in all that time had she contacted his wife, as he had hoped she would. Not once.

Five years was long enough to grieve. The grief had eventually given way to bitterness.

Now he was simply determined to have his rightful vengeance. He could not locate his wife and child. His eyes closed as he dared to wonder whether the child had been a boy or a girl.

His child.

One Nora Friedman had denied him the privilege of loving.

Now she would know the agony…the endless torture he had endured.

His first inclination had been to watch her die for daring to steal from him.

But then he'd decided upon a much more fitting punishment.

She would live.

As he climbed the sweeping staircase to the second floor, his mood lightened. Today would be a thrilling victory. The plan was a brilliant masterpiece. It was, in part, his reasoning for waiting until the lovely Nora was back within his dominion.

Oh, yes. This day was well worth the wait.

He paused at the first door to the right of the spacious landing and rapped twice.

The door opened and his personal physician peered at him over his bifocals. "You're ready?" he asked.

Romero patted his shoulder. "Not just yet, but within the hour we will proceed."

His old friend nodded. "I'm ready. The patient has been prepared?"

The look that passed between them fueled Romero's anticipation. His old friend had anticipated this opportunity very nearly as much as Romero himself.

"Lott is taking care of that now."

Romero moved on to his suite. All was in place. As soon as he had news of the P.I.'s movements, they would begin. In his suite he crossed to the monitor and selected the underground-level surveillance.

Lott had opened the door to the cell. Nora, dressed now, faced him fearlessly. Romero had liked that about her. She showed no fear of anything. Few women possessed such a courageous nature. He wondered if that would change after today.

"Turn around and face the wall," Lott ordered the prisoner. "Put your hands flat against the wall."

In true Nora fashion, she rolled her eyes, then did as she was told. She had little other choice. Lott entered the cell with his weapon palmed this time.

Nora made a sarcastic comment, but Lott ignored her. He removed the hypodermic needle from his jacket pocket while she rambled on about kicking his butt again the next opportunity that arose.

Lott stabbed the needle into her right shoulder. She stiffened, tried to twist away, but it was too late.

The muscle relaxer was in her bloodstream now. Within the next half hour she would feel the effects, slowly but surely leaving her defenseless.

And ready for payback.

Chapter Eleven

4:03 a.m.

Ted held his position in the copse of trees and shrubbery bordering the rear patio and pool area.

The house's exterior was lit up like a runway. The landscape lighting alone prevented any hope of moving closer to the rear of the house without being spotted by anyone monitoring the property. Every light in the house appeared to be glowing. Leaving him trapped in the small island of foliage.

Luck had been on his side in the beginning. Soto had parked near the massive water fountain, between it and the iron gates protecting the driveway from unauthorized entrance. She had explained that no guard was posted at the gate. Surveillance and access were controlled from inside the house. She had felt confident that surveillance would be focused on her as she emerged from her car and walked to the front entrance, giving Ted an opportunity to make a move.

Even before she had gotten out of the car, something unexpected had gone down inside the house. Security personnel had flooded the yard, front and back, surrounding the house. Soto had frozen, certain that Romero had somehow recognized she was not in the car alone. Ted had persuaded her to remain calm from his position hunkered down on the rear floorboard.

Finally, she had comprehended that whatever was happening wasn't about her and had given Ted an all-clear sign as the search appeared to move fully to the rear of the house. She'd gotten out of the car and moved toward the front entrance. Ted had slipped out of the car and disappeared into the landscaping.

Thankfully most of the exterior lighting in the front of the house was focused on the fountain, leaving an avenue of cover within the shadows. Soto had given him the layout of the property, including as much knowledge as she possessed regarding the underground tunnels. One entrance inside the house. Romero had an elevator in his bedroom suite that stopped on the first floor for access, then lowered directly to the tunnel underground.

Another entrance was near the pool. That access was used by certain guests who had the distinct honor of being invited for a round of private gaming in the massive underground entertainment room that had made Romero a favorite among the Vegas celebrity visitors.

Ultimately the purpose of the tunnels was to provide an avenue of escape for Romero. A direct route away from the property to emergency transportation. The entertainment feature merely served as a cover.

A private physician also served on Romero's staff. According to Soto, he trusted no one else with his health care. Evidently the man had made numerous enemies.

Friedman sure knew how to pick them when she was making enemies herself.

Ted banished the thought. She was in serious trouble here. Lethal trouble. He had to find a way to get her out. Waiting on backup was out of the question. The contact Simon had arranged had provided Ted with the necessities to make a move. He wasn't waiting. She could be dead by then. According to what Soto had admitted, Romero had been waiting for an opportunity to enact his revenge for Nora's past involvement with him.

Braced to move, Ted watched as the last lingering member of Romero's security team moved inside once more. Ted's worry now was the possibility of electronic surveillance. Soto knew Romero had an elaborate setup but she wasn't privy to the specifics.

Once Ted made his move, he had to move quickly. No hesitation. No miscalculations.

Getting in wouldn't be a problem.

Getting out would be the challenge.

He made the move from the copse of lush foliage to the equally mature and thick shrubbery closest to the side of the house—mansion—where Soto had assured him the exterior entrance to the tunnel would be found.

Ted held his breath. Listened. Nothing other than the night sounds and the low hum of the outdoor lighting. The three sets of French doors leading into the back of the mansion's first floor remained clear.

Go!

Ted eased along the perimeter of the landscaping bed until he had no choice but to break away and head for the wide tunnel entrance with its open iron gates.

Down the steps.

Halfway down he spotted a small overhead camera.

Damn.

Don't slow down.

No hesitation.

Pulse thumping in his ears, he kept going.

He passed the first turn to the right. That one led to the private gaming room and to the house entrance. Soto had instructed him to continue forward. Two more turns. The first was to a corridor that dead-ended and the second continued to the emergency transportation setup.

The dead end was his destination. Soto had no idea what was along that corridor since no one was allowed to that point. But she'd gotten the impression that anyone who crossed Romero ended up there. She knew for certain that the final turn led to the helipad because she'd had a short-term relationship with a member of Romero's security team when she'd first moved to Vegas. She'd overheard a conversation between him and his boss, Quinton Lott. Not once had she ever breathed that information, for fear of ending up scavenger bait in the desert. But she loved Vandiver and was willing to take the risk now.

Ted hesitated. Two steel doors lined the corridor but nothing else.

The first door was open.

He eased closer to door number one, his weapon palmed and ready.

Empty.

Ted took a breath and moved silently toward door number two. Unlike number one, the door wasn't standing fully open, but it wasn't completely closed, either.

He held his breath. Listened.

"Go ahead. Kill me. You still won't have your wife back."

Ted froze.

Friedman.

She laughed loudly. "Or your kid."

"You'll soon know just how that feels."

Romero.

Adrenaline blasted Ted's muscles. Would Romero be in there without a bodyguard?

Not likely.

"Proceed."

Tension tightened in Ted's muscles. Was that an order Romero had just issued?

"She isn't properly prepared for surgery."

Male voice. Not Romero.

What the hell? Surgery?

"She's prepared enough," Romero commanded. "Place the gag in her mouth and get started."

The sounds that followed were mostly of Friedman ranting at someone not to touch her.

Ted leveled his weapon and kicked the door inward. "Don't move," he ordered.

The man he recognized as Romero stared at him in abject surprise.

Ted moved quickly into the cell, getting his back to a wall to prevent anyone from coming up behind him. "Release her," he commanded the man dressed in scrubs and attempting to put the gag in place. The doctor, Ted presumed.

Keeping the larger part of his attention on Romero, who made no move to rush Ted, he couldn't restrain the astonishment washing over him at the idea of what the other guy, the doctor, appeared about to do.

What kind of maniac tortured his enemy with surgery?

Ted didn't even want to go there.

"My security team is on the way down," Romero said with utter calm. "Put your weapon down and perhaps I'll allow you to live."

"I don't think so," Ted argued. He pushed off the wall, careful to keep a bead right between Romero's eyes. "Maybe I'll let you live if you cooperate." Ted wrapped one arm around his throat and burrowed the muzzle of his weapon into the bastard's temple. "Now, tell your man to release her."

God in Heaven. Friedman was strapped to a gurney. A stainless-steel tray lined with surgical instruments and a portable overhead light, as well as numerous other gadgets one would see in a hospital O.R., surrounded the gurney.

This was like some sci-fi movie setting.

"Continue," Romero said. "He's not going to kill me."

As if to reiterate his words, the sound of running footfalls echoed in the corridor.

Time to take a risk.

Ted rushed the gurney, Romero in tow. He dared to shift the weapon's aim from Romero to the man in the scrubs. "Let her loose. Now!"

The man—doctor, whatever the hell he was— quickly loosened the straps holding Friedman down. Romero struggled against Ted's hold, shouting for his associate to cease. The doctor loosened the last strap, raised his hands in surrender and started backing away.

"Fool!" Romero roared.

"On the floor," Ted said to the man in scrubs, who immediately scrambled to obey. Then he stabbed the muzzle back into Romero's temple. Just in time for two security jerks to rush into the room.

"Kill him!" Romero squeaked out around Ted's choke hold.

"You even breathe," Ted growled, "and he's dead." Two beads had settled on him but Ted held his ground. He might just die today but Romero was going with him. "Hurry up!" he shouted to Friedman, without taking his attention off the two armed men.

Friedman scrambled off the gurney.

"Get behind me," Ted told her.

She bumped into his back as she got into place behind him. "Sorry," she muttered.

What was wrong with her?

"What's it gonna be, gentlemen?" Ted asked the two staring him down. "You can join the guy on the floor or you can shoot me after I splatter your boss's brains all over his nice suit. Up to you."

Romero tried to speak but Ted clamped down harder on his throat. The bastard clawed and pulled at Ted's arm, frantic squeaks accompanying his desperate movements.

"Now!" Ted commanded, ramming the muzzle deeper into Romero's skull.

Whether it was uncertainty or Romero's high-pitched squeals, the two held up their hands.

"Put your weapons down on the floor," Ted instructed, "and kick them this way."

The first weapon settled on the floor, then slid in Ted's direction.

"Facedown on the floor now," he urged as the second weapon scooted his way.

Friedman snagged one of the weapons and stuck it into Ted's waistband at the small of his back. Then she reached for the other one, almost falling on her face as she bent down. What was wrong with her?

"Let's go," Ted urged. There was no time to analyze her actions.

Friedman was out the door first, then shouted, "Clear!" over her shoulder.

When Ted had dragged Romero into the corridor, Friedman closed and locked the door, leaving the three men stuck inside until help arrived.

"The best way out of here?" Ted asked her.

She started forward, her movements somehow uncoordinated and sluggish.

He wanted to ask what they had done to her or given her, but there was no time.

Romero fought him every step, but Ted kept dragging him forward. It wasn't that difficult. Friedman was moving damned slow.

Ted was no fool. The two guards he'd locked in that cell were likely only a small portion of Romero's security team. There would be others…watching their every move.

What felt like two miles later they reached another steel door. She tried to open it, shook herself and then reached back toward Romero. She grabbed him by the wrist; he resisted. Then Ted realized what she was doing. He moved in closer to what was a scanner of some sort. Friedman pressed Romero's palm against it and the door opened.

More steps waited on the other side.

Friedman closed the door, set the lock. "They won't be able to get through." She blinked, then gave her head a little shake. "But they'll have others on the ground headed this way."

Which meant they still didn't have much time.

Friedman stumbled twice on the way up the seemingly endless stairs.

She'd assuredly had some kind of drug.

They went through the same routine at the next door. It opened into an enormous garage-style hangar. A helicopter and a military-style SUV waited beneath a collage of overhead fluorescent lights.

"This area is monitored, as well?" Ted asked her.

She nodded, pointed to four overhead cameras.

The first shot echoed in the space as he took out one camera. Then two, three and four.

"Helicopter takes an access code to navigate the pad out the overhead door," she said as she swayed, then recaptured her balance. "And a key." She pointed a ferocious glare at Romero. "We need both."

Romero managed a rusty laugh. "Go to hell."

"What about the SUV?" Ted suggested.

"They'd find us in nothing flat with the helicopter."

"What if we disable the helicopter?" Ted offered,

determined to make this escape happen before the rest of Romero's team got here.

"Tracking system," she said. "All Romero's vehicles have them. They'd find us almost as fast that way."

"Then I guess we have no choice but to head out on foot." He nodded toward the walk-through door at the end of the building, opposite the oversize garage door.

More of that hoarse laughter from Romero.

Ted had had enough of him. He adjusted his hold, applying the pressure just so until the bastard stopped squirming. When he was fully unconscious, Ted allowed his limp body to drop to the floor.

"You should've killed him," Friedman said, her speech slurred.

Ted started to remind her that they were the good guys, but she promptly spun toward the door. The gun she'd been clasping clattered across the floor and then she dropped like a rock.

He rushed to her side, checked her pulse. Strong. Respiration steady. He lifted her arm and let it drop against her side. Limp as the proverbial dishrag.

She was out.

Not much time.

Ted glanced at the SUV.

She'd said there would be a tracking device.

A quick check on Romero assured he was still out.

Only one thing to do.

Ted fired off a few more rounds, putting out the overhead lighting. He double-timed it over to the walk-through door and shoved it open. He listened for sounds of arriving company. Nothing yet. Retracing his steps with the same swiftness, he reached down and hauled Friedman up onto his shoulder, snatched up the weapon she'd dropped. He straightened and surveyed the interior of the large building. Two doors. One to a room with windows across the front. Likely an office. One with no windows. Supply closet? Maintenance shop? Weapon storeroom?

He turned to get a look at the other side of the building. Shelves lined with supplies. And another door. He moved toward that one since it was closest.

Locked.

Damn it.

He hustled over to the door next to the office. It opened with one twist of the knob.

A smile slid across his lips.

Bathroom.

That could work.

He stepped inside, careful not to whop Friedman's head on the door frame. Two stalls, urinal and two sinks. And another door. He didn't have high hopes when he reached for the knob with its keyed lock. Surprisingly it was unlocked. Supply and cleaning closet.

Quickly, he cleared an area on the floor in the closet and lowered Friedman there. Then he closed the door leading from the hangar into the bathroom. Moving carefully, since it was as dark as a cave now, he settled in the closet with Friedman and closed the door.

Though this would prevent him from seeing the movements of anyone who arrived or hearing any conversations, it was the safest bet. They wouldn't have gotten a mile on foot.

All he had to do was keep Friedman quiet if she roused.

Not wanting to be less than fully prepared, he went down on one knee, keeping his weapon palmed. If anyone came through that door, they were going to get a chest full of lead.

He pulled out his cell phone to give Simon Ruhl an update and to check on backup from the local police since Trinity Barrett wouldn't have arrived as of yet.

No service.

Damn it.

He'd have to wait it out.

Regularly checking Friedman's pulse and respiration, he attempted to relax to the degree possible.

The screech of the overhead door rising warned that they had company.

He swallowed back the doubt and focused on listening for an approach.

Shouts and the thud of boots on concrete reverberated through the walls.

It sounded as if an entire army had descended upon the garage-style hangar.

His pulse reacted to the nearness of danger. With Friedman in the condition she was in, he'd already done all he could do to protect her.

He tamped down the worry to clear his focus.

The walls shook with the slam of a door. As best he could determine, the office door.

They were searching the building.

The bathroom door opened with an audible groan. Ted stilled. The door banged against the wall. He held his breath.

Light seeped beneath the closet door. Disabling the bathroom light would have garnered suspicion.

Stall doors slammed into sidewalls, first one, then the other.

His mind abruptly jolting into gear, Ted reached up and turned the toggle that locked from the inside the door that stood between them and whoever was searching the bathroom. He unclenched his fingers just in time for the knob to turn.

Sweat beaded on his forehead as the knob twisted a second time. Though it was too dark to see, he could hear the metal-on-metal slide of the turning knob and then the wood-against-wood pressure against the door.

"Clear!" followed by the fading clump of footfalls allowed him to breathe again.

The last Romero had heard before Ted rendered him unconscious was that they would head out on foot. If they were lucky, Romero would order his men to initiate a search of the surrounding area.

That would buy Ted some time.

He strained to listen.

A swoosh and a bang accompanied the bathroom door flying open once more.

Ted tightened his grip on his weapon, prepared for battle.

The next sound sent some amount of relief searing through his veins.

Someone had needed to relieve himself.

"Hurry up, Elliott!" a male voice shouted. "We're heading out! They can't have gotten far."

The swift drag of a zipper, then, "Yeah, yeah, I'm coming."

Friedman moved.

Ted groped for her mouth, flattened his hand there.

She stiffened.

He leaned his face close to her ear and whispered, "Shh."

Dead silence echoed for one, two, then three seconds.

The toilet flushed.

The shuffling of boots across the concrete signaled the man's exit.

Ted squeezed his eyes shut and thanked God for small miracles.

She was moving again.

He put his face close to hers. "Don't make a sound. They're out there."

She went immobile.

Ted resumed his vigil, listening intently.

All they had to do now was remain perfectly quiet.

And wait until the building was clear.

Chapter Twelve

"Barrett just checked in."

Victoria Colby-Camp looked up from the report she and her son, Jim, had been reviewing. "And?"

Simon's grim expression warned that the news was not good. "He's been detained."

"Detained?" Jim Colby countered. "By whom? For what reason?"

Tension tightened in Victoria's chest. Her son had asked the questions knowing full well the answer. Ivan Romero. They had learned, as had Simon, in the last two hours that Romero manipulated law enforcement in and around Vegas. Simon's contact with the Bureau had warned that Romero was not only extremely dangerous but also ruthlessly vindictive.

Having a private aircraft detained would be child's play to a man like Romero.

"According to the detective in charge," Simon explained, "he received an anonymous tip regarding the abrupt, middle-of-the-night arrival of a private aircraft from Chicago. One that, according to the anonymous source, was part of a drug operation."

Meaning Romero had learned that backup for Ted and Nora was en route.

"Has Ted checked in?" Victoria asked, hoping against hope.

Simon shook his head. "Nothing."

"What about Soto and Vandiver?" Jim asked, concern mounting in his tone. "Are they still in Vegas or have they made a run for it?"

"According to my contact, they returned to the Palomino Hotel." Simon checked his cell phone. "The last text I received indicated that Soto's sedan remains in the personnel parking area. I called half an hour ago and spoke with Ms. Soto, and she assured me they were safe in one of the VIP suites."

"She believes they are in no danger of repercussions from Romero?" Victoria found that difficult to accept since Ted had used Camille Soto as a way onto Romero's property. A man as cunning as Romero surely had seen through the ruse…unless he had not

learned of Ted's presence. That was perhaps too much
to hope for under the circumstances.

"She insists that is the case," Simon confirmed.
"The suite is one set aside for special guests. She
claims no one, not even a member of her staff, is
aware of her and Vandiver's presence there."

Jim shook his head. "Impossible considering the
high-tech security system in place. She's not being
totally up-front with us."

"I agree," Simon went on. "I've asked my contact
to get as close to the Romero property as possible.
We have to assume that both Ted and Nora are still
there."

Simon didn't have to say that his contact's hands
were tied. Overstepping his bounds in any manner
could set in motion serious recriminations. He'd already been a great deal of help despite the risks. With
no authorization or compelling evidence—other than
Simon's word—he had taken it upon himself to do
what he could to be the Colby Agency's eyes and ears
on the ground in Vegas.

"Is there anything your contact can do to speed up
the process at the airfield for Barrett?"

Jim had an excellent point. If Barrett could get past
this stall, his hands would not be tied as were those
of Simon's contact.

"He's made a call, but there's no guarantee. Loyalty

to Romero runs deep." Simon hesitated a moment. "Ian is running down any additional information regarding Nora that might prove useful."

"I provided a full dossier on all my Equalizers," Jim challenged.

The ensuing tension threatened to push the oxygen right out of the room.

"Everyone has a history," Victoria put in quickly to defuse the escalating pressure. "We all have skeletons in our closets. Events from the past that perhaps were thought to have remained in the past. When they come back to haunt us, it's always a surprise. I'm certain Nora had no idea that Romero still carried such a grudge."

The frustration etched along every line and angle of Simon's face was in direct contrast to the cold-stone stare emanating from Jim's. These moments were impossible to avoid but now was not the time to be distracted.

"Of course," Simon agreed, breaking the ice first. "Nora would never knowingly endanger Ted or herself. I'm simply suggesting we take the steps we can to head off any future incidents of this nature."

Jim said nothing.

Victoria nodded her agreement. "That's an excellent suggestion, Simon. Every member of our staff is well experienced and has, undoubtedly, made enemies."

The merger of the Equalizers with the Colby Agency had been smooth for the most part, but the transition still had a ways to go. Victoria had complete confidence that all would be as it should soon.

Barring an unfortunate outcome with the Vandiver case. She couldn't help feeling genuine concern for her cousin, despite the fact that the situation wasn't quite as one-sided as she had represented. The continued infidelity of her husband was a painful hardship. Yet recent developments would indicate that things were somewhat different than Heather had painted them.

Time would tell.… All parties involved needed protection until that end.

"Von will put together a risk assessment of all cases and/or situations involving my people." Jim shot Simon one last daring look as he turned away. "It'll be on your desk in twenty-four hours."

Victoria watched her son leave the office she hoped he would one day call his own. *My people.* Jim had worked hard to fit in…to give his mother what she had wanted since the day he was born—to be a part of this agency. This was difficult for him. More so than perhaps even she understood.

He was a proud man, a stubborn man. But he had

earned every ounce of that pride and determination the hard way. A way no human should have to.

"I apologize, Victoria," Simon offered when the sound of the door slamming had stopped echoing in the otherwise silence. "It was not my intention to overstep my bounds or to elicit tension."

"Your suggestion was fitting given the current circumstances." She mulled over the idea a moment. "Why don't we put together a similar report on our entire investigative team?"

Confusion flared in his eyes. "We have a thorough evaluation on everyone already."

Victoria nodded. "We do. Let's pull the evaluations together into one encompassing report for Jim to review." Her son was studying the files on investigations for the past five years. He'd reviewed the dossiers on all staff members. He was no doubt aware of the agency's stringent employment guidelines. Still, if such an act would smooth over this latest ripple, why not?

Simon gave her a nod of understanding. "I'll have Mildred take care of it as soon as she arrives this morning."

One step at a time. The merger would come full circle one step at a time.

"Simon," Victoria said, slowing his departure, "one last question."

He turned to face her again. "Yes?"

"Our supplier in Vegas." The Colby Agency had a supply or incidentals contact in every major city across the country. In this day of airline security measures, there was no way to transport the necessary equipment required for unforeseen complications. "Is there anything he can do to assist us in this precarious situation? Any support whatsoever?"

"Unfortunately, he, too, is hesitant to step on Romero's toes."

Who was this man that he wielded such power? Victoria had known such men in the past…*Leberman*. The mere name had the power to send a chill through her heart. But, in her experience, a man like that amassed power over time—a great deal of time—and by arming himself with like allies.

Though Ivan Romero possessed great wealth, his dossier read like a bedtime story compared to that of a bastard like Leberman. How had he accomplished such loyalty in such a short, somewhat unremarkable period?

No matter, Nora had, it seemed, made herself a ruthless and significantly powerful enemy. Victoria hoped Ted could salvage the situation.

For now, it appeared the case could wait. Heather, Victoria's cousin, was safe under the watch of Leland Rockford. Her errant husband, Dr. Vandiver, had been released by Romero and was, to their knowledge, safe for the time being. Determining the source of his and Heather's domestic trials would keep until lives were no longer at stake.

Victoria dismissed the nagging instinct that all was not as it should be where her cousin was concerned. "Thank you, Simon. I'm certain Trinity will find a way to rendezvous with Ted and resolve this situation. Waiting may be our only option for now."

"I'm afraid that is our only recourse at the moment."

Even the Colby Agency was bested at times.

Victoria's door swung inward with Jim's abrupt return. "We have another complication."

Victoria bolstered herself for the news. "What now?" This case had taken more sudden twists and turns than any other she could readily recall.

"Heather Vandiver is missing."

That unsettling feeling that had been nagging Victoria since receiving the first troubling call from her cousin grew stronger now, spread through her limbs with icy intensity. "But her husband and his mistress are still at the hotel in Vegas."

"As far as we know," Simon qualified. "We haven't had a visual in almost two hours."

"Without access to a private jet," Victoria countered, "that's not time enough to have made such a move." Even then it would have been difficult for

Brent Vandiver to have made the journey from Vegas to L.A.

"Rocky can't be certain this wasn't Heather's doing," Jim explained. "He's checked in on her every half hour since midnight. She appeared to be sleeping soundly. Twenty minutes ago he went to her door, felt something looked a little off and entered the room. As soon as he'd stepped past the open door, he was hit by a Taser. When he recovered, she was gone. There's evidence that the security strip on an exterior side door was tampered with. The door was left standing open. Heather's purse, keys, everything was still in the house. Only she was missing."

"But he isn't convinced that this is a true abduction," Victoria said, reading between the lines of her son's assessment.

"Not one hundred percent. The security system at the Vandiver home is top-notch. No one would have gotten past Rocky," Jim declared. "That I can guarantee one hundred percent."

"She could simply be worried about her husband," Simon offered with little enthusiasm. "The idea that he was in actual danger may have made her see things in a different light. Perhaps she decided it would be best if she sought him out without outside interference. Panic may have motivated her to set such a ruse in motion."

"Or," Victoria offered, "she could actually be missing. And in danger."

"Or," Jim countered once more, "intent on ensuring she has an alibi for carrying out her true plan."

Vandiver had claimed when he'd spoken to Nora that Heather was the one who wanted him dead, not the other way around.

"Either way," Jim recommended, "we need someone watching Vandiver and Soto every bit as much as we need someone providing backup to Nora and Tallant."

And their hands were tied.

There was no time to get another investigator on the scene. Local Vegas law enforcement couldn't be counted on where Romero was concerned.

"I'll touch base with my contacts once more," Simon offered, "but I wouldn't count on anything more than what we've gotten already."

"We need Trinity on Vandiver and Soto now."

Jim was right. Victoria banished the fear that wanted to harden like stone in her stomach. That would leave Ted and Nora on their own.

Against an enemy like Ivan Romero.

Las Vegas, 5:20 a.m.

THE WHOP-WHOP-WHOP OF the helicopter did nothing to soothe Romero's fury. For almost half an hour they had been sweeping the landscape with the spotlight. Back and forth, round and round.

Nothing.

Three SUVs combed the terrain, as well. Not a sign of Nora and her accomplice had been spotted.

Romero had checked in with the two guards who'd remained at the house and still nothing.

The two had to be hiding. Nora knew the area fairly well. But did she know it well enough to find her way in the dark under the circumstances?

The muscle relaxer had to be playing havoc with her ability to think and focus.

A new wave of fury tore through Romero's chest. He should have killed her when he had the chance. Should have killed her accomplice, as well.

Hell, he should have killed them all.

There was only one way Tallant had gotten onto Romero's estate.

Camille.

She would pay for her deceit.

So would her new lover.

No one crossed Ivan Romero and lived to tell about it.

Why had he ever allowed Nora to live this long? Why had he needed such an elaborate plan of revenge?

Because no one else had ever hurt him the way she

had. He'd needed her payback to be special…to last longer than the few minutes required for life to drain from her dying body.

She and her brave partner couldn't possibly have gotten far. They had to be hiding amid the desolate terrain below.

What he needed was a larger and more ambitious search party.

He activated the mic attached to his headgear. "Call my dear friend Medlock," he instructed his head of security. "Let him know that we've chased intruders from my property. There are certain documents they may have obtained copies of. He'll know what to do."

Romero relaxed. The sheriff would respond to the call for help instantly and with full force.

There wasn't a secret in this entire county that Romero didn't know.… Many he possessed tangible evidence of. No one, *no one,* wanted those secrets revealed.

This time he wouldn't bother with his elaborate plan.

Nora would die.

And so would her friend.

Chapter Thirteen

5:25 a.m.

"I can carry you."

If Nora's eyes had responded to the command sent by her brain, they would have rolled. "I can walk. Get off my back. We don't have time for this." She'd told Tallant five times she could do this.

Even as she roared the argument, she swayed.

He steadied her. "I'm not so sure about that."

"Are we going to stand here and argue about this until they come back?" They needed to get out of here!

He didn't look happy but he put up his hands in defeat. "Okay. Let's do it."

Both the helicopter and the SUV were gone from the massive hangar. They'd heard the helicopter overhead as it tracked from north to south in a steady, relentless pattern. Romero wouldn't stop until he found them—that she knew for sure. Standing here, waiting around for him to realize they weren't out there anywhere, was not a brilliant idea.

With the helicopter sweeping its spotlight over the terrain, and the SUV and likely other vehicles combing the area by ground, it wouldn't take that long for Romero to come to that realization.

Their only option was to go back into the tunnel and take their chances back at the house. Romero would have most of his security force involved in the search with him. Minimal guards would remain at the house. One or two maybe.

She and Tallant were armed. Those were odds they could live with.

Tallant snagged her right hand in his left and moved toward the tunnel entrance.

Nora stumbled after him, her gaze glued to the way his big hand engulfed hers...the manner in which those long, strong fingers curled around hers.

He hesitated at the steps leading downward. "You're sure you can do this?"

Nora blinked back the pharmaceutical haze that still fogged her vision and glared at him. "Go!" She was fine. His grabbing her hand had distracted her, put her even more off balance...sort of.

As he dragged her forward, she reached around to the small of her back and pulled the weapon from her waistband. She wasn't a lefty, but she'd rather have the weapon in hand than not. Tallant had already palmed his and held it in a readied position. He was braced for confrontation. And confrontation was a given.

Focusing on each step was necessary. Her equilibrium wasn't back to normal by any means. Whatever they'd injected her with—a muscle relaxer of some kind, she believed—it hadn't fully worn off yet. The walls shifted a little, but only in her mind. Oddly, she was glad for Tallant's strong hold on her hand. He kept her moving forward. She was pretty sure that a couple of times she would have stopped otherwise, particularly on the descent of the steps.

Her throat and mouth felt sand dry. Her vision wasn't anywhere near up to par. And her balance was way off. But she was upright and moving forward. Tallant lugged her along behind him, his determined steps barely a whisper of sound and in sharp contrast to her drunken shuffle.

If they got out of here alive, it would be entirely his doing.

Tallant halted.

Nora bumped into his back. Though she'd realized he had stopped, her depth perception was suffering from the drug, as well.

Tallant held the barrel of his handgun to his lips, cautioning her to remain silent.

The branch of the tunnel that led to the two holding cells was up ahead. If a member of Romero's security team waited around that bend, there was no way for them to know until it was too late.

Struggling to keep her steps silent, Nora stayed close behind Tallant as he moved forward once more. When they were less than five yards from the door, he indicated for her to sit tight.

She didn't like it but she didn't argue. Frankly, she was in no condition to trust her judgment.

He eased closer and closer to the intersection of the two tunnels. Nora held her breath, braced to move into firing position.

Tallant checked the adjoining corridor, then sent her an all-clear sign.

Relief made her already wobbly knees a little weaker. She hurried after him, surprised at how quickly she could move now that it was safe to do so. Adrenaline probably. She needed more of it to neutralize the effects of the drug.

However, getting it by the usual methods—fear, anger, panic—wouldn't exactly be a good thing just now.

When he closed his hand around hers once more, a little shot of heat seared through her. She shouldn't have enjoyed it…but she did.

No sound up ahead or behind them. The coming

fork would take them to the house. One route led to the pool and entertaining area, and the other to Romero's private entrance that led to his study on the first floor and on up to his bedroom suite on the second.

Nora tugged on Tallant's hand. He hesitated, stared down at her. She gestured to the left, which would take them to the pool and entertaining area. He nodded his understanding and started in that direction. Another of those small heat bursts accompanied the idea that he trusted her to make that decision.

Maybe he wasn't such a bad guy, after all.

That he'd risked his life to rescue her spoke volumes. The way she'd treated him, it was a miracle he'd bothered. Then again, she would have done the same for him—complaining the entire time, of course. And in the end either one of them would have been required to answer to Victoria Colby-Camp. That alone was motivation enough to do the right thing.

She hadn't really paid any genuine attention until now, but Tallant's shoulders were seriously wide. Blocked her view of anything else. His curly blond hair was boyish, yet there was nothing boyish about his muscular body. Or those intense gold eyes.

Apparently the lingering effect of the drugs was making mush of her brain.

The private gaming room was dark, the door

closed. Only a few more yards now. Her pulse reacted to the potential for danger.

As they neared the top of the steps leading to the pool and entertaining area, Tallant hesitated once more. Nora listened, as did he. The trickling of the water fountain was the only sound.

But that didn't mean a guard wasn't standing just on the other side of the shrubbery shrouding this entrance. Again, Tallant signaled for her to stay put. Not arguing, she leaned against the wall while he rose to the landing and surveyed the area behind the house.

That he moved away from the landing and the meager cover of the shrubbery had her heart kicking into a more rapid rhythm.

She shifted her weapon to her right hand. Her palms were sweating, but her mouth and throat remained intensely dry. Cocking her head, she listened for noise beyond the water sound.

Seconds turned to a full minute. Had he run into trouble beyond her hearing range?

One step up. She was still several from the landing. It couldn't hurt to get a little closer.

One more.

Another.

Two steps from the top.

Deep breath.

She reached the landing and took stock of the situation.

The area was deserted. Ambient lighting sparkled against the water and highlighted the elegant plantings around the natural stone patio.

Where the hell was Tallant?

All sets of French doors along the back of the house remained closed, while the interior glowed like a shopping mall open for business.

But there wasn't a human to be seen.

Somewhere beyond the walled entertaining area a dog howled. Another excellent reason they hadn't tried that route for their escape. Her ankle burned with the memory of her close encounter with the K9 kind.

Okay. No Ted Tallant.

If he had been captured, she owed it to him to help despite her handicap at the moment.

Gripping her weapon with both hands, she moved toward the back of the house.

That soft trickle of water now sounded like a raging waterfall roaring in her head.

Keep moving. Focus. Listen for any sound. Look for any movement.

Her head suddenly swam. She stalled, regained her equilibrium before taking another step.

Foliage moved next to the French doors leading into the kitchen.

Nora blinked, lost her breath.

Tallant motioned for her to get back.

The French doors opened.

"Stop right there!"

Damn.

One of Ivan's jerk patrolmen.

Since his weapon was aimed at her, she decided not to toss out the smart-aleck remark on the tip of her tongue. Instead, she held still, offered a caught-in-the-headlights look of distress but didn't lower her weapon.

"Slow and easy now, honey," he said as he took another step in her direction. "Bend your knees and ease down until you can lay your weapon on the ground. Then slide it toward me."

Tallant moved.

Nora dove to the ground and rolled to the right.

A grunt echoed as the men tumbled to the ground in a heap. One weapon lay a few feet away from the struggle. Tallant's remained in his hand, but the guard was attempting to simultaneously keep it away from his body and to bang it loose from Tallant's grip.

Nora scrambled to her feet, staggered a step or two. When the muzzle of her weapon was flat against the enemy's skull, she ordered, "Put your arms flat against the ground."

Both men stopped moving, but the guard hesitated before obeying her command.

"Now," she snapped, pressing the business end of the gun deeper into his hard head.

His fingers unclenched, releasing Tallant, and with obvious reluctance he spread his arms out on the ground on either side of him.

Tallant got to his feet and picked up the other man's weapon. "Do you always ignore your partner's orders?" he demanded as he belted the extra weapon.

Nora didn't have to wonder who he was talking to. How long would he have waited for this dude to come outside if she hadn't appeared? She shot him a look. "Only when my partner leaves me hanging."

"Let's go." Tallant motioned for the man to get on his feet.

"There'll be at least one more around here somewhere," Nora related as she scanned the area around the pool. "Ivan never leaves less than two on duty."

"We'll check the front first before going inside," Tallant suggested. Only it didn't sound like a suggestion; it sounded like an order.

Which was precisely why Nora ignored him. She

shoved the muzzle of her weapon into the guard's groin. "How many? And where are they?"

Nora didn't have to look to know Tallant would be rolling his eyes. It was a cliché move, but if it worked, who cared?

"I'm not afraid of you." The scumbag punctuated his haughty statement with a less than polite term directed at her character.

Tallant grabbed him in a choke hold and shoved his weapon into the soft underbelly of his throat. "Afraid of me, hotshot? Guys like you don't do well in prison, and I promise you, if either of us ends up dead, that's where you're going."

Just for the heck of it, Nora gave him a jab in the family jewels with her weapon.

"One more. He's out front," wheezed the guard.

Nora smiled. "See how easy it is to play nice?" She didn't wait to see what Tallant intended to do with the guy; she strode directly into the house.

WHAT THE HELL WAS SHE doing?

Ted disabled the guy, lowered him to the ground and looked around for a way to secure him.

Nothing handy.

He removed the man's belt and fastened his hands behind his back. Wrenched off his shoes and used his socks to secure his ankles. That would hold him for a while. On second thought, he grabbed a towel from the neatly folded stack on the bar near the pool and shoved a portion of it in his mouth to keep him quiet when he regained consciousness. With another quick glance around, he opted to drag the guy into the shrubbery so he wouldn't be readily noticed if anyone came around to the back of the house.

Since he hadn't heard any gunshots or breaking objects, Ted had to assume that Nora hadn't encountered anyone inside.

Still, he went in silently.

The house was well lit. Quiet. No sign of Friedman.

The kitchen was clear.

He moved toward the wide entry hall.

Friedman waited, a finger pressed to her lips.

Ted surveyed the soaring two-story hall. No sound. Nobody.

She pointed to the door across the expanse of gleaming marble from where she stood.

He tapped his gun and sent her a questioning look. She shook her head no in response to his query as to whether there was another guard.

A voice beyond the towering front entry doors yanked their collective attention there.

The polished brass knob turned.

As if they had choreographed the move, both Ted

and Friedman rushed the door, took a position on either side, careful not to make a sound.

When the door opened, Ted hesitated before ramming the muzzle of his weapon into the man's temple.

"Yes, sir. All clear here." The guard's hand dropped to his side, cell phone clutched in his palm.

Ted moved in. "Give me the cell phone."

Before the guy could react, Friedman had reached beneath his jacket and snatched his weapon.

"The phone," Ted demanded.

The guy reached out, dropped the cell in Ted's palm.

"On the floor," Ted ordered.

"They'll be back here any minute," the guy warned as he dropped down to his knees.

"And we'll be gone," Friedman taunted.

"Hands behind your back," Ted ordered.

Friedman, weapon leveled for confrontation, eased back toward the door she'd initially been watching.

Listening for any trouble she might encounter, Ted quickly secured the man on the floor the same as he had the one outside. He dragged him to the coat closet and shoved him inside, then grabbed a pair of gloves from the overhead shelf and gagged him.

Friedman was speaking, not the slightest bit softly, either.

Ted moved cautiously to the door she'd entered. A study or library. The gray-haired man who'd had Friedman strapped to that gurney stood in the middle of the room with his hands up. He'd exchanged the scrubs for an elegant suit. A cell phone lay on the floor between his feet.

"Check that phone and make sure he didn't put a call through," Friedman ordered.

Ted picked up the phone and checked the outgoing calls. "Not in the last two hours."

"Good." Friedman gave a satisfied nod. "I guess I don't have to kill you, Doc."

So he was a doctor.

"We should get out of here," Ted urged. "Romero could show up anytime."

"He will," the gray-haired man said, his head moving up and down with the same panic flashing in his eyes. "You don't want to be here if that happens." He looked directly at Friedman and said, "Trust me."

"We won't be here," Friedman assured him. "And neither will you."

Ted frowned at her. He had no intention of taking a hostage.

"He's our way out of here," she explained. "He knows the gate code. He's Romero's private physician." She glared at the old man. "And he knows what he gave me."

Ted could understand her reasoning. "Let's go."

Friedman pushed the doctor out the door, her gun jammed into his back. "I hope you have your keys, Doc."

The doctor nodded.

"Which pocket?" Ted demanded.

"Right jacket pocket."

Ted fished out the man's keys on the way out the door.

"That one." The doctor pointed to the luxury automobile parked to the right of the grand stairs leading up from the parking patio.

Ted disengaged the car's security system, careful to keep watch in all directions around them. There was only supposed to be two of Ivan's guards hanging around the house, but that could have been a lie.

Friedman ushered the doctor into the backseat, where she joined him.

Ted slid behind the wheel. When he'd started the engine and rolled up to the gates, the doc spouted the code. Hoping like hell he hadn't provided some kind of panic code, Ted entered the numbers and relaxed significantly when the gates swung open.

As soon as they were out the gates and moving at

a nice speed along the highway, Ted pulled out his
cell and checked for missed calls.

Five from Simon Ruhl.

As he put in a call to his superior, he asked Friedman, "Where're we going?"

"Back to the Palomino to find Soto." Friedman's
gaze collided with his in the rearview mirror. "She had
to have sold me out. I don't know how she knew—"

Ted launched into a conversation with Simon, cutting her off for the moment.

The news was not good, on any count.

This entire investigation had unraveled.

"Yes." Ted nodded. "I understand." He closed his
cell and dropped it onto the seat. "We have several
problems."

"You mean besides Ivan Romero and this old
geezer?" Friedman bopped the doctor in the back of
the head. "Just what the hell were you planning to do
to me? And what kind of drug was I given?"

The doctor leaned slightly away from her, as if he
feared she might whack him again. "A muscle relaxer.
Only enough to relax you for…surgery. I would have
given you an anesthetic for that."

"Surgery?" Friedman shouted. "Are you crazy?
What surgery?"

"Since you deprived him of his only child," replied the doctor, his voice shaking with fear, "he

ordered me to ensure you were never able to have any children."

God Almighty. Ted gave himself a mental shake to dislodge the idea of what would have happened had he not gotten to her before…

Friedman whacked the guy in the head again. "Idiot," she muttered. "Don't you know better than to work for a thug like that?"

"Nora."

She met Ted's gaze in the mirror. He'd known that calling her by her first name would get her attention. "I just spoke to Simon. Trinity Barrett is here, but he's been detained at the airfield. While we were incommunicado, Camille Soto and Dr. Vandiver apparently went underground. They're not answering calls and presumably are in hiding at the Palomino."

"That's where we're going," she said, fury rising in her voice. "I'm getting the truth out of that blond—"

"And Heather Vandiver has disappeared."

"What?"

Ted nodded. "She's gone."

"How the hell did she give Rocky the slip?"

"Taser. When he recovered, she was gone."

"She's on her way here," said Friedman, surmising.

Their gazes bumped once more in the mirror.

She didn't have to elaborate.

Dr. Brent Vandiver had insisted his wife had been trying to kill him. Maybe he'd been telling the truth.

Chapter Fourteen

Palomino Casino and Hotel
6:30 a.m.

"If you go in there, someone may recognize you," Tallant warned.

"You just take care of him." Nora tossed her head toward the doc in the backseat. "I'll take care of me." Just because she'd gotten ambushed once in the past twenty-four hours didn't mean she was incapable.

Tallant glanced at the rear window. They'd left Romero's pal in the car while they discussed the right way to enter the hotel and locate Vandiver and Soto.

"No offense, Friedman," Tallant countered, "but I'm not so sure you're up to the task. That drug may not have worn off fully yet."

Smart. He'd used the drug as an excuse rather than her lack of ability. "We don't have time to argue the point." Romero was likely back at the house by now. He would be livid and out for blood.

Specifically hers.

"Are you going to check every room?" he asked when she hesitated. "How long will that take? Chances are this will be the first place Romero checks when he finds we've given his security the slip."

All true.

Nora smiled. "Give me a minute." She opened the car door and scooted in next to the doctor. Why hadn't she thought of this before? "Camille Soto knows you, doesn't she?"

The doctor nodded. "Occasionally I attend to a guest here at the hotel. I do the same for others, as well."

The man was scared. That was good.

"If you called her and explained that you needed to speak with her in person, does she trust you enough to give you her location?"

He shook his head. "She knows that my first allegiance is to Ivan...Mr. Romero."

Think! There had to be a way. Nora turned back to the old man. "What if you told her that Ivan had forced you to give Dr. Vandiver a slow-acting poison? If you don't give him the antidote immediately, it might be too late."

"That's ludicrous." He made a face that showed just how crazy he thought Nora to be.

"Ivan has done worse things," Nora said. She knew this for a fact. No doubt this man did, as well. He'd been planning surgery for her this very morning! "Things for which you are likely an accomplice." No need to point out the aforementioned scheduled surgery.

That seemed to get his attention. His demeanor shifted into defensive mode. "I don't know what you're accusing me of, but I can assure you—"

"Assure me of what?" she tossed back. "That you wouldn't have cut out my uterus if my friend here hadn't intervened?"

He blinked twice. "You can't prove that."

"Probably not," she admitted as she tapped her cheek with the cold steel muzzle of her handgun. "Any more than the police could prove I put a bullet in your head and dumped your body." She looked first at one side of the gun she held and then at the other. "This isn't even my weapon. It belongs to one of Ivan's men. The police wouldn't even investigate if they thought it would lead back to him. The two of you had a difference of opinion, and he needed you out of the way. Completely understandable."

Fear glittered in his eyes as he hesitated, likely searching for some way to save himself.

Nora shrugged. "Too bad for you." She started to climb out of the car.

"Wait."

She paused for him to gather his courage.

"I can show you where she is, but you have to let me go...unharmed once I've done so."

"Absolutely," Nora assured him without reservation and despite Tallant's questioning look. At the moment she didn't care why the doctor would have this knowledge; she only needed to find the lovebirds. If Vandiver's wife was indeed on the way here, she could be in danger or the other woman could be the target. Even Vandiver himself, for that matter. Nora and Tallant still had no clear evidence who was telling the truth in this fiasco.

If they could keep Romero off their backs, it was past time to clear up this mystery.

7:15 a.m.

"ARE YOU SURE ABOUT THIS, Doc?" Ted had taken the highway into the desert. For the last ten miles or so there had been nothing but that desert.

"Yes. Another mile or so and there's a right turn."

Dawn had made its appearance, and now the

sun was gearing up to bake the sand and towering mountains.

"Tell me, Doc," Friedman prompted, "why would you know about Soto's plan to come here? Your excuse that you treated a guest who'd stayed at this isolated retreat just doesn't cut it for me."

Ted glanced at the man via the rearview mirror. He looked nervous as hell. Whatever came out of his mouth, it wouldn't likely be the whole truth.

"She told me that she and Dr. Vandiver came here quite often to get away from the hotel…from prying eyes," the doctor said knowingly.

Possible, Ted decided. "Is this the turn?"

"Yes." The doc nodded with far too much enthusiasm.

Ted had a bad, bad feeling about this. "How far until we reach the place?"

"Only a couple of miles. It's the second of only three properties on this road."

Friedman studied the landscape. "I'm not familiar with this area."

She was suspicious, too. Ted heard it in her voice.

"It's private," the doctor explained.

"Does Ivan own this property?" asked Friedman.

Ted had considered that possibility.

"Yes," the doctor replied. "He purchased the properties for those who prefer some distance from the constancy of the Strip."

"Why would Soto come here?" Ted demanded. Time to get the real scoop. "Is she that close to Romero?"

"She owes him a great deal," the doctor confessed. "She rose to manager because of him. She's no fool. This is the last place he would look for her if he suspects she's double-crossed him."

Maybe so. One thing was certain, Friedman had been right. Soto had likely sold her out. The question was, how would Soto have known who Friedman was?

"There!" The doctor pointed up ahead. "It's the next property."

Ted made the turn into the first property.

"What're you doing?" the man demanded. "This is the wrong place."

"And that's the one where Soto is, right?" Ted pointed to the small Southwestern-style house on the right a little farther down the sandy road.

The doctor nodded. "Yes…but…"

"Then we're good," Ted told him.

"Looks like no one's home," Friedman said aloud as they rolled up to the house across the road from the one Soto occupied.

Ted pulled the car around to the backyard and got out. While the doctor argued with Friedman, Ted checked out the place. Definitely no one home.

He circled the wraparound deck, paused at the front door long enough to take a good look at the place across the road. Soto's sedan was parked out front.

Then, because humans were creatures of habit, he reached down and checked beneath the welcome mat. No key. Then he reached up to check the molding across the top of the door.

A key.

He opened the door and went inside.

Smelled of disuse.

Large great-room-style space that combined the living room, dining room and the kitchen. Massive stone fireplace for those cold desert nights. Down a narrow hall were two bedrooms and a bathroom. No linens on the beds. No soap or shampoo in the tub. A partial roll of toilet paper sat atop the toilet tank.

Nope. There hadn't been anyone here in a while.

By the time he'd returned to the great room, Friedman and the doc had made their way inside.

"Anything?" Friedman asked.

Ted shook his head. "I need to get closer, to make sure they're both in there."

"And alive," Friedman suggested.

"And alive," Ted agreed.

"I don't understand," the doctor said. "I thought you intended to—"

"Secure him," Ted told Friedman. "I'll be back as soon as I've had a look."

"Come on, Doc." Friedman pushed the older man toward the narrow hall.

The doctor's incensed complaints followed Ted out the door.

He opened his cell to put through a call to Simon, but again, there was no service.

Damned desert.

There wasn't a lot to use for cover, but Ted utilized what was available. Rocks, sand, a few scrub bushes. Mostly he used a wide berth. If Soto and Vandiver were inside and worried about unexpected company, they would be keeping an eye on the road.

The closer he came to the neighboring house, the more care he took in his movements. He wasn't aware of Soto or Vandiver carrying a weapon, but there was a lot in this case that no one had been aware of.

In the rear a deck and basic landscaping foliage provided a small amount of cover. He chose what he hoped would be a bedroom window for taking his first look inside and eased closer.

No television or music sounds inside. No conversation, either.

He hoped the two hadn't been executed.

Drapes were drawn over the window with just enough of a crack between them for him to get a narrow view inside. He studied the scene a moment to ensure he had a firm visual on both Vandiver and Soto.

Definitely.

The two were not only there. They were very much alive and in bed, expressing their mutual desire.

One window at a time, Ted checked them all. Like the house across the road, two bedrooms, a bath and a great room. No one else appeared to be in the house. The only sign of occupancy was the trail of clothing the two had made starting in the great room.

Somehow he had to figure out a way to get word to Simon that he'd found the missing lovers and there was no sign of the spurned wife.

If necessary, he would send Friedman back out to the main highway to make the call.

As he made his way back across the road, a number of questions crossed his mind. If Soto had no fear of repercussions from Romero, why hide out? And if she did, this was not exactly the best hiding place. Romero owned the place.

Lastly, at this point would one of them actually be afraid the wife was onto them?

Or after them?

And why the hell had Heather Vandiver Tasered a representative of the agency she'd hired to help her?

Had it been someone else? Someone who'd slipped in beneath Rocky's radar and abducted the woman?

Too many questions.

No answers.

Chapter Fifteen

"Something is way, way wrong with this whole scenario," Nora repeated as she paced the main room of the house. The effects of the drug had finally worn off, or maybe she'd worked them off. At least she felt like herself again.

Despite the fact that neither of them had eaten in hours. They were utterly exhausted and things just kept getting more complicated. This investigation stunk to high heaven. No doubt the good doctor tied up in the back bedroom thought, so as well.

"I agree." Tallant plowed his fingers through his hair.

Nora shouldn't have been so captivated by the move but she was. She was tired. Closing her eyes, she gave herself a shake. She needed sleep. And food.

"Our first priority," he said, drawing her attention back to him, "should be contacting the agency. Right now we're operating in the dark, and no one can help us if they have no idea where we are and what we need."

He had no service on his cell. She had none on hers. He'd suggested she drive out to the main highway and try it from there. She supposed that was the only logical thing to do.

"Wait." She didn't realize she'd said the word aloud until he turned to face her. "The doctor's a local. His carrier may have service out here in the middle of nowhere."

That nice mouth of his tilted upward on one side. "You may be onto something, Friedman."

Tallant dashed out to the car and retrieved the doc's cell, as well as the one he'd taken from the guard. "The guard's has a pass code, but the doc's has full service," he said as he entered the necessary numbers.

About time they had an actual break.

She collapsed on the plaid sofa while he gave Simon Ruhl an update. It would have been nice if he'd chosen the speaker option so she could hear the other end of the conversation, but he hadn't.

After a few more questions and pauses, Tallant finally ended the call. He placed the doc's cell phone on the table and sat down next to her.

"Trinity will supposedly be released from detainment within the hour."

"He's coming here?" They could use some backup. Particularly if Romero's people showed up.

"Yes." Tallant propped his forearms on the knees of his spread thighs. "Unfortunately, that's where the good news ends."

"Great." They couldn't call the police. One guy— *one*—was on his way to provide backup. As soon as he was released at the airfield, that was. She and Tallant couldn't just leave, considering their job was to determine what the hell was going on with Vandiver and Soto and the missing wife. Speaking of which, she asked, "What about Heather?"

"The wife is still missing. There've been no hits on public transportation. If she left L.A. via public transit of her own free will, she didn't do it under her own name. We can't be certain she's headed here, but that seems the most logical move."

Which could possibly mean she hadn't done anything of her own free will.

Nora exhaled a big breath. "What're we going to do about Ivan?" He wouldn't give up. As long as they were within his reach, he represented a lethal threat. Yet they couldn't leave with this investigation unfinished. With more questions than they'd had before coming to Las Vegas.

Tallant stood, walked over to the dining table. "I've been thinking about that." He picked up the keys to the doctor's car. "I want you to drive out of here. Don't stop for anything but gas. Get back to Chicago as quickly as you can. Trinity will be here before long. I'll be fine until then."

Nora pushed to her feet. Didn't say a word until she got toe to toe with him. "Do you really believe I would ditch you? Just drive off into the sunset and leave you with this mess to clean up? Then you don't know me the way you think you do."

"Technically you would be driving away from the sunrise."

"Look." She stabbed him in that broad chest with her forefinger. "Just because you have a problem with me is no reason to play stupid."

He folded his hand over hers, capturing the offending finger in a strong grip. "This isn't about our bickering…before."

Somehow—maybe she truly had gone stupid—his eyes looked sad…worried. For her. She had to be imagining things. Yeah, he'd saved her butt back there. But she knew exactly where she stood with this guy—at the top of his frustration and irritation list.

"Then what is it about, Mr. I-have-to-prove-I'm-better?" This whole merger had been a bad idea. The Colby Agency investigators always had to come out on top, had to be right, had to be the heroes.

"It's about saving your life."

If he hadn't said it so softly, hadn't looked at her as if she were his top priority, maybe she wouldn't have had that deep ache tear through her chest. He couldn't possibly care what happened to her one way or another.

"If I go back, you win."

He closed those unusual gold eyes for a moment, as if it hurt too much to look at her. "You win. That's the way we'll write it up. I don't care about that."

"Forget it." She pulled her hand free of his and folded her arms over her chest. "I'm not leaving you here to face this insanity alone." She shook her head. "Not happening."

"You didn't want to work with me in the first place," he offered. "This is your chance to cut your losses. No one will think less of you for doing the smart thing."

She stared at those nice lips of his, wanted to pretend that she wasn't desperate to see what they tasted like. "Maybe I will." She lifted one eyebrow in challenge. "What do you say to that, Mr. Tallant?"

"That it would be the right decision. The smart decision."

"You really are crazy." She shook her head, told herself not to do what her entire body was urging her to do. "Fine…I'll…" She snatched the keys from his hand. "I'll just go."

"Stay off the beaten path," he advised.

He was willing to let her go—to let her run to safety while he stayed here and played the decoy.

She shoved the keys into his pocket. "No way. I'm not going anywhere."

He said nothing, just stared at her lips as if he didn't understand the words she had uttered.

"Stop."

His gaze lifted to hers. He blinked. "What?"

"Stop staring at my mouth."

He swallowed visibly. "I...was thinking."

Yeah, so was she. Usually that was a good thing, but in this case it was a problem.

He said nothing.

She said nothing.

They just stood there staring at each other.

"This is ridiculous." She grabbed him by the shoulders, went up on tiptoe and kissed him firmly on the mouth.

When she eased back down onto the soles of her feet, he just kept staring at her.

Maybe she should have left.

His arms suddenly went around her waist, pulled her against him, and he kissed her hard...long... deep.

The kiss was worth every moment of frustration and irritation and waiting.

His mouth was hot and firm and damned skilled. He tasted as good as he looked. Her arms found their way around his neck. Her fingers threaded into his hair. She'd wanted to do that for so long.

He lifted her against him. Her legs instinctively wrapped around his waist as he turned and lowered her on the table.

She was already unbuttoning his shirt. She needed to touch his skin. The fire he'd ignited raged through her. Made her want to rip off every thread he wore. But just touching his chest…smoothing her palms over that rippled terrain was enough…for now.

Using both hands, he slipped off her shoes, then reached for the zipper of her slacks. She wiggled, the need swelling so fast, she could scarcely control her body's determination to meld with his.

He dragged the slacks down her legs, off one foot and then the other. He hesitated, stared at her injured ankle. "What happened?"

"It's nothing." She didn't want to talk.… She wanted him to continue what he'd started. When he still hesitated, she muttered, "One of Ivan's dogs."

"We need to take care of that."

"Later." She moved his hand up her thigh. His fingers splayed on her skin, made her gasp.

He burrowed two fingers beneath the silk of her panties.

She bit down on her lip to hold back a cry of sheer want.

For one long moment he hesitated again. When her eyes fluttered open, she realized that he was staring out the window, checking the house across the road.

A smile tugged at her lips. He wanted her. No doubt about that. She could feel how hard he was. But he wasn't about to fall down on the job. She liked that a lot. He was a man after her own heart.

Convinced there was no immediate threat, he wrenched open his trousers. She helped, sighing with satisfaction as her fingers wrapped around his full arousal.

He pushed the damp panel of her panties aside and thrust inside her. Her body contracted, drawing him more deeply inside.

He leaned down, braced an arm on the table on either side of her, then kissed her. Softly at first. He held still when she desperately wanted him to move. To kiss her harder. To start that rhythmic friction her body was screaming for.

She loved the feel of his skin…the sensation of how completely he filled her. And the taste of his lips. She'd told herself she wanted to slap his face so many times. But it wasn't true. She'd wanted to kiss him. To shut that smart mouth of his by covering it with her own. To have him just like this…someplace wholly inappropriate and dangerous.

The waves of completion started deep inside her. She bucked to get him moving. She couldn't wait any longer. She needed him to…to keep touching her. His hands began to slowly trace her body. Rubbing, squeezing her breasts. Lifting her hips just enough to bury himself more completely inside her. Then those skilled fingers flowed over her bare legs, positioned them forward for deeper penetration.

She couldn't stop it. She came.

He held still and watched.

When she could think again, she grabbed him by the back of the neck and pulled his face to hers. She kissed him so hard, their teeth scraped together. She wrapped her legs around his waist and started a rhythm of her own. He growled into her mouth. She didn't slow, just kept pumping, dragging her hot, slick walls along that hard, solid length.

He tried to slow her frantic movements, but he couldn't control her…. She couldn't control herself. She was lost to the rhythm and to the new rise of pleasure.

He pulled her against his chest, carried her to the wall next to the window.

She was gasping for air as he took yet another

seemingly endless moment to check out the house across the road.

How could he have that kind of discipline?

She couldn't think, much less see anything but *him*.

His gaze collided with hers once more and he gave her his full attention. He pressed her back against the wall and set his own ruthless pace. Her nails buried into his back. His mouth sealed over hers.

He drove into her over and over until she came yet again before he finally gave in to his own pleasure.

When his body was spent, he sagged against her, gasping for air just as she did.

"I wanted to do that," he murmured as he teased her lips with his teeth, "every time I watched you walk down the hallway at the agency. Every single time you lashed me with that wicked tongue of yours. I've wanted you so damned bad. I didn't want to…I called it a lot of other things. But *this* is what I wanted."

"I knew you'd be good," she confessed with a soft, breathy laugh. "I've watched you move." She rocked her pelvis into his. "Until I thought I'd go crazy if I didn't figure out a way to get you out of my system."

He searched her eyes. "Is that what we just did?"

She had to smile at his uncertainty. Usually it was

the woman feeling uncertain about now. "No. I think you just planted yourself as deep as you can get."

He lowered his lips to hers, kissed her with infinite tenderness. How could a man capable of doing what he'd just done to her against the wall kiss so sweetly?

"I suppose," he said finally, when they both needed air, "we should get focused on the case again."

"Yeah." She rubbed his nose with her own. "We wouldn't want to get caught with our pants down." She squeezed his bare bottom with both hands. "Now, would we?"

He smiled. "Guess not."

She really, really liked the way he smiled.

She lowered her feet to the floor but hated so badly to let him pull away. That connection had felt more right than any she'd shared…ever.

Strange. He was the last person she'd expected to connect with.

Her abdomen clenched at the idea of what Ivan Romero had had planned for her.

If that vicious animal had his way, she would never know just how right things between her and Ted Tallant could be.

Chapter Sixteen

9:00 a.m.

Ted stood at the corner of the wraparound deck. Soto's sedan remained in front of the house across the road. That she'd parked in front felt wrong. Was it a signal?

There had been no traffic on this stretch of desolate road.

The only good news was that Trinity had been released after hours of detainment at the airfield. The problem now involved his getting here without being followed. Romero's people would be watching him. To come straight here would no doubt bring trouble right to their door.

None of that included the fact that Ted had stepped way out of line.

He'd made love to Nora…Friedman.

A knot of mixed emotions tangled in his gut. What the hell had he been thinking?

They couldn't stand the sight of each other. Working together had been the dead last thing either one of them had wanted to do.

But that had been before…before he'd known just how brave the sassy woman was. The risks she dared to solve a case.

And the way she'd stood up to a man like Romero.

She'd risked her life to save the life of another woman and her unborn child. Nora Friedman had sacrificed more than Ted could ever have imagined her capable to ensure the safe and happy future of a victim.

Incredible.

How could he have not known this about her?

Because he'd chosen not to look past the kick-butt facade she chose to wear. He now understood that, too. Self-preservation. She'd understood that she could never allow herself to be that vulnerable again.

He should have recognized the depth behind those exotic dark eyes.

He'd read the background on her. Born and raised in the L.A. area by a mother who kept a roof over their heads by selling herself on the street. An absentee father and no options for a future others took for granted.

Nora Friedman had raised herself, had made a life and a future without any foundation...without any help from anyone.

Ted hadn't given her an ounce of credit for that feat.

He'd been too busy fueling his frustration with her attitude.

He was a class-A jerk.

There was no other excuse.

"Look."

Ted turned to face the object of his disturbing musings. She'd managed to get within three feet of him and he hadn't even heard her approach.

Their situation was far too precarious to be so damned distracted.

"Everything okay?" He'd cleaned and bandaged her ankle with a first-aid kit he'd found in the doctor's car.

"Yes."

The way her arms were folded protectively over her chest and the somber expression on her face signaled otherwise. She was as lost in all this as he was.

She lifted one shoulder in a half shrug. "I wanted to dispel any misconceptions about what just happened."

Maybe it was her choice of words, but the idea that she would compartmentalize what they'd shared in such a way rubbed him the wrong way. Ticked him off, actually, and he didn't know what she intended to say yet.

"Let's hear it." He hadn't meant the words to come out in that harsh tone, but it was too late to take it back now. That she flinched tied some more of those knots in his gut.

"The last twenty-four hours have been insane." She lifted one hand and made a vague motion of incredulity. "We've both been wired to the max, totally running on adrenaline."

Here it came.

"Sex is a natural survival instinct. We shouldn't feel awkward about it…or try to dissect it."

"I can't argue with that." Ted turned to scope out the place across the road. There was no reason to debate the point. She obviously didn't feel anything remotely related to a connection—other than the physical. And he…well, he didn't know how he felt.

Now wasn't the time to delve into personal affairs. He knew better.

"I'll check on the doc."

Ted didn't say anything to that or even spare her a glance. Time to get back on track. Without, as she had so eloquently put it, making more out of the moment than it was.

The thought left an emptiness inside him.

He pulled the doctor's cell phone from his pocket and checked the time. Trinity should contact him soon. Simon's Bureau contact hadn't seen any sign of Romero's people sniffing around the Palomino Hotel. By now he had likely given up the search for Ted and Nora. He would be checking flights, buses, rental car agencies. Eventually he would realize that the two of them were still here somewhere.

Romero would pull out all the stops then. He would shake out every sandpile and turn over every rock for fifty miles around Vegas until his gamble paid off.

And he'd found them.

The case—Heather Vandiver's case—kept them from making a move to protect themselves.

They were squarely between a rock and a hard place.

Definitely.

THE OLD GRAY-HAIRED GUY kept moaning and groaning until she removed his gag. "You need water?" She should have asked him that already. He wasn't really an evil person, just a greedy old bastard who'd gotten drawn into Romero's ugly games.

"There's no time."

"What're you talking about?" Nora didn't like the look of him. Paler than before. Feeble almost. "You need water."

"No." He shook his head, tried to wiggle his hands free of the bindings. "I tried to tell you before but you stuck that sock in my mouth." He made a face.

"It was your sock." No "six pairs for a few bucks" special, either. Silk socks. He shouldn't be so incensed.

"Please—" he searched her eyes with his own "—just listen to me."

She felt a little sorry for him, but not enough to untie him or get close enough for him to bite her or something. "Talk fast. I have things to do." Like wash the scent of Tallant off her skin. That her body trembled at the thought of his name made her want to scream.

She would kick herself for this later. When she had Romero off her back and this case was settled.

"He'll come after us. It's a miracle he's not here already."

Now she recognized what it was that looked so different about the doc. He wasn't sick or feeble. He was scared to death. "What do you mean? He doesn't know where we are." Just because Romero owned the place didn't mean he would look here first.

"The car—" he swallowed with effort "—there's a tracking device on the car."

Adrenaline roared through Nora's veins. "Your car?" She knew this without asking.... Her mouth just hadn't caught up with her brain.

He nodded. "He'll kill me, too. You were supposed to let me go."

Holy... "Tallant!"

Nora raced to the front door, ignored the doctor's frantic shouts behind her.

Tallant stopped her bolt out the door with his wide shoulders. "What?"

"The car." She hitched a thumb toward the back of the house. "It has a tracking device. Romero knows exactly where we are."

As if her words had summoned it, the military-style SUV, a trail of dust in its wake, barreled into view on the long sand and gravel road.

"Back in the house," Tallant ordered.

This was her fault. Other people were going to die because of what she'd done five years ago.

"I have to hide the doc." She didn't wait for Tallant's approval. When she reached the back bedroom, the old man had managed to get into an upright position on the bed and was ranting at her to help him. She shook him to get his attention. "Listen to me."

Miraculously his mouth closed.

"I'm going to untie you so you can hide." When he would have started his tirade again, she put a hand over his mouth. "Do what I say and you'll be fine. We'll tell Ivan that we tossed you out on the road without your cell phone or anything. Okay?"

He nodded. She dropped her hand away from his face and quickly untied his hands and feet. With a quick shove, she hid the bindings, including the gag, between the mattress and box springs. Then she considered the limited options for hiding the old man.

The doc was a smallish man. Not any taller than her and thin.

The one decent possibility that came to mind might just work.

"Come on." She grabbed him by the arm and headed to the great room.

Where the hell was Tallant?

In the kitchen, she opened the doors beneath the sink. The base cabinet would be a tight fit, but if he curled up and stayed put, it could work. She gestured inside. "Get in."

He started to argue but decided against it. The task wasn't easy, but he curled up and got himself jammed into the small space.

"Do not make a sound," she warned. "No matter what you hear."

He tried to nod but there wasn't enough room to do it right.

She closed the doors, palmed her weapon and moved to one of the windows that looked out across the front of the property.

The SUV pulled into the driveway and stopped midway between the road and the house. What were they waiting for?

Then she saw the first of Romero's team.

Another one…then another.

The three circled the house.

A fourth man remained at the SUV.

Romero was in there. Otherwise all four would have been surrounding or busting into the place, rather than only three.

Where was Tallant?

She moved noiselessly through the house to check out the views from other windows. Approaching each window carefully in the event one of those bastards had the same idea about getting a peek inside, she moved from one room to the next.

If Ted was…Tallant…if Tallant was out there, the odds were stacked seriously against him.

Nora moved back to a window that offered a view of the SUV and its vigilant guard. Romero had to be in there. It was her he wanted. Getting Tallant killed was wrong. Just wrong.

If she provided a diversion, at least he'd have a shot at getting away.

It was her only option.

From her position to the right of the front door, she reached for the knob, gave it a twist, then swung it toward the opposite wall.

The continued silence surprised her. She'd expected the guard posted at the SUV to take a shot.

Keeping out of sight next to the door, she pulled the weapon from her waistband at the small of her back, checked to see that it was on safety, then tossed it out onto the deck.

Still no reaction from the guard.

"I'm coming out," she shouted.

No response. No sound at all.

Taking a deep breath, she sidestepped into the open doorway.

The guard leveled a bead on her, center chest.

The red spot from the laser beam confirmed her assessment.

Hands up, she started across the porch.

She felt fairly confident that he wouldn't shoot her. No, Romero wanted to savor that duty himself.

Down one step, then two.

Still no sign of Tallant or the other three from Romero's security team.

Strange.

But then, every damned thing about this investigation had been strange.

Third step. And then the final one to the ground.

She kept an eye on the guard as she approached him.

"Round up your friends and let's go," she suggested.

She didn't have to see his glare, couldn't since he wore sunglasses, but she could feel his contempt.

"Get in. Rear passenger seat."

"Whatever you say."

She walked around him to the passenger side and opened the back door.

"I'm really quite annoyed, Nora."

She smiled at Romero. "That—" she climbed into the seat next to him "—actually makes me happier than you know." She closed the door.

Before she could settle into the seat, the back of his hand slammed across her face.

Her cheek and nose stung, eyes watered. But she refused to make even a whimper of distress. She settled into position and stared at him. "You always did enjoy torturing those weaker than you." The whole getting knocked around thing was getting old.

"Only those who lack the discipline to follow my orders." He rapped on the window.

The guard posted at the front of the SUV immediately stalked to the driver's door.

Nora stole a glance at the house. Had Tallant been taken down? If so, where were the three jerks who'd arrived with Romero?

"What's the status of the others?" Romero asked the man as he slid behind the steering wheel.

"Nonresponsive."

Hope bloomed in Nora's chest. Had Tallant managed to take down all three?

"Let's go," Romero ordered.

"We dumped your doctor," Nora said, more to distract him from the windows as the SUV backed toward the road than to give the doc a cover. "Hope you don't mind."

Romero shot her a glower. "My staff is fully expendable."

Nora wondered what his driver thought of that. "Where's your number one bully, Lott?" It struck her as odd that he hadn't arrived with Romero. Usually he would have been the one providing his personal security.

"He had an unfortunate accident," Romero replied.

The driver snickered.

Romero had killed him. Or had him killed. Nora's stomach clenched. For allowing her to escape.

"One day someone will stop you, Ivan," she warned. "It's only a matter of time."

He smiled at her. That repulsive, sinister expression that screamed of evil victory. "But not today." He reached into his jacket and withdrew a small-caliber handgun. Elegant pearl handle. "I've been saving this for a special occasion."

Nora's pulse skipped into a rapid staccato. "For blowing your brains out?" She couldn't think of anything more special than that.

That evil gaze narrowed.

"Oh, wait." She bopped the heel of her hand against her forehead. "What am I thinking? You have to have a brain before you can blow it out."

He jammed the shiny muzzle against her forehead. "You are not nearly so smart as you think, Nora. Your luck just ran out."

"What the hell?" echoed from the front seat.

The gun still boring into Nora's skull, Romero glanced at his driver. "What?"

"There's a car—"

Something hit the back of the SUV. Hard. Nora bumped the back of the seat in front of her. Romero did the same. The SUV sped up, propelling them both back into their seats.

Nora grabbed Romero's wrist, shoved his arm upward.

An explosion echoed inside the vehicle. Glass shattered behind her.

She shoved harder, pushing him into the door on his side of the vehicle. There was nothing she could do but try to keep the business end of the weapon pointed away from her.

Another jolt against the back of the vehicle, throwing Nora on top of Romero. His surprise gave her enough leverage to push his hand fully away from her.

A second explosion rent the air.

The SUV swerved...bumped across the ditch.

The weapon flew out of Romero's hand.

Nora scrambled onto the floorboard after it.

Romero climbed over the seat.

Nora's fingers wrapped around the pearl handle.

The SUV lurched.

A jolting stop.

Suddenly the vehicle was falling...onto its side.

Her stomach rocketed into her throat as she rolled with the momentum.

The crash seemed to echo forever.

For a moment she lay there, attempting to gather her wits. The engine still hummed.

Her fingers remained clasped around the butt of the weapon.

Where was Romero?

She got herself into an upright position and peered over the seat.

The driver's head was bleeding.

Romero lay crumpled between the steering wheel and the windshield.

Nora blinked. He was still breathing. No blood that she could see. His right leg was in bad shape. Twisted at an odd angle. When he regained consciousness, that was going to hurt like hell.

Only the driver was bleeding.

She reached around to check his pulse.

Shock radiated through her.

He was dead.

Then she saw the reason.

The blood had oozed from a small hole in the back of his head. She leaned down to get a look at his face. No exit wound that she could see.

Even though she didn't care if he was dead or alive, she checked Romero's pulse, as well. Just to be sure. She made a disparaging sound. You couldn't kill an evil bastard like that.

"Nora!"

Her heart leaped. Tallant…Ted. "Yeah, I'm okay!"

It took him a minute to get a door open, but he managed. Tears welled in her eyes. If he hadn't given chase and rammed the SUV…

He pulled her out, dragged her into his arms.

"What the hell did you do that for? You should have stayed in the house."

She hugged him hard, the damned little gun still clutched in her hand. "I didn't want him to kill you because of me."

Ted drew back and stared into her eyes. "I had things under control."

She shook her head. Swiped at the moisture on her cheeks. "I didn't know. I was afraid…for you."

"Come on." He pulled her against him. "I called for emergency medical support. They'll be here soon. Trinity Barrett is on his way, as well."

She glanced back at the overturned SUV. "Maybe that bastard will die before they get here."

"He's not going to get away this time," Ted assured her. "The Colby Agency won't stop until he's finished."

That was one thing Nora understood now with complete certainty. The Colby Agency was a force to be reckoned with. Even if they did play so close to the rules.

She stalled. "There's another vehicle at the house where Dr. Vandiver and Camille Soto are hiding out."

Before the words were fully out of her mouth, Ted was running in that direction.

A little wobbly at first, Nora raced after him.

To Nora's knowledge, Mrs. Vandiver had not been found. The idea that Dr. Vandiver was convinced his wife was trying to kill him sent a new fire into Nora's muscles.

If she had given Rocky the slip…had gotten here somehow…

She might have killed Vandiver and his mistress already.

Chapter Seventeen

Ted pressed his ear to the wall near the front entrance in an attempt to make out the shouted words from inside.

Female. Two different voices.

Confirmed his assumption that Heather Vandiver was here. The rental in the driveway bore a California license plate.

He held up a hand as Nora neared the steps, then motioned for her to go around back. She hustled around the corner of the house.

Male voice.

Dr. Vandiver.

Whatever was happening inside, it was growing increasingly tense as Ted listened.

He reached toward the door, rapped hard.

The shouting stopped.

Ted banged on the door a second time.

Scrambling sounds inside had him reaching for the knob.

More shouts. A scream.

Weapon drawn, Ted burst through the door.

Heather Vandiver waved a handheld device at him.

Taser.

That certainly answered one question.

Dr. Vandiver stood next to the bed, his boxers hanging on his hips.

Camille Soto, the other woman in this awkward triangle, stood at the other end of the bed, a sheet draped around her.

"Who're you?" Heather demanded.

"He's from the Colby Agency," Soto said, her expression reflecting the terror in her voice. "He's here to protect Brent."

"Put down the Taser," Ted said firmly. "Put it down and we'll talk."

Heather shook her head, waved the Taser. "No." She glanced at the gun but seemed unaffected by it.

"Dr. Vandiver, step away from the bed." Ted hitched his head toward the front of the house. "Move toward the door."

Vandiver sidled away from the bed.

"Don't you dare," Heather howled at him. "You're not going anywhere, you bastard."

Ted couldn't exactly shoot the woman. Her weapon wasn't exactly deadly—in most instances. In an effort to lessen the tension, he lowered his weapon. "Mrs. Vandiver, I understand you're upset. But this isn't the answer. Put down the Taser and let's call Victoria." He hoped the mention of her cousin's name would snap her out of this irrational state.

She turned her attention to Soto. "Do it."

Soto's eyes widened. "I...don't know what you mean."

Ted studied the woman wrapped in the sheet. She was lying. She looked scared as hell, but more than that, she looked as if she'd been cornered.

"I paid you," Heather shouted. "I paid you a lot of money."

Soto was shaking her head and inching away from the foot of the bed.

"You paid her for what?" Ted asked quietly. No need to amp up the anxiety level.

Heather jerked her attention toward him. "To kill that bastard." She nodded toward her husband. "He cheated on me one time too many. I wasn't about to give him a divorce and end up with only half of what I'd earned putting up with his indifference and infidelity all these years."

"She's crazy!" Soto shouted, stumbling back a

couple more steps. "I don't know what she's talking about."

"That's impossible." Vandiver moved toward his wife. "You're lying."

Ted grabbed him by the arm and hauled him back. "Let's not get excited here. Look." Ted tucked his weapon into his waistband. "There's no need for this to get out of control."

Heather laughed. "I might be crazy, but at least I'm not stupid." She laughed again. "You thought she cared about you." Heather shook her head. "She was going to kill you." Her expression turned dark and angry. "But when she stopped returning my calls and the two of you disappeared, I knew I'd been double-crossed."

"Prove it," Soto challenged. "No one's going to believe you."

Heather nodded. "I thought you might say that." Heather reached into her pocket.

Ted's hand went back to the butt of his weapon.

Heather pulled a mini recorder from her pocket and waved it. "How's this for proof?" She pressed Play.

"I have a plan for taking care of him."

Camille Soto's voice.

"Make the deposit and this will be his last trip to Vegas."

A damning statement by Ms. Soto.

"I can't believe this," Vandiver muttered.

"You stupid, stupid man," Heather taunted her husband. "The only thing any woman would want from you is your bank account."

Sirens wailed in the distance.

"We'll let the authorities sort this out," Ted suggested, thankful help was close.

"I'm not taking the fall for this," Soto shouted. The sheet dropped to the floor, revealing her nude body and the handgun she'd been hiding under the wrinkled linens. "We'll just all go to hell together."

"Lower the weapon, Ms. Soto," Ted warned.

"You bitch!" Heather screamed. "You promised!"

"Since your antidepressants and sedatives didn't work," Soto said, leveling a bead on Heather, "maybe this will."

Ted dived at Heather, knocked her to the floor.

A bullet zinged past his ear, lodged in the wall next to the door.

"Get down!" Ted shouted at Vandiver.

Another gunshot.

Vandiver hit the floor.

Ted moved to scramble toward Heather.

A series of shots hit the ceiling.

Nora was struggling with the woman, the still discharging weapon's muzzle pointed upward.

Where the hell had Nora come from?

Ted grabbed the Taser and lunged into the fray.

He pushed Nora aside and jammed the Taser against Soto's naked torso.

She stiffened. The weapon clattered to the floor. Soto crumpled into a heap.

Ted turned to check on the others. Heather was crawling toward the weapon Soto had dropped.

Ted kicked the weapon out of her reach.

Nora jerked Heather to her feet and restrained her.

Vandiver hadn't moved.

Ted knelt down next to him. The man had covered his head with his arms. Blood spilled from his shin. He was hit, but it didn't look serious.

"Help is here, Dr. Vandiver," Ted assured him. "Let's get you out of the path of the door." He'd heard the slamming vehicle doors outside.

Vandiver shook his head, tears rolling down his cheeks. "I loved them both."

Ted glanced up at Nora, who still had a grip on Heather Vandiver. Nora rolled her eyes.

Ted stifled a laugh.

This wasn't funny.
It was crazy sad.
But, for this case, it was over.

Chapter Eighteen

Colby Agency, Chicago
Thursday, 2:00 p.m.

Victoria closed the file on her cousin's case. She still felt some amount of astonishment at the news of her deadly deception.

Jim heaved a heavy breath. "I'm certain the psychological analysis will reveal the motive for this incredible turn of events."

Victoria nodded sadly. Jim was correct. Heather would be evaluated to determine if she was fit to stand trial. "I can't help feeling as if I should have kept in touch. Perhaps I would have noticed something was very wrong."

"Mother." Jim eased forward in his chair, braced his clasped hands on her desk.

It still made her smile when he called her "Mother."

She should be accustomed to it by now, but perhaps she never would be.

"As much as you want to," Jim went on, "you cannot save the world."

"*We* can attempt to save our clients," she suggested, emphasizing the *we*.

He nodded. "One case at a time." He paused. "Simon's contact passed along the news that Ivan Romero is now facing a number of federal, as well as local, charges for his crimes. Camille Soto turned state's evidence against him to secure a lighter sentence for her part in the conspiracy against Dr. Vandiver."

"That's certainly good news." Victoria was immensely thankful that Nora had not become another of his victims. That monster deserved to spend the rest of his sadistic life behind bars.

"I've given Tallant and Nora a few days' R & R," Jim added.

"They made an excellent team." Victoria was quite impressed at how well yet another Equalizer–Colby investigator team had worked together.

Jim reclined in his chair, studied Victoria a moment. "*We* make an excellent team."

"Yes," she agreed. "We do."

"Tasha and I thought we'd host the annual agency barbecue at our house this year."

Tasha, Jim's wife, was a true jewel. Victoria

couldn't be happier with her daughter-in-law. "That's an excellent idea."

The Fourth of July was coming up next week. Jim's suggestion was yet another step toward the complete cohesion of the merger.

"Perhaps Ian and Nicole will be able to attend," Victoria noted, "and show off the new baby." Ian Michaels was one of Victoria's seconds in command, along with Simon Ruhl. Ian and his wife, Nicole, had welcomed their third child only four days ago. Tasha, Jim's wife, was due any day with their second child. Life at the Colby Agency was truly blessed.

"Tasha would love that. She's so ready for our son to be born."

A recent visit to the doctor's office had confirmed that the baby was indeed a boy. Victoria was beside herself with joy. Her son couldn't possibly love his daughter, Jamie, more, but she knew how very much he wanted a boy.

"You and Tasha are still set on the name you've chosen?" Victoria felt giddy each time she thought of how thrilled her husband would be when he heard the news.

"Lucas James Colby," Jim confirmed. "Luke."

Victoria's heart filled with pride. "Lucas will be ecstatic."

The intercom on Victoria's desk buzzed. She

pushed the button for the speaker option. "Yes, Mildred." Mildred, her longtime personal assistant, wouldn't have interrupted a meeting between Victoria and Jim had it not been urgent.

"Victoria, Jim," said Mildred, sounding a little giddy herself, "Tasha and Jamie have just left the Pier with one of Chicago PD's finest."

Victoria's breath hitched.

Jim sat up straight. "What happened?"

"Labor, dear boy," Mildred enthused. "The two of you need to get to the hospital now."

The next few seconds were a blur of grabbing keys and phones and shouting orders to Mildred as she followed them to the elevator.

Once they were in Jim's SUV and headed for the hospital, Victoria managed a deep breath. She turned to her son and smiled. "We are so very fortunate."

He braked for a traffic signal, sent a return smile in her direction. "Yes, we are."

She reached over and placed her hand atop the one he had resting on the console. "Finally." A realization struck Victoria. "Oh, my." She grabbed her purse. "I'd better call Lucas!"

Jim laughed. "He's former CIA, Mother. He probably already knows and is at the hospital, waiting for us to catch up."

Victoria entered his number all the same. "You could be right."

She relaxed in her seat and waited for her husband to answer her call.

Together they would witness this miracle and welcome the newest member of the Colby family.

3:00 p.m.

NORA SHUT OFF THE VACUUM cleaner and listened.

Rapping on her front door confirmed that she'd heard something.

She hurried down the hall and to the door. A quick peek through the security peephole made her smile.

Ted.

He'd called her at midnight last night just to ensure she was okay.

How could she have ever thought he was anything less than sweet and...well, handsome as hell?

Truth was, she'd recognized the latter the first time she laid eyes on him. She just hadn't wanted to admit it.

She started to open the door but hesitated. With a quick glance in the mirror by the coatrack, she adjusted her wild ponytail. She looked a mess. Shorts. Cutoff tee. Barefoot.

This morning had brought a burst of energy. She'd gotten up in the mood to clean her apartment.

Not a normal inclination for her.

She blew into her hand to check her breath. Decided she was good to go. And opened the door.

"Hey."

He leaned against the door frame, the short-sleeved button-down shirt and faded jeans making him look even hotter than the suits he wore at the office.

"Hey, yourself," he said, the deep sound of his voice sending shivers along her skin.

"Come in." She backed up a step and opened the door wider.

"If I'm interrupting," he countered, hesitating to cross the threshold.

"Yeah, right." She gestured to the vacuum cleaner. "Like I wouldn't take any excuse to get away from that." Not exactly what she'd meant to say. "Come on." She grabbed him by the arm and dragged him inside.

"I didn't have you pegged as the domestic type."

Nora closed the door and turned to face him, hands on hips. "How exactly did you have me pegged?"

One corner of that sexy mouth tilted wickedly. "I'd better take the Fifth on that one."

"Would you like something to drink? A beer?" Was it too early to be offering beer? "Juice?"

No man ever made her feel awkward. Somehow this one did.

"No, thanks."

"Then sit." She gestured to the sofa.

Thankfully she'd picked up before she'd started vacuuming. Her place had been a mess. Clothes and take-out boxes strewn all over the place.

He swaggered over to the sofa and settled on one end. She draped herself on the arm of the other end.

"So, what're you doing today?" They'd both been given rest days. Definitely a good thing, considering how exhausted she'd been when she finally climbed into her own bed last night.

"Went to the market. Picked up a few things." He shrugged those really nice shoulders. "Went for a run. Worked out at the gym."

God, she hated people who could work forty-eight hours straight and then still go to the gym. "I'm glad you had the energy."

"Habit."

She wasn't about to get on the subject of habits. Chocolate. Wine. Shopping. She had far too many habits in which she liked to indulge.

"I thought maybe you might like to have lunch."

That tingle that started each time she thought of him—even when he wasn't in the room—buzzed to life. "That could work." She stood. "But I need to change first."

"Actually—" he stood as well "—I meant *here*."

Her fridge was distinctly empty.

Before she could say as much, he added, "There's this great place just a few blocks from here that delivers."

"Chinese?" she asked, hoping he was thinking of her favorite take-out joint.

"Definitely. A sort of hole-in-the-wall, but the food is fantastic."

She reached for the phone on the table by the sofa. "I know their number by heart." She entered the number and made a mental note of what he wanted as she waited for an answer.

When the order had been placed and an assurance that it would be twenty to thirty minutes had been given, Nora dropped the phone back into its charger and rummaged around in her brain for what to say next. "Twenty to thirty minutes."

"Good. We can—" he shrugged "—talk for twenty to thirty minutes."

Her head was moving up and down in affirmation. "Talking is good."

"Get to know each other better," he said, clarifying.

"Yeah," she agreed. "There's a lot…to know, I suppose."

"I have two brothers," he said. "And my parents."

She nodded again. "No siblings. A mother somewhere in Cali." She probably should have explained that last part, but she couldn't stop watching his lips.

"I bought a house over in Hyde Park a couple of months ago."

"Nice." And his hands. He had the greatest hands. Broad, powerful…long, blunt-tipped fingers.

"I'm still trying to figure out the whole decorating and furnishing thing."

"Yeah, me, too." Her apartment, other than her meager furniture, looked exactly as it had the day she rented it three years ago. She wouldn't mention that, though.

"I guess we have about fifteen more minutes."

"Fifteen to twenty probably."

Not nearly enough time for what she would love to do with him.

Her heart bumped against her sternum when his gaze settled on her lips.

Their eyes met…and the polite conversation was over.

They lunged into each other's arms.

He kissed her. She loved the way he kissed. The

way his hands moved over her body, lifted her against him.

"We don't have enough time," he murmured against her mouth.

"Fifteen minutes of foreplay." She nibbled on his chin. "We can save the main course for after the delivery."

He eased her back down on the sofa. "Sounds like a plan."

He cupped her breast, made a path down her throat with those amazing lips. She did not want to wait.

"Forget the foreplay." She reached for the fly of his jeans.

"I was hoping you'd say that," he whispered as he slipped his hands into her baggy shorts.

Ten seconds of stripping and he was inside her.

She closed her eyes, relished the incredible sensation.

She couldn't get enough of touching him…of having his weight against her.

It felt so good.

Just like the dream she'd had last night.

Hours and hours of making love with him.

She'd awakened with the strangest urge…the urge to make babies.

Maybe it was all the chatter about new babies at

the agency.… Or maybe it was knowing how close she'd come to losing that precious capacity.

Whatever the case, Ted Tallant was definitely the man she wanted to make babies with.

As his lips melded with hers and his hips began that rhythmic pumping, she had one last fleeting thought.

She'd have to marry him first…make a decent man out of him.

Maybe she'd run that by him later…after this appetizer…and the main course…and maybe even dessert.

* * * * *

COLBY VELOCITY

BY
DEBRA WEBB

This book is dedicated to my two dearest friends,
Vicki Hinze and Peggy Webb. Two of the most amazing ladies
I have ever had the privilege to know and love!

First published in Great Britain 2011
Harlequin Mills & Boon Limited,
Eton House, 18-24 Paradise Road, Richmond, Surrey TW9 1SR

© Debra Webb 2010

ISBN: 978 0 263 88512 5

46-0311

Harlequin Mills & Boon policy is to use papers that are natural, renewable
and recyclable products and made from wood grown in sustainable forests.
The logging and manufacturing processes conform to the legal environmental
regulations of the country of origin.

Printed and bound in Spain
by Litografia Rosés S.A., Barcelona

Chapter One

Kendra Todd surveyed the deserted street. The last of the lingering Fourth of July revelers were only a few blocks over. The fireworks at the Pier crackled in the air, sending sprays of light over the city.

She had attended the agency cookout at Jim Colby's home. Afterward she'd anticipated a quiet evening at her apartment…but that hadn't happened.

Talk about ghosts from the past…. The frantic call she'd received had taken her back several years. Three, to be exact.

To a place she'd just as soon not revisited.

9:04 p.m. He was late.

Kendra tucked her cell phone back into the holster on her belt and surveyed the street once more.

Ten minutes more of hanging around this street corner alone and she was out of here. Whatever her old friend's latest drama…it wasn't hers. Kendra

Todd was no longer a part of the D.C. world of ruthless ambition and colliding egos. In three years she hadn't looked back once.

The move to Chicago was the smartest choice she'd made in a very long time. Working with Chicago PD's community affairs division the first two years of her new Windy City life had been very useful in acquainting herself with this new environment. Last year's offer to join the staff of the Colby Agency had come after working closely with Ian Michaels during the abduction attempt of Victoria Colby-Camp's granddaughter. The opportunity had proven the perfect prompt for Kendra to make a major move toward personally recognizing and professionally achieving a true career goal.

Reaching out to those in need and using the interactive skills she'd honed so well to solve a case satisfied her in a way nothing else about her professional history had. The camaraderie at the Colby Agency surprised her still. For someone who had no family left and who'd walked away from her lifelong friends three years ago, the atmosphere at the agency was spot on. She not only liked her job as an investigator, she also liked being part of something real.

Real life. Real people.

To say this jolt from the past was unwelcome would be a vast understatement. Not that she hadn't kept in touch with a few of her former associates. Christmas cards and the occasional birthday card were exchanged. At first she'd even exchanged e-mails with her former boyfriend, but that had fizzled out after only a few months. But this—tonight—was far from a mere unexpected call from an old colleague.

This was trouble in big, bold letters.

Headlights flashed, drawing her attention to the west end of the block. A dark nondescript sedan had made the turn at the intersection and now rolled slowly in her direction.

She maintained her position against the wall of the closed boutique and watched as the sedan pulled up to the curb directly behind her smaller, two-door sports car. The snazzy red car was her one visible capitulation to vanity. And maybe to independence from all the *red* tape and chaos of so-called organized government.

The driver's door opened and she held her breath. As soon as the head and torso rose from behind the wheel of the car she squinted to identify the driver. The street lamp's glow spread across the hood of the sedan but fell short of providing sufficient illumination beyond the windshield. But she would know that tall, slim frame anywhere…even in the dark.

Yoni Sayar straightened his suit jacket and shoved the car door closed.

Kendra couldn't deny some sense of sentimentality at seeing him. Three years was a long time and they had been good friends.

"Kendra." He smiled as he strode toward her.

"It's good to see you," she confessed before accepting his quick, firm embrace.

Tall, thin and dark, Yoni was a natural born American but his parents were Israeli immigrants. Both had worked hard to ensure he received the best education possible and were extraordinarily proud of his accomplishments. A master's degree in global communications was complemented by his ability to speak a number of languages with incredible ease and fluency. He'd turned down numerous lucrative corporate offers to pursue his goal of making a difference in the merciless world of politics. A lobbyist who supported the rights of main street Americans over those of corporate America.

Yoni was one of the good guys. He'd worked hard to earn the respect of the most powerful senators and congressional members, including Senator Judd Castille, Kendra's former boss.

After a thorough scrutiny of her face, he said, "You look very happy." He nodded his approval. "Happy and stress-free."

A moment's hesitation passed before she admitted, "I'm very happy." Old habits died hard. Even with a good friend like Yoni, the political arena had made her wary of the slightest personal confession. "The Colby Agency is great. It's the best move I could have made."

He surveyed the deserted street. "I'm very pleased to hear this." His tone gave away his distraction more so than his not so discreet surveillance of their surroundings.

"Would you like to have coffee while we talk?" He'd insisted on meeting someplace where they wouldn't be seen. Another learned trait of the political life. Still, surely he didn't expect to talk right here on the street, deserted or not. He'd come all this way, the least she could do was buy him a cup of coffee.

He shook his head. "I can't risk being seen."

With you. That he didn't verbalize that part disturbed her on some level. She and Senator Castille had parted on less than favorable terms. That was no secret. The rumors that had at first buzzed in the media were quickly squashed by Castille's people. It was completely understandable that Yoni would not want to be spied collaborating with the enemy.

Even three years later she remained the enemy.

"All right." She gestured to her car. "Why don't we sit in my car?"

He glanced nervously at the vehicle parked in front of his rental. "Well…we can do that."

That his uneasiness continued to mount triggered the first, distant alarm. Kendra led the way, hitting the remote and unlocking the doors as they reached the vehicle. She settled behind the steering wheel and waited until he'd slid into the passenger seat next to her before locking the doors once more.

"You bought a new car." He looked around the interior, surprise in his expression. "It's very nice." He managed a lackluster smile. "It suits you."

"It was time." The interior lights dimmed automatically, leaving them in darkness.

It was his turn to speak. This was his rendezvous after all. Yet the silence dragged on several seconds adding to Kendra's uneasiness. "Why don't you start at the beginning?" No point beating around the bush. He'd asked for this meeting, had taken a flight, rented a car and met her in an out-of-the-way location. A scene right out of an espionage movie.

Yoni released a big breath. "You know how Castille is. If he smells trouble…"

Trouble. There it was. She'd known it was coming. "I thought you and Castille were still tight." The truth was, when Castille had targeted her, Yoni hadn't gone out of his way to back her up. She'd understood at the time, still did actually. Once Castille had decided she was out, no one or nothing was going to change his mind. Yoni sticking his neck out

Did you know you could have received this book before it hit the shops?

Visit www.millsandboon.co.uk

MILLS & BOON

For access to all the latest Mills and Boon titles before they hit the shops visit www.millsandboon.co.uk

For a limited time only, we are offering you **15% OFF** your order when you enter the code 15MAR11 at the checkout. **But hurry**, this offer ends on 31st May 2011.

PLUS, by ordering online you will receive all these extra benefits:

- Be the first to hear about exclusive offers in our eNewsletter

- Try before you buy! You can now browse the first chapter of each of our books online

- Order books from our huge back list at a discounted price

- Join the M&B community and discuss your favourite books with other readers

MAR

and damaging his own position with the arrogant senator wouldn't have helped Kendra.

Political life was ruthless.

A frown furrowed across her brow as all those frustrating memories tumbled into vivid recollection. How the heck had she allowed herself to be dragged back into this vicious cycle?

"What sort of trouble?" And what did it have to do with her? Kendra tamped down the frustration. She reminded herself that she'd heard something in his voice that concerned her when he'd called. She couldn't just ignore him if he really needed help.

"I'm certain you've heard about the Transparency Bill."

She'd heard. Anyone who read the newspaper or watched the news likely knew of it. The bill was a very progressive action that had raised lots of eyebrows, particularly on Capitol Hill. Ultimately if the bill was passed, the way lobbyists and special interests groups worked would be forever changed. For the better. Though those lobbyists and special interest groups didn't see it that way.

"Castille supports it," she acknowledged. That she knew based on the headlines. "He's taken a lot of heat from the groups he once allowed to bolster his nest egg." Oh, yes. Castille was one rich old man. He'd reveled in the fringe benefits of those who lobbied for his support. Now that he was nearing retirement he'd opted to man-up and do what no other senator before him had had the courage to do. Limit the behind-the-scenes influence and reach of all those very groups who fueled the power.

"He has persuaded a number to follow suit," Yoni mentioned, not that it was necessary. Kendra knew very well how much influence Castille wielded.

She turned to her old friend, searched his face. Her eyes had grown accustomed to the low light. "I can see where you might not be a supporter of the proposed legislation."

He shook his head. "I helped design the bill."

"Are you serious?" It was difficult to imagine Yoni, a lobbyist, proposing anything that would limit his ability to do his job. Though his efforts were always forthright and just, there were necessary strategies that those outside the political playing field might not fully understand if those efforts were exposed. Serving the greater good came with a cost—usually associated with providing benefits for certain private groups. It was simply the way the world worked.

Yoni dropped his head back against the seat and released a weary breath. "The whole process has gotten out of control. Someone has to draw a line somewhere. I admire Castille for having the courage to do so."

No question about the need for stronger

boundaries. She'd thought as much three years ago. That was just one of the subjects about which she and Castille had butted heads.

"I can see where that move would make you more than a few enemies." Was that why he'd come to her? Didn't make a whole lot of sense considering she was many degrees removed, but he hadn't actually given her any real specifics yet.

"Frustration, anger, resentment—all those things I anticipated," he explained, "but not the hideous threat of blackmail."

"Blackmail?" Her confusion cleared. "Someone is attempting to blackmail you?"

He nodded. "I have until ten Friday morning to ensure the senator ushers through a couple of amendment attachments or, according to the note I received, I'll face the consequences."

Tension tightened her muscles. "Do you have the note with you?"

He reached inside his summer-weight jacket and pulled out an envelope.

Kendra tapped a button to illuminate a console light. She accepted the envelope and inspected the exterior. His name was carefully printed on the front and nothing more. "Where was it delivered?"

"To my office. It was pushed beneath the door before we opened. I found it this morning."

Which meant anyone could have delivered it.

Yoni's office was in downtown D.C. on a public block with little or no security measures. She opened the envelope and withdrew the single page typed note.

You know what you need to do. Friday, 10:00 a.m. is the deadline. Meet the demand or face the consequences.

"Have you been to the police?" The answer would be no, otherwise they wouldn't be sitting here going through the cloak-and-dagger motions.

"I can't go to the police."

"Why not?" That made no sense. "This threat could be more than an opportunistic scare tactic. You need to take it seriously." He'd been in this business long enough to know this already. Power and money were strong motivators; some would do anything to get their hands on one or both.

"There's another note."

That he didn't make eye contact was more telling than he realized. She'd understood there surely was one or more other notes since this one did not state the precise demands or consequences. "Did you bring that note, as well?" Was he really going to make her ask for every iota of information?

He retrieved another plain white envelope from his interior jacket pocket and handed it to her. When her fingers tightened on the envelope, he hesitated before letting go. "I don't want this ugliness to color your opinion of me." The worry in his eyes backed up the voiced concern.

"You know me better than that." She pulled the envelope free of his hold.

Yoni's name on the front. Inside, the letter was typed just like the other one, except this one was actually a copy of a press statement dated for Friday. The statement explained how a highly respected D.C. lobbyist had more than his share of skeletons in his closet. Kendra felt her jaw drop as she read the accusations that ran the gamut from illicit sexual behavior to fraternizing with known terrorists.

She carefully folded the letter, tucked it into the envelope once more and passed it back to him. "First, I need to know one thing."

"Anything."

'How many of those accusations are true even in the remotest sense?"

"You can't be serious."

The barely restrained inflection of outrage in his tone was without doubt authentic. She knew him well enough to know it when she heard it. Despite how strongly she felt about him as a person, she also fully understood that no one ever knew anyone *completely.* "Not a single word of it?" she pressed.

He moved his head side to side solemnly but firmly. "Not one word."

"I take it you want me to find out who's behind this threat."

Another of those weary sighs escaped his lips. "I didn't want to drag you into this, Kendra. But I'm desperate. There can be no evidence of these accusations because they are irrefutably false. But you know what a scandal like this could do to my reputation. False or not, I would be ruined on too many levels. Not to mention it could serve to undo much of what I've worked so hard to accomplish. I believe it is related to the bill Senator Castille and I are pushing. The bill is far too important to allow extortion to stop it. Can you and this Colby Agency you love so much help me?"

Kendra didn't allow herself the time to think about how she had sworn she would never go back to D.C. This was the trouble she had fully expected when the call had come. Yet, this was Yoni, her friend. A genuine hero of the people.

She couldn't turn her back on him.

"You understand that this will require your complete cooperation?"

"Yes, yes. Whatever you need."

"And we may have to bring the senator into it."

"Whatever we have to do," he reiterated.

"All right. I can help you," she said, determined to make it so, no matter that the voice of reason shouted at her that it was indisputably a mistake. "More important, the Colby Agency can help you."

Chapter Two

Chicago, Wednesday, 5:00 a.m.

The vibration of metal on wood jarred Leland Rockford from a dead sleep. He rolled over and plopped a hand on the table next to his bed. His eyes refused to open as he fumbled across the table top for his cell phone. It shimmied in his hand as he grasped it.

With a flick of his thumb he slid the nuisance open. His eyelids reluctantly raised and he stared at the digital numbers on the alarm clock. 5:01 a.m. Who would call him at such an ungodly hour?

"Rockford," he mumbled, then cleared his throat.

"Rocky, it's Jim. We need you here ASAP."

His boss. Jim Colby's tone was clipped, tense. Not good. After last week's false labor alarm, his boss was seriously on edge. Rocky threw the sheet back and sat up, dropping his feet to the carpeted floor. "What's up?"

"I'm sending you on assignment in D.C. Come prepared to leave immediately."

Rocky scrubbed a hand through his sleep-tousled hair. "On my way."

He closed the phone and dropped it back onto the table. Okay. D.C. That meant he had to pack a suit. He hated suits. Hated dealing with rich hotshots who thought they owned the world.

Exhaling a blast of frustration, he pushed up from the bed. First a quick shower and a cup of coffee to boost his sluggish brain.

"You getting up?"

Damn. He'd forgotten that he had a guest. "Gotta go out of town for work."

The lamp on the right side of the bed switched on, highlighting the blond tresses spread across the pillow next to his. "Now?" she asked, squinting at the light.

"Now. I'll call you when I get back." He didn't wait for additional questions. Time was limited. Jim would be waiting for him.

Hurrying through a hot shower, he dried his hair with the towel then wrapped it around his waist and hesitated before stepping out of the bathroom and into his bedroom. When he did he experienced a distinct sense of relief that his guest hadn't hung around to chat. She'd left a note on his pillow.

I'll be waiting....

Rocky couldn't help feeling a little guilty. She was a nice lady. They'd gone out several times over the past couple of months and he liked her. But he just couldn't see the attraction between them as anything beyond basic lust. To be fair he'd tried. More for her sake than his own. She deserved his respect and at least a half-hearted attempt. Maybe when he returned from D.C. they would have that uncomfortable it's-not-working talk he'd been putting off.

These days he wasn't into pursuing dead ends. Or lust…just for the sake of a good time.

Not that he didn't like bachelorhood or hadn't enjoyed his share of no-strings-attached relationships, but at thirty-five it was getting a bit old. Time to think about a permanent relationship. Maybe even kids. His parents would love that.

That thought kicked his brain into gear.

Had he just used that particular four-letter word?

Kids.

Guys didn't have biological clocks, he was relatively certain, but it sure as hell felt like he could hear one ticking inordinately loudly in some mutinous region of his brain.

He hesitated as he pulled on a pair of jeans. A part of him wanted to deny the concept, but he wasn't into denial, either. Came with the territory when a guy was raised by parents who were practicing psychologists. Denial of one's feelings equated to fear. Suck up some courage and face the facts.

It was time to settle down and do the family thing.

All he had to do was find the right woman. He'd bought the house with the big yard. His finances were in order. Seemed as good a time as any.

All he needed was a good woman who respected his idiosyncrasies and his work. He had plenty of the former, like being a slob around the house. Watching sports and shouting at the refs on the television screen. Preparing gourmet meals. Something he and his father had in common. His entire life Rocky had remained convinced that his father the shrink was in fact a closet chef.

Rocky didn't want anybody in his kitchen. And his work was his top priority. Finding a woman who didn't mind relinquishing control in the kitchen likely wouldn't be a problem. Finding one who could live with him gone for days on end more often than not was another matter altogether. That was going to be the tough hurdle.

He grabbed a shirt from the top of the stack on the chair next to his closet, which was generally about as close to the closet as his laundry made it.

He wasn't worried about finding the right woman. One of these days when he least expected it, he would stumble on the one for him.

He glanced at the note on his pillow. But he wasn't going to hold his breath.

Colby Agency, 7:05 a.m.

"SINCE YONI SAYAR," Jim Colby explained as the briefing in Victoria Colby-Camp's office came to a conclusion, "was murdered outside his Crystal City apartment at three o'clock this morning—not even four hours ago—there's no word from the police as to the suspected motive. If they know anything, which is doubtful, they're not telling. I've asked the liaison to keep us informed but there are no guarantees. This is a politically sensitive situation and I don't expect to be kept in the loop beyond what the rest of the world will see and hear in the media."

Rocky divided his attention between his boss and Victoria, the head of the Colby Agency. Despite this year's merger, Rocky couldn't help considering himself and the other Equalizers, including Jim, as separate from the rest of the Colby staff. The transition had moved along smoothly for the most part so far. He supposed it would simply take time to feel as if he "fit in" here the way he had in the old brownstone a world away from this ritzy location.

Victoria gestured to Kendra Todd, the Colby investigator who sat on the same side of the small conference table as Rocky and with whom he would be working on this assignment. "Kendra, do you have anything else to add?"

Kendra had explained Sayar's position in D.C. politics and his unexpected meeting with her less than twelve hours ago. She remained clearly shaken by the news of his murder. That fact had not stopped her from plunging into a strategy for determining the truth about this tragic event. She'd spoken with Sayar's parents an hour ago to pass along her re-assurances that she would personally see that the investigation was conducted without bias and in a speedy manner.

"Nothing more as of yet," Kendra began, her voice weary. "I want you and Jim" she glanced from her boss to Rocky's "to know how much I appreciate the agency's support in this…investigation."

Typically the agency—as had been the case with the Equalizers—had at least one client who was very much alive before delving into a case. This situation was a little outside the norm since the client was now dead, but both Victoria and Jim felt strongly about finding the truth, particularly since Sayar had come to Kendra just before his murder.

"You have our full support," Victoria reiterated. "The Colby jet is standing by. Whatever resources you need on this end will be available."

"Going in blind like this," Jim took up where his mother left off, "and with the murder of Mr.

Sayar, we believe it wise to be fully prepared. With that in mind, we're recommending you both carry your weapons. D.C.'s new handgun regulations are somewhat more relaxed, so there's no worry on that count."

Carrying personal protection was standard operation procedure for Equalizer cases, but the Colby Agency saw things differently. No weapons unless absolutely necessary. Rocky felt a sense of relief at this news. He much preferred being armed.

"Thank you." Kendra stood. "I'm ready," she looked expectantly at Rocky, "if you're all set."

Rocky pushed to his feet. "I'm good to go." He didn't have to ask who would be serving as lead on the case. For now, the Colby investigator assigned was in charge. That was fine by him. He had a reputation for being a rogue when it came to strategy in the field, and though he liked to bend the rules he rarely broke those rules. Not his style.

Within ten minutes they had picked up their weapons and bags, loaded into the agency car and headed for the airfield. Since Kendra didn't appear to be interested in conversation, Rocky passed the travel time reviewing Sayar's dossier a second time. Mostly he needed a distraction to keep his mind off how good she smelled. The scent was soft, subtle and sweet. Womanly.

But he was ignoring that.

She was friendly enough in a very professional way, but she paid little or no attention to him on any other level. Why should she? They were colleagues, nothing more. Obviously he wasn't her type.

He reread the last paragraph he'd perused. Sayar had no criminal record, not even a parking ticket. Top of his class at Vanderbilt University. Hardworking family. No ticked off ex-girlfriends. According to his family, Sayar never complained about work or any of his professional associates. This tragedy was a complete shock to all who knew him, again, according to the family. The tragedy was too fresh. Later when the shock wore off a little, one or both parents might remember little seemingly insignificant details they couldn't recall now.

Rocky closed the file and slid it into his bag. Whatever the victim's family thought or recalled, something was going on. Otherwise Sayar wouldn't have come to Kendra. Problem was, he was dead and all Rocky and Kendra had were questions.

Kendra stared out the car window at the passing cityscape. Rocky took advantage of her preoccupation to study his partner for this assignment. She was young, twenty-eight compared to his thirty-five. Long hair, more blond than brown. Smooth skin that seemed to be perpetually tanned. High cheekbones, thin nose and extra full lips. Big, brown eyes that reflected utter brilliance and deep compassion.

Always conservatively dressed, but those modest skirts did nothing to disguise her tall, slender, well-toned frame. During the siege of the agency back in January he'd caught himself staring at her more than once. A very attractive woman.

But what he liked about her most was her extraordinarily ladylike manners. She reminded him of his mother. Prim, proper—classy—and always going out of her way to be helpful. He'd asked around about her social life and he'd learned a sad truth. Kendra Todd was all work and no play. She rarely dated. Never looked at him as anything other than a fellow investigator. Never looked at any of the males around the office in an unbusinesslike manner.

He'd asked her to lunch once but she'd declined, opting to remain at her desk with a sandwich from home. She was the first woman he'd been attracted to who wasn't attracted to him first.

Strange.

Even stranger, he was attracted to her and she wasn't actually his type. Kendra Todd possessed all those traits that he respected in his mother, but she was way too focused on business at this stage in her life.

Way too uptight for him.

She turned in his direction, her questioning gaze colliding with his.

Rocky blinked. Busted. "Sorry about your

friend." Shaky recovery but at least he'd gotten out something rational.

"Thank you." She smoothed a hand over her cream-colored skirt and cleared her throat, simultaneously shifting her gaze forward.

The awkward silence that followed squeezed the air right out of the car.

Only one way to alleviate the tension. "You had time to lay out a preliminary strategy?" Safe enough question, he supposed.

A moment passed while she chewed her bottom lip. "I'm going straight to the top."

He lifted his eyebrows in question. "Senator Castille?"

"Yes."

Could prove dicey. "You think he'll see you?" At the briefing she'd mentioned that her parting with the senator had been less than pleasant.

"No."

"I guess you have a plan B." Rocky knew enough about her to fully understand that she wouldn't take no for an answer without a fight.

Kendra turned her attention back to him. "He will see me. He won't like it. He'll evade my attempts, ignore my questions, but he *will* eventually admit defeat."

Approval tugged at one corner of Rocky's mouth. Oh yeah, this lady was a ferocious tiger despite her sweet little kitten appearance. Something else he appreciated about her. "So you're fairly certain the senator is involved somehow."

"I'm certain of nothing," she pointed out. "I feel confident that he is well aware of whatever rumors are traveling the grapevine regarding the murder. Those rumors might provide leads."

"What about other lobbyists? Personal friends?" Judging by the stack of notes she had in that brief-case of hers, she'd done some serious research in the hours after her meeting with Sayar. Rocky doubted she'd gotten much sleep.

"There are two close associates, Stanford Smith and Ella Hendrix, who have publicly slammed his support of a controversial bill." Kendra took a deep breath and appeared to consider her next words before continuing. "It would be too easy, not to mention stupid," she glanced knowingly at Rocky, "for either one of them to be the one we're looking for. But, like the senator, they will be privy to rumors, incidents, that we need to know that might propel our investigation in the proper direction."

Rocky hadn't thought of it until now but he wondered if a lack of a real social life was a lingering side effect of D.C. politics. According to the dossier, Sayar had no notable social life. Rocky opted to ask about that later. To ask now might back up any suspicions she had about catching him staring at her. Every time he had the opportunity to study her he noticed something new.

Like the small sprinkling of freckles across her nose. He'd never noticed that before. Then again, he'd never sat this close to her in a confined space for this length of time. When she smiled, those extra full lips revealed gleaming white teeth that were far from perfectly straight. Just a little crooked. Just enough to give her smile special character.

He liked that about her. Gorgeous but not too perfect.

He seemed to like a lot of things about her.

"Did you have suggestions on where to begin?"

It wasn't until she asked the question that he realized she was openly watching him stare at her. He swallowed. Told himself to say something. "We should, of course, check out his residence. Often when someone feels cornered or afraid, he or she will hide information in a safe place in hopes of keeping a secret." He didn't look away when he ran out of logical suggestions. No point pretending he hadn't been staring. She'd caught him red-handed. Twice now.

"We'll go there tonight when the police have finished their investigation," she agreed. "The property will assuredly still be a crime scene, but hopefully the police will choose not to post a guard once their techs are finished."

"They'll take his computer." Rocky was a whiz with computers, but the chances of the cops leaving that behind were slim to none.

"They will," Kendra echoed. She relaxed in the seat, turning her attention front and center once more. "But they don't know about Yoni's backup drive or where he keeps it hidden."

Now that was a stroke of luck. "You obviously do."

"I definitely do." She shot Rocky a triumphant smile. "He recently moved it, but he gave me the location last night. Just in case."

"He was aware on some level that the threat might go beyond a reputation assassination?" In Rocky's opinion the idea that the victim felt he was in physical danger put a slightly different slant on the case.

"He didn't say as much, but I got that impression. Yoni wasn't one to break protocol. He played by the rules." She gave Rocky another of those pointed looks. "All the rules."

Rocky studied her eyes, the certainty there, and the determined set of her jaw. "Once in a great while a true innocent is mowed down in a scenario like this, but only once in a great while. I'd wager your friend has at least one secret that'll surprise you." He didn't have to spell out the glaring fact that Sayar did not want to go to the police.

Another of those long, awkward pauses lapsed with her staring directly into his eyes.

"Maybe," she admitted.

"If I'm right, you owe me lunch." A long-awaited lunch, he didn't mention.

Her assessing gaze narrowed slightly. "You're on."

He grinned, leaned into the headrest. Lunch was a given. Rocky had never met a man or woman, dead or alive, who didn't have at least one secret. Yoni Sayar surely had his.

"If you're wrong," Kendra said, cutting into his victorious musing, "you have to wear a suit to the office every day for a week."

Surprised, he looked her straight in the eye. "Something wrong with what I wear?" He was a jeans and boots kind of guy. Sure he wore the requisite button-down shirt and sports jacket, but never suits. Well, almost never. Occasionally he had no choice.

She shook her head. "Nothing a little polish and silk won't take care of."

"Ha-ha." He pretended to be annoyed but deep down he was kind of happy that she'd bothered to observe what he wore. She sure hadn't given the first indication that she'd looked at him long enough to notice. "Nice to know you care."

"Appearances are everything, Rocky," she said,

surveying the entrance to the airfield as the driver made the turn. "At the Colby Agency appearances are extremely important."

His anticipation flattened. Her attention was related to business.

Like always.

Chapter Three

Kendra waited through the lengthy hold. When Castille's secretary returned to the line, Kendra didn't give her time to pass along the no she knew the senator had likely given. "I have to talk to him, Jean. It's urgent, as I'm sure you know."

Rocky lounged on the other side of the booth they'd claimed once the lunch crowd started to dwindle, his expression resigned to the idea that she was butting her head against a brick wall. But he had to hand it to her; she didn't give up easily.

"Kendra, I wish I could help you," Jean offered, her voice hushed. She wouldn't want to be overheard consorting with the enemy.

"I understand that an appointment is out of the question," Kendra put in before the woman who'd worked with the senator his entire senatorial career could continue, "but if you can give me some hint of his schedule for this afternoon I'll catch him on the run." Kendra had some idea of Castille's daily agenda. Two years as his personal aide had provided significant insight into his usual activities. But it had been three years.

Things changed. So did people.

"What about his three o'clock at the club?" she prodded. During Kendra's tenure as his aide, Castille hadn't missed a Wednesday afternoon sit-down with *the boys* at the club. The Summit catered to high-level D.C. politicians and businessmen, providing classic luxury along with a three hundred percent markup on beverages. Membership was required for entrance, but the sidewalk outside was fair game as long as one wasn't a reporter. If any of the old staff remained, she might just get inside. But she wasn't betting on it.

"I can't confirm that he'll make that standing appointment today, considering what's happened," Jean advised, her tone somber.

That was all Kendra needed. "Thanks, Jean. I owe you." Kendra closed her cell phone and gazed triumphantly at the man waiting across the table. "I can catch him around three." The club was barely twenty minutes away. Arriving ahead of schedule wouldn't be a problem. In fact, it might work to her advantage.

"I'm impressed. The secretary must remember you more fondly than her boss does."

Jean Brody had no children of her own. The sixty-year-old and Kendra had bonded very closely, but even that bond had never breached the woman's loyalty to the senator. What she had given today was a confirmation of something Kendra already knew. It was their mutual respect that kept Jean off Kendra's list of persons to interrogate. As well as the knowledge that no amount of persuasion would prompt the secretary to speak ill against Castille. She was a rare breed.

"You could say that, yes," Kendra said in answer to her partner's assessment.

Rocky made an agreeable sound and resumed his monitoring of the street outside the wall of plate glass that ran the length of the diner's storefront. He was slightly out of his element but he hadn't let that cloud his attitude.

Kendra studied the man seated across the table from her. She didn't yet have a complete handle on his thought process regarding the case of her connection to the players. That he continued to act cooperatively went a long way in easing her concern about working with him. Not that he was a bad guy, he absolutely wasn't. But he was a former Equalizer and the merger with the Colby Agency had been a difficult pill to swallow to some extent for Jim

Colby's entire team. Most of the bumps were behind them now.

That her attention, despite the current situation, settled on the usual details about him annoyed her, but it was what it was. An unexpected attraction that could not be allowed to proliferate.

Rocky was tall, heavily muscled. Coal-black hair and unsettlingly vivid blue eyes. Everything about him somehow refuted his background. Reared and educated in Tampa by medical professional parents, he dressed like a cowboy—sans the requisite hat. From the first time she'd met him she'd fully expected the man to drawl out a "yes, ma'am" to match that swagger of a champion that attracted the eye of every female he encountered—including Kendra's. When he walked into a room he owned it, insofar as female interest was concerned.

As if she'd made the statement out loud, her partner swung his gaze back to her.

She rerouted her thoughts. "I left a voice mail for Wayne Burton." Keep going with the details. Rocky had been in the restroom when she'd made that call. "He's a contact in D.C.'s homicide division I reached out to on occasion…before." Before she'd recognized the writing on the wall and the hard cold fact that she was not cut out for this world. And before she'd tried a relationship with him that couldn't have fit in a million years. "I'm hoping he'll agree to brief us on the path the investigation is taking at this point."

Those startlingly blue eyes searched hers a moment as if looking for the motive behind her words. "A reliable enough contact you have reason to believe he would go out on a limb to give you a break in a potentially sensitive and high-profile case?"

Rocky wasn't asking about reliability. What he had actually asked was had she slept with Wayne Burton. His eyes confirmed her analysis. "Yes," she said, unashamed. Wayne was reliable and she had slept with him. But that was history. History Leland Rockford had no need to know. She hadn't communicated with Wayne in three years...other than the occasional e-mail.

"That should make life a lot simpler." Rocky plucked a cold French fry from his plate and popped it into his mouth. "For the case anyway."

Kendra let the innuendo slide. She moistened her lips, shouldn't have stared at his, but it was difficult not to. He had very generous lips for a man. Everything about him was a contradiction. His appearance gave away nothing of his past life. His slow, methodical manner of conversing totally belied his state school academic record. The man was incredibly smart and far more insightful than he apparently wanted anyone to know, including his current partner.

And yet he didn't seem to get how this was going to play out. "Nothing about this investigation will be simple," she warned. "This is a community filled with secrets and powerful people who know how to keep the important ones—unless it benefits them somehow to share those secrets. We'll have to dig deeper and work harder for every single detail."

Rocky propped his forearms on the table and leaned forward. "Good thing neither of us is the type to surrender without a fight."

She resisted the impulse to recline deeper into the faux leather of the booth to regain those few inches of distance he had claimed. He'd done this at the hotel when he'd insisted on opening the door to her room and seeing her inside before going to his room next door. He'd gotten closer than he'd dared before, had looked her directly in the eyes and spoke quietly as if what he had to say wasn't to be overheard. That it was somehow intimate. Maybe it was her imagination but she hadn't noticed him doing that before.

She would be lying to herself if she didn't admit that he'd made her shiver. Something no other man had done with such ease.

Quite possibly she was making too much of it. She'd had zero sleep and Yoni's murder had her on an emotional ledge. She stared at her untouched food. Her appetite was AWOL. But she needed to eat. Coffee alone wouldn't keep her on her toes.

She kept replaying every moment of last night's meeting with Yoni. What had she missed? Had he said anything at all that should have clued her in to the fact that he was in imminent danger?

How could she call herself a private investigator when she'd completely misread the urgency in a potential client she knew so well?

"You shouldn't beat yourself up."

Kendra blinked. So now he was a mind reader? "I was just—"

"Thinking how you should have seen this coming?"

Definitely a mind reader. "Maybe." Surely she'd missed something relevant in last night's meeting. Something he'd said…

"He failed to tell you everything."

She wanted to challenge that assessment. To defend her friend…she had known Yoni as well as anyone who'd worked with him could have. But logic told her that Rocky had pegged the situation. Yoni had been worried enough to contact her, to draw her from her new life. Yet he hadn't once mentioned fear for his safety…only for his professional reputation.

"It's possible he had no idea the source of the

threat would go this far," she proposed. "Frankly, his murder may prove unrelated to his reasons for coming to me. There's no way to guess."

"But you don't believe that," Rocky suggested with equal conviction.

"No." Rocky was her partner in this assignment. Choosing not to be completely honest served no purpose. "I believe there is more…that he didn't tell me." It pained her to say as much, but it was true. "If that proves the case, then he had a compelling reason for leaving me in the dark." Yoni wouldn't knowingly put anyone in danger.

Rocky pulled out his wallet and dropped payment for their lunch on the table. "All we have to do is determine what that reason was."

Kendra reached for the check the waitress had left, then for her purse.

"It goes on the same expense log," Rocky reminded before sliding from the booth.

Giving herself a mental kick for again being slow on the uptake, she scooted across the bench seat and stood. "We should get into position to intercept Castille."

"Since you know the way, why don't you drive?" He gestured for her to go ahead of him.

She inhaled a whiff of his aftershave as she turned to go. The scent caught her off guard. She'd spent the last several hours in his company, seated right next to him and it wasn't until this moment she noticed the earthy masculinity of it. Despite the abundance of food smells surrounding her, his scent abruptly reached out and permeated her senses.

Sleep deprived. Frayed nerves. Too much caffeine.

After a good night's sleep she would be more herself.

But her friend would still be dead.

Summit Club, 2:50 p.m.

THE BROODING ARCHITECTURE of the exclusive club blended into the row of brick and limestone structures that flanked the tree-lined street far enough from Pennsylvania Avenue to allow some semblance of separation.

Luck appeared to be on Kendra's side as she leaned against the bar on the side of the expansive dining room opposite the lobby entrance. The afternoon shift bartender who'd worked at the club three years ago was still on staff. He'd not only allowed Kendra and Rocky inside, he'd seated them at the bar with a wide-angle view of the entrance Castille would assuredly use.

"I'm still in shock." Drea James shook his head as he checked his stock of liquors and whiskeys. "Yoni always made it a point to stop at the bar and say hello whenever he was here." Drea shrugged, the shock he spoke of evident in the listless move. "It's crazy. What's happening to this world?" He reached down for a replacement bottle of bourbon.

"Was he still dating that girl…?" Using a cliched ruse, Kendra tapped her forehead as if she was attempting to recall the name.

"Leigh?" Drea frowned. "I don't think so. He always said he was too busy for a real social life." After a moment's contemplation, he added, "She still asks about him though."

"Really?" Kendra feigned surprise. Yoni not only hadn't mentioned a girl, neither had his parents. "Maybe she hoped they would get together again."

"Wishful thinking," Drea said somberly. He glanced around, then leaned across the bar. "Don't get me wrong, Leigh's a cool chick, but Yoni was way out of her league. That dude was going places." He pointed to Rocky's glass. "More sparkling?"

Rocky held his hand over his glass. "No thanks."

The bartender turned his attention back to Kendra. "I figure that's the only reason Leigh worked so hard to get a job waitressing here. She's looking for a sugar daddy. Know what I mean?"

Definitely. "I'd like to ask her a few questions. Will she be working tonight?" Whether she was seeing Yoni now or not, anything this Leigh person had noticed or overheard could prove useful.

"Not tonight." Drea furrowed his brow thoughtfully. "Tomorrow night for sure."

"Maybe I could call her?" Kendra prodded. She wanted the woman's last name and address if she could get one or both.

Drea shook his head again. "I can't get over you being a PI now. That's wild."

"It's a different world," Kendra agreed. Telling Drea that Yoni had visited her in Chicago hadn't been on her agenda but the detail had compelled the bartender to open up. Yoni spent a lot of time in places like this meeting with colleagues and contacts. Any information she could obtain from this man might fill in numerous gaps. "The work has taught me that even the most seemingly insignificant detail can make all the difference in an investigation."

Again Drea appeared to contemplate her words. As if he'd suddenly remembered something he picked up a pen and grabbed a cocktail napkin. "This is Leigh's cell number." He scribbled on the napkin. "And her address." He pushed the napkin across the bar. "You tell her I said she needs to share anything she knows with you."

Kendra read the name. Leigh Turlington. "Thanks. This helps a lot." She gave the bartender a smile as she withdrew a business card from her purse and presented it to him. "And you call me if you hear anything at all related to Yoni."

Drea examined the card. "You know I will."

"Right on time," Rocky said under his breath.

Kendra followed his gaze to the mirror behind the bar. The reflection of the room behind them showed Castille and two other men following the hostess to a table near one of the towering windows with a view of the street below. For added privacy, the dining room was located on the second floor.

"He only allows one member of his security inside," Drea explained, keeping his voice hushed. "He's the one in the black suit. The other guy is Bernard Capshaw. He's the CEO of Capshaw Enterprises."

A waitress approached the other end of the bar, drawing Drea in that direction.

Kendra wasn't acquainted with Capshaw the man, but she knew the company. Aerospace technology. The industry, like many others, was on the edge of financial collapse and in need of government support.

Castille hadn't changed much. If anything he looked younger. The wonders of modern cosmetic procedures. She couldn't see the man going for full-blown surgery but there were other, more convenient procedures that provided ample benefits.

Appearances were supremely important in this high-stakes arena.

The other man, Secret Service no doubt, was an unknown to her. No one from three years ago but that changed nothing. Kendra was well aware of SOP. The senator wouldn't be allowed out of the man's line of sight except to visit the men's room and only then after the facility had been checked for hidden threats.

"I'll be waiting in the ladies' room," Kendra said to Rocky. "Send me a text if Castille wanders in that direction."

"You might be in for a long wait," Rocky noted.

That was true, but it was the only way to ensure she got one-on-one time with the senator. And that she didn't attract the attention of his security. "Text me if he leaves the table."

"Will do."

Rocky watched her in the mirror behind the bar as she slid off the stool. As she made her way to the ladies' room she wondered how long his total cooperation would last. So far he hadn't actually questioned any of her decisions, but then they'd scarcely begun.

The ladies' room had been renovated since Kendra's last visit here. Opulence remained the mainstay of the decorating theme. Nothing but the best for the power players. At one point some newly elected senator had suggested that popular gathering spots like the Summit were subsidized by wealthy lobbyists who wanted the atmosphere conducive to persuasion.

No one paid any real attention to the accusation, yet everyone understood that it was in all likelihood true on some level.

Money talked.

Most anything else walked.

Kendra's cell vibrated in its leather holster. She checked the display. The text was from Rocky and read: Security headed your way.

The man in the black suit would check the men's room then return to the table to let the senator know it was all clear. Since both the men's room and the ladies' were stationed in a short corridor that led to nothing else, entry was possible only from the dining room. Permitting security to feel comfortable allowing the man to do his business in private.

Let me know when security returns to the table and Castille heads this way, she entered before hitting the send button.

Kendra checked her reflection. Smoothed a hand over her suit jacket. She looked as tired as she felt. The weariness particularly showed in her eyes. Never a good position from which to strike. This would be her first face-to-face with Castille since the day she'd walked out of his office. He wouldn't be happy to see her.

"Tough," she muttered.

Her cell vibrated. Security has returned to table. Your mark is en route.

Kendra tucked her phone away and took a breath. She pressed her ear to the door and listened for the neighboring hinges to whine. The carpeted floor prevented her from hearing Castille's approach.

A soft metal-on-metal rub signaled the senator had entered the men's room directly across the narrow corridor. Time to move.

She eased open the ladies' room door and quickly surveyed the corridor all the while knowing that Rocky would have warned her if anyone else had approached the area.

Clear.

Though no one had come this way while they sat at the bar, she still felt uncomfortable barging into the men's room. Putting manners aside, she crossed the corridor in two strides and entered forbidden territory.

Castille stood before the row of marble sinks admiring his thick head of gray hair in the mirror. Apparently satisfied, he reached to adjust his silk jacket. As the door whooshed closed behind Kendra his gaze collided with hers in the mirror.

"Afternoon, Senator." Kendra closed in on his position, her head held high, her shoulders square.

He stilled. Fury flared in his eyes. *"You."*

That he didn't immediately go for the call button on the belt at his waist surprised her. Security would have descended upon the men's room in ten seconds or less. And she would be spending hours under federal interrogation.

"It's been a while," she commented as she leaned one hip against the cool marble about three feet from where he stood. Crowding him wasn't the goal.

He cut her a look that warned exactly how he still felt about her. "I don't know what you think you're doing, but you're making a very serious error in judgment. This is stalking."

"Yoni was my friend." That his primary worry was her presence infuriated Kendra. "I want to know what happened to him."

"His murder," Castille said in a matter-of-fact tone, "had nothing to do with his work." His attention shifted back to the mirror as he straightened his purple tie yet again. "You should have checked your facts before you bothered to make an appearance."

"Why don't you enlighten me?" she suggested while he openly admired the fit of his charcoal suit.

He faced her, the lack of compassion in his

expression fueling her fury. "The official conclusion at this point is that the homicide that occurred early this morning had nothing to do with Sayar's political position. Preliminary results of the homicide investigation will be released tomorrow morning. You, like the rest of the world, can catch it on your preferred news channel."

"He came to me with concerns," she countered. Let him offer an explanation for that. "I'm here to follow up on those concerns."

Castille puffed. "Yoni was losing his edge. Confidence in his ability was on a downward trend. Surely you haven't forgotten how it works in this town. There are two kinds of folks."

The bastard took the time to wash his hands before continuing. Kendra's fury rushed unimpeded toward the boiling point.

Castille selected a meticulously rolled hand towel from the basket on the counter and dried his hands then settled his condescending gaze upon her once more. "Those who rise to the mountaintop and those who tumble over the edge of the cliff. Yoni was stumbling. He was on his way down. There was nothing I could do to help him."

"Because of the Transparency Bill?"

The brief glimmer of surprise in those cold eyes sent triumph rocketing into her chest. He knew

Kendra well enough to understand that if she knew that, she knew much more.

"The bill is brilliant," Castille confessed. "But the weight of taking such a stand helped to push our friend off that ledge, Kendra. The pressure under these kinds of circumstances is immeasurable. Yoni buckled under that tremendous weight."

The senator shrugged. "There is no mystery here. Tomorrow's press conference will set the record straight for any conspiracy theorists. Such as yourself," he accused.

"I'll make my own determination as to whether there's a mystery or not," she challenged, not put off one bit by his condescension. She wasn't going anywhere until she had the whole truth.

"Then consider yourself on notice." Castille tossed the hand towel aside. "If you attempt to connect Yoni's troubles to me or my office, you will be profoundly sorry you made the mistake of coming back."

He walked past her.

"Consider yourself on notice, Senator." She turned, surprised that he'd hesitated at the door, his back to her. "I'm not afraid of you or your position. If the facts lead back to you, that's where I'll go. And *if* that's the case, you will be the one profoundly sorry."

He opened the door and walked out, the whoosh of the closing door underscoring his departure.

The gauntlet was on the ground.

Let the battle of wills commence.

Chapter Four

Judd Castille glowered at the lobby entrance long after Kendra and her cohort had departed.

He should have known Sayar would go to her. Judd had kept up with the self-righteous witch in part because of Sayar's occasional comment in regards to her professional rise in the field of private investigations. She had landed herself a position at a widely acclaimed agency. But Judd hadn't cared. He'd only been thankful she was out of his hair. She had been a thorn in his side the last year of her tenure with him.

Now she was back.

And it was that nervous fool Sayar's fault.

Judd had actually expected her to show up after hearing the news of her friend's murder. However, he certainly hadn't expected her to have the unmitigated gall to confront him on his own turf. Who did Kendra Todd think she was?

She was no one.

No one who mattered.

"Is there a problem, Senator?"

Judd shifted his attention to the man seated next to him. "Why would there be a problem?" The situation with Capshaw was precarious enough without an appearance from the likes of Kendra Todd. Distraction could crush a man's best efforts. Judd could not allow anything or anyone to distract him at this pivotal juncture.

Far too much was at stake. Sayar had recognized that immensity, as well. What had he been thinking going to Kendra?

"You seem distracted," Capshaw offered, a hint of victory already shining in his beady eyes.

"And rightly so," Judd returned, restraining the infinite derision he felt for the man. "Yoni Sayar was murdered this morning. He was a trusted colleague. He'll be greatly missed."

Capshaw sipped his scotch—scotch paid for by Judd and ultimately the taxpayers. "I'm not so sure the architecture of the Transparency Bill will withstand this tragic loss."

As if the bastard gave one damn. Again, Judd curbed his baser urges, like reaching across the table and strangling the man. "I have full confidence the bill will be moving forward." If it was the last thing Judd did, he would get that piece of legislation passed. Men like Capshaw proved all the motivation necessary.

This vicious cycle had to stop.

Regret trickled through him but he banished it. He would not permit failure.

Truth was Judd was tired. Feeling his age. At sixty-three he had one or two more terms at most in him. He needed to leave his mark. To accomplish something that would put him in the history books.

He was on the verge of doing exactly that…if he could keep Kendra Todd out of his way until this ugliness passed. She would stir the pot…make things worse.

Confidence welled inside him. He had a plan in place to divert her attentions. By the time she recognized that she was on a path going nowhere, Judd's position as an American hero would be sealed.

His gaze settled on Capshaw as the greedy bastard scanned the menu. And men like him would no longer be able to steal from the ordinary citizens of this country to feather their own nests.

This was a war. Sacrifices had to be made.

If Kendra wasn't careful she could very well join others already on that casualty list.

Chapter Five

Crystal City, 5:20 p.m.

"When we get inside, I'll keep him talking while you look around."

"Got it." The lady had moxie, Rocky had to give her that. The meeting with Castille had visibly shaken her but she'd come right out of that confrontation ready to move on to the next step. She'd put a call in to Leigh Turlington, a woman Sayar had dated. But it turned up to be a dead end. They'd only gone on one date and Turlington hadn't even known Sayar's phone number, much less what he was into.

Rocky had offered to drive from the Summit to Yoni Sayar's residence just outside Crystal City, allowing Kendra time to decompress rather than fight rush-hour traffic.

Yellow crime-scene tape draped the sidewalk and small patch of grass in front of the town house, a blatant warning that bad things had happened on the other side. In this case, Sayar had been shot as he started up the short walk from the street to his front door. At least that was the story they'd gotten from the grieving parents. No official word had been released by the local authorities. According to Castille that wouldn't happen until tomorrow morning. Unless Kendra could get something out of the guy they were waiting for.

Rocky had parked across the street from the victim's residence. The late afternoon sun glinted against the windows of the two-story home. Wide brick steps led to the nondescript front door. Rocky squinted at first one window then the next. All appeared to be closed up right with blinds or shutters. No sign of the cops or any lingering crime-scene technicians.

"Your friend is late," he noted aloud as Kendra checked the time on her cell phone yet again.

"He's a homicide detective," she reminded Rocky, her own impatience showing. "I'm certain sticking to a time schedule isn't always his top priority." She returned her attention to the town house that had belonged to her friend. "Wayne will be here."

Wayne. That was right, they were friends, too. Rocky had his own theory about that particular friend. He'd picked up on the subtle change in the inflections of her voice when she'd spoken to her *contact*. Not that it was any of his business, personally or professionally, or his concern insofar as this case stacked up or how they conducted their investigation.

The concept just bugged him.

No use denying it...the idea of Kendra and another man, any man, got under his skin somehow. Didn't seem to matter that they hardly knew each other beyond the workplace. Dumb, yeah. But a fact nonetheless. He'd learned at an early age that denial was less than constructive and totally unproductive.

A black SUV rolled to a stop in front of the town house. The driver's door opened and a tall man wearing a suit stepped out.

Had to be Burton. *Her contact*. Rocky disliked him already, mostly because of the suit.

"That's him," Kendra reached for her door.

Rocky did the same, giving her ample time to round the hood across the street ahead of him. Kendra hadn't mentioned whether she'd informed Burton she was bringing along a partner.

Waiting through the requisite embrace, Rocky stood back until the reunion formalities were out of the way. *"It's been forever." "God, you look good."* He rolled his eyes. Primarily because Burton had it right. Kendra did look good.

Rocky closed the final couple of yards between his position and theirs. Burton dragged his focus from the lady and pointed it at Rocky. Rocky stuck out his hand. "Leland Rockford," he announced.

Burton gave Rocky's hand a challenging but brisk shake. "Lieutenant Wayne Burton, D.C. Homicide."

Maybe he misheard but Rocky could swear the man had emphasized the lieutenant part. Rocky jerked his head toward Kendra. "Her partner."

Burton ignored that last part, resting his attention on Kendra once more. "You may have been the last person to see Sayar alive," he said as he turned to the town house, placed a hand at the small of her back and ushered her in that direction.

Rocky bit back the compulsion to say "Besides the folks at two airports and the car rental agency." Just another reason he didn't like the guy. Another dumb reason.

Except that Kendra looked at Burton as if every word coming from his mouth were the gospel that would show her the way to the promised land. He couldn't recall once having her look at him that way.

Burton lifted the official crime-scene tape for Kendra to duck beneath. Once on the other side, they walked wide around the bloodstained section on the walk where the victim had fallen. At the stoop the overly friendly detective removed the crime-scene seal from the door and unlocked it.

Rocky stayed two steps behind. He figured he would learn more by watching and listening than by attempting to insert himself into the conversation.

Kendra moved slowly around the living room, visually inspecting the space. She'd told Rocky that she'd been here before and hopefully would recognize anything glaringly out of place.

"So Sayar didn't give you any details about why he wanted to hire your agency?" Burton asked.

For a second Rocky was sure he'd misunderstood the question.

"He promised to give me all the details when I arrived in D.C. tomorrow," Kendra said, clearing the confusion for Rocky. She turned to face Burton. "That was to be our first official meeting."

Rocky restrained the smile that tugged at the corners of his mouth. The lady wasn't as smitten as he'd first thought. She'd kept the details of the final conversation with Sayar to herself. Good deal.

"He simply said," she added, "that it was urgent and personal."

Burton assessed her at length, obviously not fully buying her story. "He came all that way and didn't give you anything?"

She moved to the table next to a recliner and bent down to view the framed photo there. "He said he couldn't discuss the situation by phone. Showing up to talk to me was his only choice. He wanted a commitment from me that the Colby Agency would take his case and then we would move forward." She straightened and looked Burton straight in the eye and lied. "He wasn't willing to share anything until I had the backing of the agency."

Rocky was impressed.

"Puts a whole new spin on what we know."

Kendra inclined her head and studied her old friend. "What exactly do you know?"

"Allowing you and your partner access to the property is breaking the rules," Burton hedged.

"The techs have finished," Kendra challenged.

"You wouldn't be here otherwise," Burton tossed right back.

"Touché," Kendra conceded.

This part Rocky was enjoying more and more.

"What I'm about to tell you won't be released until tomorrow morning's press conference," Burton began. "I'm counting on you" he glanced at Rocky with no lack of suspicion "to keep this quiet until then."

"You have our word," Kendra assured him.

A brief hesitation no doubt for the effect, then Burton announced, "We have evidence the shooting was the result of Sayar surprising a burglar."

Rocky hadn't noticed any sign of forced access at the front door.

"Solid evidence?" Kendra wanted to know.

Rocky decided to wander around the room as the two hashed out the theory. That was the plan Kendra had laid out. All indications so far suggested that Sayar lived frugally, Rocky decided. Minimal furnishings. Minimal decorating. Nothing on the walls except a calendar over the desk. No laptop or desktop sat on the desk, confirming Rocky's conjecture that the police would have confiscated it right away.

"His wallet was missing as were his computer and a flat-panel television that hung over the mantel." He pointed to the fireplace.

Rocky's attention moved from the cop to the mantel and back. So, the techs hadn't gotten the computer. Interesting. Maybe Sayar's murder was a coincidence after all. Part of a robbery. It wasn't totally outside the realm of possibility.

Just highly unlikely considering his meeting with Kendra.

While Kendra launched more questions at Burton, Rocky seized the opportunity to drift into the kitchen. Dirty dishes in the sink, despite the built-in dishwasher. Counters were clear of clutter except for a can opener and a microwave. Stove top and oven looked unused.

Rocky opened the fridge. Carton of milk and orange juice. Sandwich meat, which was out of date. Same with the cheese. Freezer compartment was empty.

A few cans of soup in the cabinets. One half-empty box of crackers.

A definite bachelor.

Rocky listened to ensure there had been no break in the conversation in the other room, then checked the back door. Again, no indication of forced entry. When he eased it closed once more, he didn't lock it.

Just in case.

With Kendra and Burton still deep in intense conversation, Rocky moved to the only other room downstairs. The bathroom. Toilet paper and hand soap. Pedestal sink and toilet. Empty medicine cabinet. Like the rest of the walls downstairs, a generic shade of off-white coated the walls and trim. Floors were covered with faux-wood flooring.

A cell phone erupted into chimes. Rocky stopped in the tiny square of a hall between the living room and bath to listen. Burton reached into his jacket pocket and then his gruff voice replaced the chimes. Kendra's gaze collided with Rocky's as he approached the stairs leading to the second floor. Her nod of encouragement was so subtle had he not been staring so intently at her he would have missed it entirely.

She would keep Burton occupied.

By the time Rocky had reached the upstairs landing Burton had ended the call. Kendra tossed out another demand for information.

Upstairs four doors lined a short, narrow hall, two on either side. The beige carpet hushed Rocky's footfalls. Door one led to a bedroom furnished with only a futon. Nothing in the closet. Doors two and three opened to a bathroom and a linen closet respectively. The final door opened into the bedroom Sayar had used.

More of the generic paint. Double bed with tousled linens. Clothes hung neatly in the closet. Shoes lined the floor beneath. One chest of drawers with a flat-panel TV resting on top. Rocky quickly and efficiently rifled through each drawer. Socks, T-shirts, boxers. That was about it.

He lifted the mattress from the box springs. Nothing under the mattress. He knelt down. Or under the bed. A few magazines, an MP3 player and two framed photos cluttered the bedside table. Along with a couple of twenty-dollar bills. Seemed a little strange that a burglar would leave cash lying around.

The drawers of the bedside table contained the usual suspects: tissue, throat lozenges and a flashlight. The only thing missing was a pack of condoms. Most single guys kept those handy.

Before exiting the room, Rocky stood back and took one last look around.

Then it hit him.

There were several items in the room that shouldn't have been if Burton's theory was to be accepted.

Rocky didn't bother quieting his steps as he descended the stairs. Burton shot him a harsh glare but couldn't drag himself away from the conversation with Kendra long enough to reprimand Rocky.

"I'm not buying the robbery theory," Kendra argued. "He was far too agitated last night. Something was very wrong in his life. Seems one hell of a coincidence that he was murdered a few hours later practically at his own door."

Burton flared his palms. "Our only option is to go with the evidence we find. Unless we discover some additional information that suggests otherwise our hands are tied. The case will be written up as a robbery-homicide."

"And go unsolved like the hundreds of others that occur in your jurisdiction every year."

Now that was cutting the guy off at the knees. This was the first time Rocky had watched Kendra in action out in the field. So far he continued to be impressed.

Another of those annoyed glances arrowed Rocky's way. Rocky hadn't made a peep. Apparently the cop in his fancy suit didn't like being dressed down by his former girlfriend in front of her new male partner.

Burton dropped his hands to his sides and said nothing in response to her accusation. "Is there anything else here you want to see that" he cut Rocky another look "you haven't already?"

Kendra met Rocky's gaze, he shook his head, then she said to Burton, "I guess that's it."

When they were on the street once more Burton exhaled a big breath. "Look, I'll keep you posted. There'll be a final decision later tonight before we go public tomorrow morning."

"I really appreciate your support, Wayne."

Rocky headed for the rental car. Kendra knew what she was doing. If she needed some space to get what she needed from this guy, Rocky wasn't going to stand in her way.

The investigation was top priority.

Still, he couldn't help looking back as he reached the car. Burton gave Kendra another of those big hugs, only this time he held on a little longer than before.

Rocky hit unlock on the remote and got behind the wheel. That part he didn't need to observe.

He stared at his reflection in the rearview mirror. *Man, you are getting desperate way before your time.*

If Kendra Todd was into him he would know it by now. She wasn't. He needed to get that through his thick skull and focus on the case.

Kendra hurried across the street and to the passenger side. When she'd settled into the seat she smiled. "Drive around the neighborhood."

"Yes, ma'am." He started the car, waited until Burton had driven away and then eased from the curb. "Any particular reason or are we just checking out the architecture?"

"I need to get to the patio."

"For?" Rocky made a left at the first intersection.

"That's where Yoni told me he'd hidden his backup hard drive."

"If the cops didn't find it," Rocky countered.

"Trust me, they didn't find it."

Sayar must have had one hell of a good hiding place. "What's your take on the robbery scenario?"

"No way," Kendra said with absolute certainty. "Someone wanted it to look that way."

"I don't think the cops are buying it, either." He slowed for another turn, this one right. "Not for real. If they are, then they're not too bright."

Kendra turned in her seat to study him. "What did you see in the other rooms besides Yoni's lack of decorating skills?"

She had that part right. "I'm guessing he ate out a lot."

She smiled, her expression—her eyes—distant. Rocky's throat tightened. The smile hadn't been for him but he'd liked it a lot all the same. "He ate out and with his parents. Cooking was not one of his fortes."

"No beer or hard stuff, either."

"Focused and unusually straitlaced."

Rocky felt a twinge of sympathy for the parents. They had raised a good, hardworking son it seemed and this happened to him. Not fair. Not fair at all.

"What about his bedroom?"

"Now there," Rocky made another slow turn, "is where things got interesting." He rolled carefully past a house where children played kick ball in the yard. "Sayar's wallet and computer were missing. But not the thirty-two-inch flat-panel television in his bedroom. An MP3 player lay right on the bedside table in plain sight. No cheapo, either. This was one of the high-dollar jobs. And if that isn't enough to convince you this was no robbery, forty bucks was next to the MP3 player."

"I knew Wayne was holding out on me." Kendra shook her head, her lips compressed in a firm line.

"That's his job," Rocky offered. He had no idea

why he felt compelled to defend the guy, but it was a reasonable explanation.

Kendra opened her mouth to argue, but then snapped it shut.

Didn't take a mind reader to know what she'd started to say. She had expected more from her former lover. Maybe the two had been a lot closer than Rocky had suspected.

"I suppose the burglar could have been interrupted by Yoni's return before he made it to the second floor," Kendra suggested, playing devil's advocate.

"Possibly," Rocky agreed. "But if he had that much notice that Sayar was coming, why not run out the back door and avoid the whole confrontation?"

"Exactly," Kendra agreed.

No way it was a robbery.

"There's an alley between the rows of town houses," Kendra said, "take the one directly behind Yoni's side of the street."

Rocky doubled back, then maneuvered down the narrow alley, careful of the garbage cans and bicycles. Each town house had a privacy fenced patio area and a parking pad designed for two vehicles.

"That's Yoni's car." Kendra pointed to the next parking pad on the left.

Rocky pulled in beside the small green hybrid. "He must have taken a taxi to the airport and then back." Otherwise he would have entered his home from the back door."

"Makes sense."

Kendra was out of the car as soon as Rocky had shifted into Park. As he emerged from the vehicle she lifted the latch on the gate and disappeared behind the eight-foot dog-eared fence.

Rocky scanned the alley. A cat pilfered through an open garbage can a few houses down. Otherwise the alley was quiet and vacant.

Satisfied that Burton or one of his buddies wasn't going to show up and arrest them for breaking and entering, Rocky stepped through the gate she'd left standing open. He'd expected to find her moving patio chairs or prowling through the two shrubs flanking either side of the steps leading to the back door.

He hadn't anticipated finding her dismantling the barbecue grill. She'd opened the lid, removed the rack and was digging through the mound of unused charcoal.

Rocky was just about to ask her what she hoped to find when she produced a large zip plastic bag. Inside was a square boxlike device.

Kendra turned to him with victory on her lips. "Yoni's external hard drive."

Like he realized earlier, the lady had moxie.

Rocky re-mounded the charcoal, replaced the

rack and closed the lid. He couldn't help eyeing the windows of the town house as he dusted his palms together. "We should get moving."

"I'll hook this up to my laptop when we get back to the hotel." Dirty bag or not, Kendra stashed her find beneath her cream-colored jacket.

"We don't need back inside for anything, right?"

She shook her head.

Being a good citizen and because Burton would know who'd unlocked the back door, Rocky locked it, then checked to ensure it was secure. No need to tick off Kendra's one official *contact*.

The alley was still deserted except for that determined cat who'd found himself an edible treasure. Once in the rental car, Rocky resisted the impulse to zoom away from the scene of their crime. Drawing unnecessary attention wouldn't be smart.

Kendra tucked the bag with its contents beneath her seat and reached for her seat belt. She hesitated, then reached for her cell phone.

"Kendra Todd."

The sound of her name made him smile. When he'd first learned that the Equalizers would be joining the Colby Agency he'd had some reservations. But now, after getting to know the staff—Kendra in particular—Rocky felt pretty much at home.

"Who is this?"

Rocky shifted his attention to her as he braked for the first intersection.

Kendra drew the phone from her ear and stared at the screen.

"What's up?" Tension rifled through Rocky.

Her gaze connected with his. "We have a rendezvous where we'll supposedly receive evidence about Yoni's murder and the identity of the killer."

Rocky checked the cross street then pulled away from the intersection. "Your caller didn't ID himself?"

"No."

The single syllable carried a truckload of confusion and disbelief.

"Did he name Sayar's killer just now?"

"Yes."

Their gazes intersected once more.

"Senator Castille."

Chapter Six

Kendra waited in the shadows of the Lincoln Memorial. Yoni Sayar deserved justice. Having his death swept under the rug as a random act of violence was wrong. Kendra intended to right that wrong.

"We've got company," Rocky whispered in her ear via the communications link.

"Black sedan," she confirmed.

Room service at the hotel had provided the fuel she'd been lacking. With no sleep, she'd been on the verge of total exhaustion. But the anonymous call along with a ham and cheese on rye back at the room had energized her. With Rocky's help she'd spent two hours attempting to make some sense of Yoni's electronic files. Her friend hadn't warned her that the files would be encrypted.

Why would he ensure she knew where his external hard drive was hidden if she couldn't make sense of the information stored there? Rocky had downloaded the files and sent them to the Colby Agency for further attempts at decoding. Two staff members from research were pulling an all-nighter toward that end.

She and Rocky had assessed their needs and selected the essential equipment, including their weapons, for this covert rendezvous. Arriving an hour early had provided the opportunity to survey the area and get into place. The minutes had dragged by like hours. Exhaustion had crept back into Kendra's bones.

A man emerged from the sedan she'd spotted and headed for the steps leading to the monument. He carried a slim briefcase or portfolio. Kendra checked the weapon at the small of her back beneath her jacket. Whatever this guy's game, she was prepared. Rocky was less than ten feet away, lost in the shadows, as well.

Before the man reached the top of the steps he reached up and ran a hand—his left hand—through his hair. Irritation burned through Kendra. She stepped forward, allowing her anonymous caller to see her.

Grant Roper.

Castille's aide. Kendra's replacement. Left-handed, arrogant, conniving jerk.

The surprise she'd felt at having the anonymous

caller name Castille as Yoni's killer evolved into equal measures of astonishment and outrage. Roper had been bucking for her position for months before she'd walked away. What the hell was he doing turning on the man he idolized now? This did not feel right.

The distinct hum of a setup vibrated the night air.

"Kendra," Grant acknowledged as he stepped closer.

"I don't know why you called and asked for this meeting." Kendra took another step in his direction, giving him her most intimidating glower. "But I don't appreciate your games, Grant. Good night."

She stared past him.

"I told you I have evidence. Do you want to see it or not?"

The question stopped Kendra's determined departure. She turned her head to stare at him over her shoulder. "Did Castille send you?" That would be just like the old buzzard to send his minion to try and spy on Kendra's investigation. He would know all the right buzz words that would get her attention.

Grant's face furrowed into an incredulous mix of shock and desperation. "Are you joking? He'd have the same thing done to me that he did to Sayar if he even suspected I was talking to you."

"Why should I believe anything you say?"

Kendra contested. He'd have to do more than talk if he wanted her to be swayed. She didn't trust him one iota. "Where's the evidence you claim to have?"

He jerked his head to the left. "Let's move away from these spotlights."

Kendra gestured for him to go first. He'd barely taken two steps before Rocky moved out of the shadows. Grant balked.

"Who's he?"

"My partner." Kendra moved in closer. "That's all you need to know. Now, let's see that evidence or I am out of here."

Grant was visibly displeased with Rocky's presence but that was too bad. Kendra had absolutely no sympathy for the slimy little snake.

He pulled a manila folder from his leather case. "I can show you what I have, but I can't let these originals out of my possession. Castille thinks I destroyed them. If he finds out…"

Yeah, Kendra got the idea but that didn't mean she believed a word of what Grant had to say. She accepted the folder. It felt heavier than it looked. She opened it, stared at the first of what turned out to be a stack of eight-by-ten photos. There were six in all. Each one showed Senator Castille in intimate conversation if not compromising positions with a young woman. Judging by the way she was dressed, a prostitute.

"Who's the woman?" Kendra banished her own conclusion and focused on Grant's face, looking for the signs of deception she fully expected.

"She *was* Aleesha Ferguson. Spent most of her time working K and L Streets. When she wasn't serving the senator's needs—if you know what I mean."

Kendra shook her head. "I find this difficult to believe." Had to be a hoax. She thrust the folder back at the man she knew from experience would beg, borrow or steal to get what he wanted. "Castille is a lot of things but not this."

"I've been keeping tabs on his extracurricular activity for months," Grant argued. "This is no one-time occurrence. The pictures are real."

"You said *was*." Kendra waited while Grant put the folder away then met her gaze. "What happened to this Aleesha Ferguson?"

"Hit-and-run." Grant lifted his chin and stared knowingly at Kendra. "Your friend Sayar helped cover up the whole thing."

The little weasel had crossed the line with that statement. "Yoni would never have knowingly participated in a criminal act of any sort." Kendra made up her mind. "We're done."

She turned her back on the wannabe player and headed for the steps. Rocky moved up beside her, adjusting his stride to hers.

"Check it out," Grant called out to her. "Aleesha Ferguson was killed by a hit-and-run driver. The case was never solved. Mrs. Castille was the driver. She called Sayar that night. Check his cell phone records. You'll see!"

"I'm telling you the truth!" floated across the summer air as Kendra reached the car.

Rocky started the engine and roared away from the curb. Kendra steamed, so angry she barely remembered to fasten her seat belt.

"Any possibility that twerp is telling some fragment of truth?"

Kendra wanted to say unequivocally hell no. No way would Castille stoop to such immoral behavior. Absolutely no way would Yoni help anyone—not even Mrs. Castille, who, he undeniably admired and adored—cover up a murder. No. No. No.

"The pictures were real," Kendra confessed. Whatever else she didn't understand or want to believe, that much was jarringly bona fide. "But there may be a perfectly logical explanation we're not aware of." There had to be one. She couldn't wrap her head around the outrageous concept otherwise.

"Then we have to make ourselves aware."

Kendra met Rocky's unrelenting gaze. Her partner was right. No one was going to willingly give them any facsimile of the truth about Yoni's murder or anything else, for that matter, he may or may not have been involved in personally or professionally.

Not here…where secrecy and diversion were ways of life.

10:31 p.m.

KENDRA INSERTED THE KEYCARD into the door of her hotel room. She would definitely need coffee to stay focused while they hashed through the pathetic clues and leads they had at this point.

"I'll grab my laptop," Rocky said as he unlocked the door directly across the hall.

"I'll put on a pot of coffee." Kendra pushed through the door, flipped the light switch and tossed her purse onto the luggage rack.

Instinct nudged her, sending her gaze sweeping across the room. Her breath stalled in her chest.

"What the…?"

Her room had been ransacked.

The side chair's upholstery was shredded. The mattress tossed off the bed…linens strewn across the carpet. Drawers had been removed from the chest and scattered haphazardly on the floor.

Her attention settled next on the travel bag she'd abandoned when they first arrived, its contents seemingly vomited from the zippered opening.

The external hard drive.

She stumbled across the room in her haste.

Dropping to her knees at the desk, she crawled beneath it and peered up at the under side of the desk top.

The compact piece of hardware was gone.

Kendra eased back from under the desk and plopped down cross-legged on the carpet. Something else she should have anticipated. Castille knew she was here. Wayne. She couldn't see what Wayne had to gain by taking the drive. Castille...the jury was still out on him.

Okay, it wasn't a total disaster, she reminded herself. Rocky had downloaded the files and forwarded all to the Colby Agency. So nothing was actually lost in that sense.

The problem was that now someone had their hands on Yoni's files. The ones he'd wanted to ensure she alone found if anything happened to him.

The most she could hope for at this point was that the agency could break the encryption before whoever had taken the external drive did so.

A long, low whistle reverberated from the door.

She looked up as her partner entered the criminal disarray. "I think it's safe to say someone suspected Yoni had discussed more with you than the idea of hiring the Colby Agency."

"Only two people were aware of my meeting with Yoni," she voiced the theories she had already considered.

"Castille could have sent his underling to distract you while another of his loyal followers did this," Rocky theorized.

"But," Kendra argued, "I'm one hundred percent certain he wouldn't have sent those pictures as a prop."

"That leaves Burton."

"Yeah," she granted.

Would Wayne have given her and Rocky access to Yoni's home if he was building a cover-up? Rocky had ensured they hadn't been tailed after they'd left Yoni's town house.

On the other hand, would her old friend have permitted their entrance into the crime scene— which was unquestionably outside regulations— for this very purpose? To determine if she knew something he didn't...like where the external hard drive was?

Kendra didn't want to believe the worst about him. Like Yoni, she'd always considered Wayne one of the good guys. Even a good man had his price. Castille was immensely powerful. Not that he'd proven a particularly bad guy, but power often brought out the worst in a person. The senator was no exception.

She rubbed her eyes, pushed her hair back. This was exactly why she'd left this world behind.

No one could be trusted when professional gain was at stake.

"Damn it." Kendra braced to get up when a hand reached down to her. She looked from the strong, wide hand to the man standing over her.

"Come on." He wiggled his fingers. "We'll move across the hall and use my laptop. See what we can find out about this Aleesha Ferguson. We'll figure this out," he hitched his head toward the mess, "later."

Kendra placed her hand in his, watched as his long fingers curled around hers. Warmth whispered through her, bringing with it a sense of relief and safety she needed more than she would dare say out loud.

Rocky pulled her to her feet in one smooth motion. "Housekeeping will take care of the mess." He gestured to the room at large and shrugged. "It's not so bad."

Another reality settled in as Kendra took a closer inventory of the room. No, it wasn't bad, the place was a disaster. Curtains, linens, furnishings had been damaged or destroyed. Hotel management was not going to be happy when they saw this.

"Okay," she relented. He was thinking a lot more clearly than she was. Kendra felt so damned tired. So frustrated. Her soul ached with regret for Yoni… for his family.

And her heart twisted with the need to find the truth…and justice.

Rocky kept her hand in his, leading the way to the door. As she stepped over her scattered clothing she hesitated, frowned. Pulling free of Rocky's gentle hold, she crouched down to inspect her favorite teal blouse. Shredded…like the chair. One piece at a time she picked up each item she'd hastily packed. Every single one was damaged beyond repair. Except the pair of jeans and the T-shirt she'd thrown in for no real reason. Maybe to blend better with her partner.

Didn't matter. Just clothes. She could buy more.

Why would whoever had come here looking for the hard drive have done this?

This part was a personal attack against her.

Rocky ushered her to her feet once more. "Don't let this scare tactic get to you. The person or persons responsible want you to be afraid."

He was right. She nodded, then followed him out the door, grabbing her purse as she went. Her attempts at slowing the whirlwind of confusion building to a hurricane in her brain proved impotent.

Searching for the external drive, then taking it, she could see. Someone had something to hide and didn't want her to find it.

But why the personal attack?

Maybe just the fear factor, like Rocky had said. Probably not personal at all. Well, whoever had damaged her things could get over it. She wasn't going anywhere. Not even across the street to another hotel. She and Rocky were showing no fear. This reaction from the enemy proved one thing for certain: someone was getting nervous.

When they were in Rocky's room, door closed and locked, he pointed to the chair, a duplicate of the damaged one in hers, and ordered: "Sit. I'll make coffee."

Kendra couldn't say how many minutes passed with her brain meandering in a shocked daze, but the smell of freshly brewed coffee drew her mind back to the here and now. "Smells good," she had the presence of mind to say.

"I don't know about good," Rocky said as he handed her a cup, "but definitely strong."

She cradled the cup in both hands, letting the heat permeate her palms. Felt comforting.

Rocky sat down at the desk and fired up his laptop. "Is that *A-l-i-s-h-a* Ferguson?"

"Try that," Kendra suggested. "If you don't get the right hit, go for *A-l-e-e-s-h-a*." She sipped her coffee, her mind replaying the images from the photos. Castille in a car with the Ferguson woman. The two in what looked to be an alleyway. Always at night. Always alone. Always deep in conversation.

But never touching or kissing…

If Castille was having an affair wouldn't whoever snapped the candid shots have caught at least one image of that behavior?

"Aleesha with the two *e*'s," Rocky confirmed. "Twenty-two. No known next-of-kin. Investigators deemed her the victim of a hit-and-run that occurred sometime between midnight and 3:00 a.m. on June 2. No suspects as of the date of this article. Maryland native. That's about it. The woman in the article photo definitely looks like the one in the shots Roper showed off."

Kendra fished for her cell phone and put a call into the agency. After giving a condensed briefing of the day's events, researcher Patsy Talley promised to do all she could to get Yoni Sayar's cell phone records for the past two months and to look into Aleesha Ferguson's background and death. Kendra thanked her colleague and ended the call.

"Anything else?" she asked Rocky who remained focused on the screen of his laptop. Another cup of coffee would provide the jump start her brain cells needed.

"Her name and photo popped up on an escort Web site based in Baltimore. Looks like there hasn't been an update in more than two years. She may or may not have still been involved with that business."

After refilling her cup, Kendra moved up behind Rocky to study the screen. In the photo Ferguson was outfitted in leather and chains. If this was the other woman, did Castille's wife learn about her and flip out? Or was Grant's accusation nothing more than an attempt to draw attention away from Castille himself? At one time Kendra's relationship with Sharon Castille, the senator's wife, had been relatively close. "Maybe we should try talking to Mrs. Castille."

Rocky glanced up at her. "Is there any chance she would willingly see you?"

Kendra wandered to the foot of the bed and collapsed. She wasn't sure how much longer she could put off getting some sleep. Even a second cup of coffee wasn't doing the trick. "I suppose it depends upon how the senator explained my abrupt departure from his staff. Can't hurt to try."

"I have a plan." Rocky pushed up from the desk. He covered the two steps between them and joined her on the foot of the bed. "You need sleep."

Kendra motioned to the door. "I should call the front desk about my room."

Rocky moved his head from side to side. "You sleep." He patted the bed. "I'll do a little more research, then I'll crash out in the chair."

She couldn't do that. It would be…inappropriate. Absolutely. Inappropriate. "I'm sure they'll give me another room." Kendra stared at her lap where her clasped hands tightened in uncertainty around the cup.

"Look. I'll call the front desk about your room. Don't worry about that." He curled his forefinger beneath her chin and lifted her gaze to his. "But, for tonight, I want you where I can see you."

His touch or maybe his voice made her tremble just a little. Could have been the exhaustion. "I'll be fine." She was perfectly capable of taking care of herself. His suggestion that she couldn't was... ridiculous. She had taken care of herself during dicey field investigations before.

He dropped his hand, gave her a patient smile. "I'm certain you would be fine either way, but I wouldn't be fine at all."

Confusion lined her brow.

"I'd spend the rest of the night worried about the possibility that whoever did that" he pointed in the direction of her room "would come back. I could conduct this investigation alone." He nodded for emphasis. "Don't think I can't. This whole partners gig is the Colby way of doing things."

She opened her mouth to argue the idea, but he kept going. "The bottom line is that I need you on this one. I don't know the players or their worlds. Your knowledge and your contacts will make what has to be done a whole lot easier and more efficient.

Not to mention I know how much this case means to you. So let's not take any chances with safety. Yours or mine. You crash here and we can keep an eye on each other."

Maybe it was the genuine concern in those blue eyes of his…or maybe it was just her need to feel protected at the moment.

As much as she'd like to claim immunity to vulnerability, that would be a lie. Determined, aggressive, she was both those things but she was also a woman and right now she felt a little vulnerable.

"I can't argue with your reasoning, partner." She exhaled the remainder of her uncertainty. "Wake me up if you find anything."

"Will do."

Rocky returned to his laptop. Kendra didn't move for a time. Instead, she watched the man whose nickname gave the impression of hard, unyielding fortitude. In the past fourteen or so hours she had learned that wasn't the case at all.

Big, tough Leland "Rocky" Rockford was soft and caring on the inside.

A smile widened her weary lips. She liked that.

She pushed up and moved to the side of the bed, kicking her shoes off as she went. Drawing the covers back, she decided that sleeping in her jacket would be counterproductive. She shouldered out of it and tossed it on the foot of the bed. Her holstered cell phone went on the bedside table.

Kendra stretched her kinked muscles, started to climb into the bed but abruptly realized that this suit was the only usable wardrobe element she had left. The jeans absolutely didn't count. Outside going shopping first thing in the morning, which was not on her agenda, she had little choice but to get under the covers and slip the skirt off as well.

With a camisole beneath the blouse, there was no reason she couldn't take that off, too. Otherwise she'd be a wrinkled mess in the morning. With a quick glance to ensure Rocky was absorbed in his work, she unbuttoned and peeled off the blouse.

Dropping back onto the pillows she pulled the covers up to her neck. It felt good to lie down. The many questions related to the case churned in her brain, but just closing her eyes was decelerating the puzzling whirlwind. Sleep dragged at her weary body, promising oblivion. She slowly let go.

Rocky would wake her if he found anything or if news came in from the agency research folks. Her lids fluttered open just enough to get one final peek at her partner…and protector.

He was no longer staring at the screen of his laptop. He was staring at her.

The image of those blue eyes drifted into darkness with her.

It was nice, she realized, not being alone.

Chapter Seven

Thursday, 6:15 a.m.

Rocky closed his laptop and turned in the chair to check on Kendra. She slept like a child—trusting and innocent. He scrubbed a hand over his face and realized he was smiling.

He liked watching her sleep.

Fortunately, he'd managed to catch a few winks himself. Around two this morning he'd moved to the more comfortable upholstered chair and stretched his legs out on the side of the bed opposite her. He'd fallen asleep watching her. Her face was the first thing he'd seen when he opened his eyes at five-thirty.

Another first for him.

Not only was she the first woman he'd been attracted to that wasn't attracted to him first, she was also the first sleeping lady he'd gotten so much pleasure simply watching.

Didn't make a lot of sense.

It just was.

Patsy T.—her name was Talley, but he liked call-ing her Patsy T.—had called with an update. She'd forwarded Sayar's cell phone records as well as Aleesha Ferguson's rap sheet to Rocky's e-mail.

Sayar had in fact received two calls from Mrs. Castille the day of Ferguson's death. Sayar had in the next hour made three additional calls to the senator's wife. The calls from Castille to Sayar were thirty seconds or less. Two of the three made by Sayar were similarly short, but one lasted a full three minutes. That didn't confirm Grant Roper's accusation, but it made for another lead to follow.

Aleesha Ferguson had numerous arrests for pros-titution and vagrancy in Baltimore as well as the D.C. area. Her mother, Alice Ferguson, had died of an overdose five years ago, leaving Aleesha alone and to, apparently, follow in the footsteps of her longtime profession. Alice had grown up in Arling-ton and moved to Baltimore after her only child was born. There was no traceable connection between Aleesha and the senator other than the photos Roper had flashed.

No traceable link between Aleesha and Sayar or Castille's wife.

Nothing.

Patsy T.'s research partner, Levi Stark, was very close to decrypting Sayar's files.

They were close to a lot of information but close wouldn't solve this case.

The only way to change that was to get this day started. He prepared a fresh pot of coffee and headed to the bathroom for a shower. Hesitating at the door, he glanced at Kendra and opted to grab his change of clothes to prevent an awkward situation after his shower in the event she awoke.

By the time he'd rushed through a shower and pulled on clean clothes, the smell of coffee had filled the room and Kendra was up with a cup in her hand.

"Good morning."

Her hair was a little mussed, the only evidence she'd just gotten out of bed. His gaze slid to the tousled linens and his gut tightened. He'd fought the urge to climb into that bed with her more than once last night. He felt relatively sure she wouldn't have appreciated that move.

"Morning." He stuffed yesterday's wardrobe into his bag and fumbled around until he found his toothbrush and paste.

"Thanks for making coffee." She sipped the hot brew. "It was great to wake up to hot caffeine."

It was great to wake up in the room with you.

He pushed the forbidden thought out of his head. "Patsy T. called."

"Did she find anything useful?"

While Kendra finished her coffee, Rocky brought her up to speed on what he'd learned. She studied the phone records and the rap sheet via his laptop, coming to the same conclusion he had. They had a lot of starts but not necessarily any that would lead them to the desired end result.

"I'll take a quick shower." Kendra sat her coffee cup on the desk. "Five minutes," she promised. "Then we'll get moving."

"I'll pack up our gear."

When she'd closed herself in the tiny bathroom, he packed up his laptop and gathered the rest of the gear they would need. Communications devices and weapons. He surveyed the room, decided that was everything.

He poured himself another cup of coffee. The sound of the water running in the shower stalled the cup halfway to his mouth.

Images of her naked, the soap gliding over her skin...the water tracing that same smooth path, rinsing the soap away.

He licked his lips, imagined how hers would taste. Nice, full lips that made the cutest bow when she was lost in thought. He liked her fingers, too.

Long, slender. When she was frustrated she rubbed at her forehead with her fingertips.

Why had he noticed so many little things about her in such a short time? The bigger question was, why had he been paying that much attention? Good thing she couldn't read his mind or she would likely think he was losing it or some kind of perv.

The roar of the blow dryer in the bathroom prodded Rocky from the distracting thoughts. He pulled on socks and boots. Threaded his belt through the loops of his jeans and fastened it. Then dragged on a sports jacket—his usual concession to the suit thing. A quick thread of his fingers through his hair and he was good to go.

The bathroom door opened, releasing a burst of sweet-smelling steam, and Kendra stepped out. "You were right," she said, looking and sounding well rested.

"Yeah?" His gaze immediately traced a path from her bare feet up those shapely legs to the hem of her skirt. He blinked, forced his attention to her face, which was every bit as distracting as the rest of her.

"Sleep was what I needed." She pulled on the cream-colored jacket she'd worn the day before. "I feel better prepared to move forward."

"Good." Efforts to banish the way her blouse had tightened against her breasts while she'd shouldered into the jacket proved futile. The more alone time he spent with her the less control he appeared to have.

"I'd like to go to my room." She stepped into her shoes, simultaneously stuffing something into her pocket. "See if any of my stuff survived." A search of her purse produced her keycard.

"Sure." He followed her out the door, annoyed that he'd slipped into one-word mode like a teenager suffering from lust overdose.

As she tucked her keycard into the slot on her door, he noticed that a hint of lace peeked from her jacket pocket. He blinked, swallowed. Pink lace. His attention instantly settled on the way her skirt molded to her backside. The way she dressed he'd expected plain white cotton undies...not pink lace.

The door of her room abruptly opened and Wayne Burton filled the space. "I tried your cell phone."

"What're you doing in my room?" she demanded.

Rocky had been about to voice the same question.

Burton backed up, allowing them entrance into Kendra's hotel room. "Management called in the breaking and entering. When I heard it was your room, I came right over."

Nice. A homicide detective for a B&E. Rocky was duly unimpressed.

Crime scene techs and a couple of uniformed cops were rifling through Kendra's stuff.

"I'll need a list of what's missing," Burton said to Kendra.

While Kendra briefed her *friend* on the missing items, Rocky watched his reaction. An occasional glance in Rocky's direction confirmed that Burton was doing the same thing.

Something Burton said had Kendra's temper rising. Rocky had missed whatever was said because his attention had abruptly diverted to where the pink lace had inched its way farther out of her pocket.

Rocky moved in closer to her and frowned at Burton. "Any thoughts on how someone discovered where Kendra is staying?" he demanded of Burton as he covertly snatched the scrap of pink lace from her jacket pocket and shoved it deep into his own.

She glared at Rocky, still furious at the situation.

"Is that an accusation, Mr. Rockford?"

Rocky looked the cop straight in the eye and answered honestly, "Yes."

The stare-off lasted about five seconds before Burton's expression relaxed and he threw out a challenge of his own. "Do you have reason to believe this incident had something to do with Kendra personally versus a random act of burglary?"

"You mean a random act like Yoni Sayar's murder?" Rocky countered.

"Just do what you have to do," Kendra snapped. Then she took a breath. "May I have whatever's left of my personal things?"

Burton backed off. "Sure."

He walked over to where her bag lay on the floor. Rocky hadn't noticed until then that the clothing items that had been spewed over the floor were now tucked back into the bag. Which meant Burton had gone through her things. Touched her stuff.

Renewed fury boiled up inside Rocky.

"Let's go." Kendra turned to him, bag in hand.

Rocky sent a final sour look in Burton's direction before executing an about-face and stalking back to the room across the hall. Inserting the keycard twice was necessary since he was too ticked off to do it right the first time.

When the door had closed behind them, Kendra flung her bag on the bed. "He's watching us." She set her hands on her hips and shook her head. "I knew it was likely but it really makes me angry to have it confirmed. Wayne is treating me like a suspect!"

Unable to stifle the assessment, Rocky opened his mouth and promptly inserted his foot. "I'm not so sure Burton keeping an eye on you has much to do with Sayar's murder case."

Kendra stopped picking through her damaged clothes and glared at him. "What does that mean?"

The taste of boot still on his tongue, Rocky shrugged. "The former personal connection between the two of you is Burton's top priority where you're concerned. At least, that's the way it looks to me."

"He told you this?" she demanded.

Rocky heaved a sighed. "No. But I'm not blind. You are," he said pointedly, "if you don't recognize his underlying motive. He's still got a thing for you."

Irritation flashing in her eyes, she swung her attention back to her stuff. "Whatever."

Yeah, whatever.

She fisted a wad of white lace and deserted her search. "I'll be ready in a minute."

He watched her storm toward the bathroom door before saying, "You might want this." She stopped and turned back to him, her free hand resting on the door. He pulled the lacy pink panties from his jacket pocket and walked over to hand the racy lingerie to her.

Her jaw went slack as she accepted the scrap of fabric. She patted her pocket, her cheeks turning as pink as the sexy panties.

Before she could demand how he'd ended up with her panties, he explained, "While you were railing at Burton, they popped out of your pocket. I grabbed them and tucked them into mine." He shrugged when she continued to stare at him in utter outrage and humiliation. "I didn't want you to be embarrassed in front of all those guys." Every tech and cop in the room was male.

She didn't say a word. She pushed into the bathroom and then slammed the door between them.

That was what he got for trying to be a gentleman.

Rocky wandered to the window and stared out at the promise of a hot, sultry day. His behavior was unacceptable. He needed to stop looking at her as a woman and start focusing more intently on the case. Difficult to do, though.

The bathroom door opened and he turned to face whatever she had to say next. He'd crossed the line to a degree and he owed her an apology.

"Look," he said before she could launch what would no doubt be a lecture about professionalism, "I apologize for making you uncomfortable. I thought I—"

"Why would you apologize?" she asked, surprising him. "You saved me from being the object of cop jokes for days. I appreciate it. Thank you."

Wow. He hadn't expected that. "Good." Back to the one-word reactions.

"Let's get going." She shouldered her purse. "We

need to eat." She pressed a palm to her flat middle. "I'm starving. Then we're going to see what we can find out about Mrs. Castille. Maybe talk to her."

Rocky picked up the bag with his laptop and their other gear. "What about the press conference?"

"We already know what they're going to say. Why waste our time?"

"Agreed."

Rocky mentally kicked himself as he followed her along the corridor. Pink lace panties shouldn't lessen his IQ. He hesitated at the bank of elevators and pushed the call button. The pink lace hadn't lowered his intelligence level, the idea that she'd worn them did that all by itself.

The warning chime that a car had arrived and the opening of the doors dragged him from the troubling thoughts. When Kendra didn't move through the open doors he followed her gaze back in the direction of her room just in time to get a glimpse of Burton ducking quickly back inside.

"He's watching us," Kendra murmured.

"He's watching you," Rocky countered.

Her gaze bumped into his. "It's way more complicated than that."

Rocky couldn't ignore the worry in her eyes. "You're right. Every aspect of this investigation is complicated. Including that cop."

She held his gaze, preventing him from drawing a breath.

With every fiber of his being he wanted to kiss her. To touch those lips with his own for just a moment…one or two seconds.

The elevator doors closed behind her. He told himself to reach around her and push the call button again, but that wasn't happening.

She blinked, turned her back and pushed the call button herself.

Rocky started mentally kicking himself again.

The doors opened and they stepped into the empty car. It was early. Not much movement from the other guests yet. Rocky leaned against the back of the car and let the tension flow out of him. Kendra selected the lobby floor and took a position against that same wall, no more than fifteen or eighteen inches between them.

Soft music whispered in the air. Elevator music. He worked to focus on the tune and not the scent of soap on her skin.

"Do me a favor, Rocky."

He braced for her censure, turned his face to hers as the elevator bumped to a stop on the lobby floor. "Name it, partner." She was his partner in this investigation. Professional partner.

"Next time you look at me the way you did a minute ago," she pushed away from the wall but kept her gaze fixed on his, "do something about it or walk away."

He watched her stride out of the elevator and across the marble lobby before he had the presence of mind to follow.

Do something about it?

He could do that.

The thought had him licking his lips.

No, he couldn't do that.

His attention lit on her once more as she waited at the main exit.

But he would.

Eventually.

It was feeling more and more inevitable.

10:40 a.m.

KENDRA LEANED FORWARD as Rocky made the turn into the private drive of the Castille estate. A limo sat in front of the stately home, the uniformed driver fitting luggage into the trunk.

"Looks like we got here just in time."

Kendra made an agreeable sound.

"No reason to expect the senator will show up?"

"According to Castille's secretary, he's in the office all morning. A lunch appointment at one, but otherwise he'll be in his office all day preparing some big presentation."

"Then the missus is going away for…" Rocky grunted as he parked behind the limo and got a closer look at the stack of designer luggage in the truck "…for a week or two."

Kendra chuckled. "Maybe for the weekend." She reached for her door. "The lady likes to travel in style with every possible accessory. A senator's wife never knows what might come up."

They rounded the hood and approached the driver together. "My name is Kendra Todd," Kendra said when the driver had finished sizing her up with a critical eye. "I'm here to see Mrs. Castille."

"Is Mrs. Castille expecting you?" a male voice behind her demanded.

Kendra's attention moved to the grand steps that fronted the house. Andrew…something, Mrs. Castille's personal assistant, descended a step or two as he waited for Kendra's response.

"Andrew, it's good to see you." Kendra used the ruse to approach the steps. "This is my friend Leland Rockford." She gestured to the man beside her. "I'm in town for a couple of days and I wanted to stop by and say hello to Mrs. Castille."

"I'm afraid she's unavailable at the moment," he said in a condescending tone.

Kendra claimed one step upward, defying his decree. "Why don't I leave my number? That way if she has the time she can call me while I'm in town."

Andrew pulled out his PalmPilot. "I'll pass along the message."

"Eight-seven-two," Kendra began.

"Andrew, is the car ready?" Mrs. Castille appeared at the door.

"Mrs. Castille." Kendra jumped at the opening, moving up the steps despite Andrew's scathing glare. "I was just leaving my number with Andrew."

"Kendra." The senator's wife pasted on a smile. "Judd didn't tell me you were in town."

Kendra accepted a quick cheek-to-cheek hug. "He's such a busy man. I'm sure he has far more on his mind than my itinerary."

"Andrew, tell the driver I'll be a few minutes." Sharon Castille motioned for Kendra to come inside. "Let's have a coffee." She managed a more genuine smile for Rocky. "Who's your friend, dear?"

Kendra made the belated introductions as she and Rocky followed the senator's wife into her parlor. Andrew disappeared down the entry hall, probably to usher the kitchen help to prepare a tray. Or to call the senator and alert him to their presence.

"You're here on business?" Sharon asked when they'd settled amid her luxurious furnishings.

Kendra chose a fairly direct approach. "I'm here

to support Yoni's family. I was devastated to hear of his death."

Hesitation. Blink. "Yes…it's just awful. The senator says he'll be greatly missed."

"I know he was a good friend to you both," Kendra suggested.

Two blinks this time. Blank expression. "I'm sorry to say I didn't know him that well. I saw him a few times at social events and occasionally at Judd's office. Still, it's tragic. Just tragic."

By the time she'd finished speaking her voice had reached that sympathetic tone she'd clearly been striving for. Too bad she'd had to work so hard to accomplish her goal.

"You saw the press conference this morning?" Another couple of rapid blinks.

"Yes." Kendra worked equally hard to restrain her anger. What was the woman hiding? Yoni was dead! Was there no one close to him who cared to see that justice was served?

"Tragic," Sharon repeated. "Just tragic."

Kendra went for broke. "Yoni mentioned to me that the two of you spoke occasionally. By phone, I believe he said."

Despite the store-bought blush applied so meticulously to her cheeks, the color drained from Sharon's face. "Really? I can't recall speaking to him by phone?" She pressed a finger to her lips, then said, "Perhaps there was that once…when Judd was out of town." She shook her head. "I'm not sure actually."

"I could be mistaken," Kendra offered, then frowned as if trying to recall the conversation. "Maybe it was someone else." She shook her head. "It was last month. I may have the whole thing confused." She feigned a laugh at her confusion. "He kept talking about some automobile accident. Doesn't matter anyway. So," Kendra stared into the woman's startled gaze, "how have you been?"

The conversation turned short and crisp from there. The coffee tray never arrived. Within ten minutes of their arrival Sharon appeared to suddenly remember that she was on her way to her sister's house in Alexandria. She really had to go. The driver was waiting after all.

Rocky guided the rental car around the circle driveway and back onto the street. "I think that's the first time I've been in a room with two other people and not said a word."

Kendra laughed, mostly because she was frustrated and disappointed and needed a break in the tension. "I assumed you were too busy analyzing the target to speak."

"It didn't require that much effort."

Kendra made another sound that couldn't quite be labeled a laugh. Rocky was definitely right about that. Sharon Castille had lied through her perfect white teeth. She was probably on the phone to the senator right now.

How was it that the people closest to Yoni could care so little for his life that they would cover up the truth about his death?

There was only one reason.

To cover up their own guilt.

"You up to a little street walking?" Rocky asked, dragging her from the painful thoughts.

Kendra turned in her seat to study his profile. "I was just thinking that should be our next move."

"Great minds and all that jazz." He shot her a smile.

She liked his smile. Liked spending time with him. She'd been alone for so long. It hadn't bothered her until now. Funny. "So," she redirected her thoughts to their next step, "that gives us a few hours."

The ladies of the night preferred the dark. "I'd like to do some research on the Transparency Bill Yoni talked about. Find out who supports it, who's against it. Maybe something will jump out at me."

"Where to?" he asked.

"The library."

"Just tell me the way."

"Take the same route back to D.C. proper that we came." That he kept checking the rearview mirror as she talked tripped an internal alarm. "Something wrong?"

"Nothing I can't handle." He made an abrupt right.

Kendra braced, keeping an eye on the side mirror for their tail.

Rocky had no more straightened out from the turn than a silver sedan skidded into the same turn.

"I hope you know this area well." Rocky stomped the accelerator.

"Fairly well." She kept her focus on the street signs. Hoped her memory didn't fail her.

"Take the next left." That would take them back to the Beltway where they could more easily get lost in the traffic.

Rocky barreled into the turn, skidding wide. Kendra held her breath. Horns blared as they crossed traffic out of turn.

They hit the Beltway, pushing well beyond the posted speed limit. A few abrupt lane changes and a last-minute exit and the silver sedan was no longer in the rearview mirror.

Rocky doubled back one exit and reentered the Beltway. He laid back with the slower traffic in the right lane.

"Good job." Kendra exhaled some of her tension.

"For now." Rocky sent her a pointed look.

"Whether it was your visit with Burton or Mrs. Castille, someone's marked you for surveillance."

Which had to mean they were getting warmer.

Chapter Eight

L Street, 9:05 p.m.

Rocky wrapped his arm around Kendra's shoulders. The move startled her at first but then she recognized that it was designed to ensure they didn't stand out. She relaxed. Most of the couples were holding hands or wrapped in each other's arms as they cruised the popular street.

If anyone had tailed them to or from the library they were very good at covert surveillance. Neither Rocky nor Kendra had picked up on a tail.

Levi Stark had completed decrypting the files and sent all to Rocky's laptop. Most of the information was related to the various bills Yoni had been working prior to his death. But one had proven unsettling. It read like a transcription of a meeting or telephone conversation with only one side of the conversation recorded. According to the transcript, Senator Castille had exchanged heated words with an unknown party related to his refusal to pay a fee in exchange for silence on a subject that was never mentioned.

Possibly the conversation was connected to the blackmail threat Yoni had spoken of. But no particular bill, or subject for that matter, was mentioned. No names were revealed. Which made no sense at all. Why had someone bothered to steal the hard drive from her hotel room if it contained nothing of significance?

Kendra could only assume that, like her, the thief had assumed something important would be in the files. That not being the case, she had no answers and nothing concrete on which to move forward.

Yet, Kendra had to presume that the information carried some sort of hidden significance that, apparently, only Yoni understood.

The most disturbing aspect was that she and Rocky had been on location more than thirty hours and they knew nothing useful to the investigation.

While at the library Kendra had looked up the Ferguson accident in a number of the local papers. In each instance the vague mention was buried so deeply one had to be specifically looking for the article to locate it—if it was reported at all. The one detail she had discovered that changed her view of Ferguson's death in any manner was the name of the detective in charge of the investigation.

Wayne Burton.

Too much of a coincidence to actually be coincidental.

Music wafted from the L Street Lounge. Kendra wished her friend hadn't been murdered…that she hadn't had to come back here for *this*. She wished she were on a date having fun like other women her age. How long had it been since she'd gone out for a night on the town with a man just for the fun of it?

Too long.

Maybe she never really had. Her relationship with Wayne had felt more like a necessary accessory that everyone expected.

It hadn't felt natural or relaxed. She'd never been involved with a man who made her feel those things.

She glanced up at the man holding her close to his side. A man like this one. Handsome. Compassionate. Considerate.

He looked down at her. Made a questioning face. "I should've shaved this morning. If we run into any of your fancy friends they might mistake me for someone you picked up on this street."

Kendra laughed, the sound came from deep in her belly. "You're right, you know." She shook her head, watched the couples drifting into the lounge.

Without warning Rocky stopped moving forward,

held Kendra even tighter. "Hang on." He ushered her to a lamppost where he basically wrapped the rest of his big body around her.

"What's up?" She wanted to lean her head to one side and look past him to see whatever he'd noticed, but that wouldn't be smart.

"Hear that?"

She listened, heard a gruff male voice. *You show up here again and I'm calling the cops.*

"Watch to the right," Rocky murmured.

Three young women strutted down the sidewalk away from the lounge directly behind Rocky's back.

The man, a bouncer evidently, had ordered the women out of the lounge.

Rocky pulled Kendra away from the lamppost, his long fingers curled around hers, and started after the women.

Kendra hadn't recognized any of the three but she understood what Rocky saw…ladies of the night. Super short miniskirts. Sky high heels and tight, revealing blouses.

"Stay close," he warned before releasing Kendra's hand.

Before Kendra could question his strategy, he'd hustled up behind the ladies. The women stopped walking and started flirting.

Kendra took a position at the next lamppost. She

didn't want to get too close. The ladies might not be as forthcoming with her.

One wrapped her arm around Rocky's and tip-toed to whisper something in his ear. He smiled.

Kendra's throat tightened.

Ridiculous.

Rocky was doing his job. When he pulled out his cell phone and showed the screen to each of the three, Kendra knew he was asking if they had known Aleesha Ferguson. He'd downloaded a photo of her from the data they'd gotten from the agency.

The move didn't go over well with one of the girls. She backed away from the huddle. When she whirled around, her bottled blond hair flew around her shoulders. Long skinny legs thrust one in front of the other as she stormed away from the huddle.

As she stamped past Kendra's position, Kendra made a snap decision and followed her.

Stay close rang in her ears, but Kendra ignored the warning. This woman's reaction to seeing what Kendra presumed was Ferguson's photo spoke volumes.

This direction might take them to a dead end as far a Yoni's murder investigation, but it was the only lead they had at the moment.

Kendra quickened her pace to catch up with the long strides of the other woman. When she'd moved up next to her, Kendra made another snap decision. "I've got fifty bucks. Do you have a minute?"

The woman stopped and gave her a cold once-over. "Make it a hundred and I might be able to help you."

Kendra didn't have that much cash handy. "Just three questions, okay?"

The woman's hard gaze narrowed. "What kind of questions?"

Kendra reached into her purse, careful not to take her eyes off the woman. "Does it matter?"

She stared at the cash in Kendra's hand. "Guess not. I get all kinds," she muttered. She jerked her head toward the next building. "This way."

Glancing back to see if Rocky was still talking to the other two would only make the woman suspicious. So Kendra followed her to a narrow alley between the next two buildings.

"This'll be fine," Kendra said two steps into the dark alley. She wanted any information she could get, but she wasn't a fool. The weight of the weapon in her purse pulled heavily at her shoulder, but she had no desire to be forced to use it.

The woman leaned against the building and reached into her tiny shoulder bag.

Kendra's hand slid back inside her own as new tension rippled through her even as she recognized that it would be difficult to conceal a weapon in a bag that small.

The woman pulled out a cigarette and lighter, lit the cigarette and after a long drag, demanded, "So ask your questions."

Kendra maintained her position square in the middle of the narrow alley. If the woman bolted it would have to be into the darkness away from the street. "I'm looking for the truth."

She laughed. "Afraid you're looking in the wrong place, lady. We don't sell the truth on this street."

"My friend showed you a photo of my sister," Kendra lied. "I want to know what happened to her."

The girl threw down her half-smoked cigarette and pushed away from the wall. "I don't need your money that bad."

"Wait." Kendra moved to the left, blocking the path she'd intended to take. "Please, help me."

The woman's glare burned through the darkness. "I can't help you."

"Three questions," Kendra reminded. She offered the money to her. "Just three."

She stared at the money. "Okay." Her gaze met Kendra's once more. " But I'm not making any promises that I'll answer all of them."

Kendra nodded. "Fair enough." Big breath. "First, and this one doesn't count, what's your name?"

One second, two, then three passed before she caved. "Delilah."

"Nice to meet you, Delilah." Kendra offered her hand. "I'm Kendra."

Delilah reluctantly accepted the handshake.

"First question, were there any witnesses to the accident?"

"What accident?"

Kendra dredged up some additional patience. "You know what accident I mean."

"Yep." Delilah lit another cigarette. Coughed. "But what you read in the papers or whatever the cops told you was wrong."

Kendra waited for her to continue. She wasn't going to waste question number two if she could help it.

"It was no accident." She looked past Kendra then met her eyes once more. "He hit her on purpose."

"He?" Damn it. The question was out of Kendra's mouth before she could stop it. But he? According to Roper it had been Mrs. Castille.

"Yeah. A guy. Dark hair. Young. I didn't see him up close so that's all I know. But I won't forget that big fancy white car he was driving."

Delilah witnessed the accident? Kendra's heart hammered in her chest. She only had one question left for the fifty bucks. Think! "This man had some beef with Aleesha?"

Delilah shook her head. Took another draw from her cigarette. "I don't think so. I guess he could have been one of Aleesha's friends, but it was the car that I recognized."

Kendra held her breath. Prayed she would keep going. Any information she could provide might kick-start this investigation.

"That old bitch had been stalking Aleesha for weeks." Delilah threw down her smoke and stuck out her hand. "Give me the money."

Was she referring to Sharon Castille? Kendra needed to know who Delilah was. Was Delilah a professional name? Did she live in the area? Finding her again was essential. "I might have more." She dug around in her purse. Pulled out her sunglasses and thrust them at Delilah. "Hold that for me, will you?"

Delilah huffed with impatience, but she wrapped her fingers around the sunglasses.

Three, five…Kendra had five more dollars. She added that to the fifty along with one of her business cards and offered it at the woman. "Will that get me one more answer?"

Her face puckered with annoyance, Delilah shoved the sunglasses back at her. Kendra accepted them by grabbing the very end with her thumb and forefinger.

"Depends on the question." Delilah stuffed the

money into her tiny shoulder bag without counting it or noticing the business card. "Make it fast. I got stuff to do."

"Do you know the woman's name? The one who was stalking Aleesha?"

Delilah held Kendra's gaze, clearly wrestling with the decision to answer. "Castille. Sharon Castille. That senator's wife."

Kendra kept the shock off her face. She wanted to ask so many other questions...wanted to know more—needed to know more. More than anything she didn't want to let this woman go but she was out of cash and pushing the limitations of her patience already.

Hesitating as she stepped around the barrier still in her path, Delilah searched Kendra's face. "Aleesha didn't have no sister."

"You're right," Kendra admitted. "I wasn't completely honest with you but that doesn't mean I don't want to right this wrong."

"She's dead. You can't right that."

"Wait!" Kendra needed to know her last name. "Delilah what? What's your last name?"

The woman kept walking. Didn't look back.

Kendra wandered back onto the sidewalk. Even if Mrs. Castille was responsible somehow for Aleesha's murder, what did that have to do with Yoni's. Yoni had dark hair and was young but he couldn't—wouldn't—have done such a thing. Kendra absolutely refused to believe that about him. Covering up a murder was absolutely not possible.

A big body bumped into Kendra, turned her around and ushered her in the opposite direction. "Keep moving."

Even if his voice hadn't given him away before Kendra's distraction cleared, his scent would have. Rocky. "Did you learn anything?" She wanted to tell him her news but she wanted to hear his first.

"We have two tails," he said without looking at her or slowing his rushed pace.

Kendra had to focus to keep up with his long strides. "They spotted you on the corner?" She was relatively certain no one had tailed her to the alley.

"Yes, ma'am. But, as I approached your position I noticed a guy hanging around who may or may not have been part of the tag team."

Damn.

"We parked in the other direction." Getting to the car seemed like the best strategy right now.

"That's a fact," Rocky agreed as he guided her between two clusters of pedestrians. "But we don't want to lead them to our means of escape if we can help it."

Rocky executed a right face and hustled her into a cafe. He bypassed the hostess and weaved through the tables until they reached the corridor where the restrooms were located.

"Kitchen." He pointed to the door labeled Employees Only.

She recognized his strategy now. "Wait." She dug in her heels. "I'll get a table." He was already shaking his head before she finished explaining. "You go out the back, get the car and when you're in front of the cafe text me and I'll come out."

"No way am I leaving you here."

"They're not going to approach me in front of all these people." She backed away from him. "Go."

She didn't give him a chance to argue. She moved back through the dining room and hooked up with the hostess. A table situated in a straight line and only a few feet from the door served Kendra's purposes for a hasty exodus. She spotted two men loitering outside the window, one blatantly watching her.

"A waitress will be right with you," the hostess promised.

Kendra thanked her and pretended to study the menu. The watcher's accomplice came inside and took a seat at the bar. Kendra calculated the distance between them, ten yards max.

A waitress approached Kendra's table. "Would you like to order a drink first?"

Kendra checked the street again, then pulled her

credit card from her purse. "Sparkling water will be all, please." She passed the card to the waitress. "Would you swipe my card now? I'm expecting someone and I may have to leave in a hurry."

"Sure."

Keeping her cell phone in hand, Kendra checked the door from time to time, covertly scanning the street beyond the floor-to-ceiling front windows simultaneously. The only obstacle standing between her and the street was the guy outside the window. She would need a distraction for him.

What about the third guy Rocky had spotted? As the minutes ticked by Kendra worried that he'd followed and overtaken her partner. Rocky was a big, well-trained guy. He could take care of himself. And he was armed.

Then again, the other guys likely would be, as well.

The two hanging around her position wore jackets with their trousers. Most any manner of lethal weapon could be hidden under a jacket.

Her phone vibrated in her palm.

I'm turning onto your block now.

"Here you go."

Kendra smiled for the waitress as she placed the

stemmed glass of sparkling water on the table, along with the check and Kendra's card.

"Thank you." Kendra quickly signed the check, providing a nice tip, and tucked the card back into her purse.

She shifted her legs, settled her purse into her lap and prepared to move as soon as she saw the rental car approach.

A car rolled up slowly. Kendra's muscles tightened in preparation for launching out of the chair and through the exit.

Silver...not black.

Not Rocky.

The tinted window on the front passenger side powered down as the silver sedan came to a stop.

Horns blared in indignation.

Kendra's mouth formed the words *Get Down!* as her brain analyzed the series of events.

She hit the floor.

The glass window exploded, showering fragments over the front of the dining room.

Screams filled the air.

Tables and chairs tumbled to the floor.

A light fixture burst and went dark.

Framed memorabilia on the wall shattered and crashed to the floor.

The blast of metal smashing into metal followed by screeching tires erupted outside.

More screams inside…shouting and crying.

Rushing footsteps.

Kendra shook off the shock. Shoved her hand into the purse she still clutched. Her fingers curled around the butt of her weapon. She came up onto her knees, the weapon leveled at the closest threat—the man who had been loitering by the window.

Gone.

She swung around, scanned the people now moving around the bar. No sign of the one who'd taken a post at the bar, either.

"Gun!" a voice shouted.

Someone tackled her from behind.

Her cheek flattened against the wood floor, pieces of glass bored into her flesh.

Her weapon was pried from her fingers.

The weight crushing into her back was a patron or an employee of the cafe…not a threat. She told herself to remain calm. Stay cool. Three more men were huddled around her. She didn't bother attempting to explain who she was and why she had a weapon.

The police would be here soon enough.

Her one concern right now was Rocky.

Where the hell was Rocky?

Chapter Nine

11:55 p.m.

Lieutenant Wayne Burton glared first at Rocky then at Kendra. "Two people are injured."

Not counting Kendra, Rocky bit back. A paramedic had treated her minor abrasions and cuts. The small bandage on her cheek had anger fisting in his gut all over again. This was unacceptable.

Yet it could have been so much worse.

He should never have allowed her to stay here alone.

The cafe dining room was wrecked. Front windows shattered. Broken chairs and tables, mostly from the panicked patrons. A bullet had left an ugly hole in the vintage mahogany bar. The mirror behind it lay in a million pieces in the prep alley behind the long bar. Whiskey and liquor bottles were shattered.

All three of the perpetrators had disappeared

into the night. But not without a little something to remember Rocky by. The silver car had whipped around him as soon as he'd turned onto the street that ran in front of the cafe. When Rocky had realized what the driver intended, he'd rear-ended the bastard. He'd managed to get part of the license plate number before ramming him.

As soon as he'd ensured Kendra was okay, including pushing aside the three idiots who'd seized and manhandled her, he'd given the first cop on the scene the information about the silver car.

Kendra pushed up from the chair she'd taken after Burton had sequestered them to the cafe manager's office. "I have a question for you," she said to her old *friend*. She shifted to regain her balance. The heel of one shoe was missing. "Why are you here?" She turned her palms upward. "There are no fatalities, thankfully. It's a drive-by shooting so far as anyone knows. There's no evidence I was a target any more than anyone else seated in the dining room."

She went toe-to-toe with the cop. "So, tell me, why are you here?"

Burton glowered at her, his face red with the frustration and anger he'd readily shown in his tone since his arrival.

"Good point," Rocky said, adding insult to injury. "Working the Sayar case makes sense. The breaking and entering at the hotel, not so much so. This," he shook his head, "surely you have homicides to work. This is D.C. after all."

The glower Burton had reserved thus far for Kendra shifted to Rocky. "Do you think I'm stupid?"

Loaded question. Rocky resisted the urge to say yes.

Burton's fury swung back to the woman glaring up at him. "Do either of you think for one second that I don't know what's going on here?"

"You have the floor, Lieutenant," Kendra shot back. "Why don't you tell us what *you* believe is going on. Clearly you have all the insight."

"You," he growled, "are trying to turn Sayar's case into something it's not. We have no evidence of anything other than a random act of violence carried out during the execution of a robbery."

"Except the robber wasn't too bright since he forgot the MP3 player and flat-panel television in the victim's bedroom," Rocky pointed out. "And the forty bucks lying on the bedside table."

Burton's gaze sharpened. "Stay out of the Sayar case," he warned. "What happened at your hotel room and here tonight should be warning enough that you're barging into territory that…could have serious consequences. You do not want to push this."

"Is that a threat?" Kendra demanded.

Burton heaved a sigh. "That's all I can tell you for now." He hitched a thumb toward the door. "I'll have one of the officers take you to your hotel."

"Not necessary." Rocky stood. "The rental agency is bringing another car." He gave the man a nod. "But I appreciate the offer."

Burton started for the door then hesitated. "If you're smart," he said to Kendra, "first thing in the morning you'll get on that fancy jet that brought you here and go back to Chicago. Don't let the past drag you down with it, Kendra."

When he'd gone, Rocky closed the door behind him. "Your friend has a point."

Kendra closed her eyes and took a deep breath as she fought the receding adrenaline. "I understand that nothing we do will bring Yoni back, but his family deserves the truth."

There was nothing left to give them…except the truth.

Friday, 1:00 a.m.

ROCKY OPENED THE DOOR to his hotel room.

Kendra hesitated before going in. "They gave me a new room."

He shook his head. "I'm not letting you out of my sight again."

"I need clothes…" She exhaled a weary breath. "I need sleep."

"I can't help you with the kind of clothes you're accustomed to." Rocky ushered her into the room and closed the door. "But the sleep" he gestured to his bed "I can take care of."

"I'm not putting you out of your bed again." She stood her ground near the door.

Rocky crossed the room and picked up her bag with its few salvageable contents. "Your toiletries are here." He picked up his own bag and poked through it until he found a clean shirt. "This'll have to do until we can do some shopping tomorrow."

She hesitated, every thought going through her head playing out on her face. Uncertainty. Temptation. Exhaustion.

Surrender.

One uneven step disappeared behind her. "Only if you're sure you can manage some sleep, as well. We're both exhausted."

"Don't worry about me." She closed the distance between them, her steps halting with the missing shoe heel, and tugged the shirt from his hand. "I can sleep anywhere, anytime."

"Okay, partner."

Rocky watched her walk across the room. How could a woman look that good with a broken shoe heel and in a rumpled skirt and torn blouse? Her jacket had been trashed, blood on the sleeve where she'd wiped her cheek. She'd taken it off in the manager's office and hadn't bothered to pick it up when they left.

The spraying of water in the shower had him conjuring mental pictures of her releasing one button after the other on that torn blouse…allowing the silky material to slide off her shoulders. Then she would reach behind her to lower the zipper of her conservative skirt. It would fall to the floor, circling her bare feet. More of those lacy panties he hadn't expected from her would drag down her thighs.

"Knock it off, man," he muttered.

He sat down on the end of the bed and pulled off his boots, rolled off the socks and tossed them aside. His wallet, cell phone and change went on the desk. The belt was next. Unbuttoning his shirt and pulling it free of his waistband was as far as he went with removing clothes. He didn't want to make her uncomfortable.

Grabbing a pillow, he pulled the upholstered chair closer to the bed and settled in. When he closed his eyes, those tempting images of her naked in the shower invaded his brain once more.

Banishing the arousing pictures, he concentrated on relaxing each muscle. One at a time. Slowly, thoroughly. His heart rate decelerated. His breathing became deeper, slower.

He'd almost succeeded in drifting off when the bathroom door opened and the clean steam, spiced with the sweet smell of her and generic hotel soap, permeated the room, awakening his senses and resurrecting those forbidden images.

He cracked one eye open just enough to watch her pad to the bed. His shirt fell to mid-thigh. This was the first time he'd seen that much of her legs. Gorgeous. The other eye opened. She climbed onto the bed and burrowed beneath the covers.

By the time she'd snuggled in, his heart rate had jumped back into overdrive. No use denying it. He was seriously attracted to the woman. Not just the way she looked, and her refreshing ladylike manners. This went way deeper than that. He liked the way she talked, the way she moved. Her way of thinking…her compassion.

"I thought you were asleep."

Her voice lugged him out of the lust-arousing thoughts. "Almost," he admitted. *Until you came into the room and made me sit up and take notice, mentally and physically.*

"I tried to be quiet."

He smiled. Wouldn't have mattered if she'd floated on the air…he would have felt her presence…smelled her sweet scent. "Don't worry about it."

"Why didn't you ever get married?"

If she'd asked if he'd actually been born a girl he wouldn't have been more surprised. "Busy, I guess." He wasn't about to go into the psychology

of his choices. His mother had a whole book of theories on his reasoning for remaining single. Rocky
felt relatively certain her analysis was part of the
reason he'd recently started feeling some urgency
on the subject.

"No siblings?"

"Nope."

"Hmm."

He considered the "hmm" for a moment. "What
does *hmm* mean?"

"Nothing."

Yeah, right. "You think because I'm barreling toward forty that I should be or have been
married?"

"No...I...yes. How long have your parents been
married?"

"Forty years."

"You're a nice guy. Good job. You bought a house
last year, didn't you?"

"Sure did."

"Seems like you've got the whole *nesting* thing
going on."

He lifted his head and stared pointedly at her.
"Have you been talking to my mother?" The remark
sounded exactly like one his mother would make.
Had made, recently as a matter of fact.

Kendra laughed. "I don't know your mother."

"The two of you would hit it off." In a heartbeat.

Silence lapsed around them, doing nothing at all to slow Rocky's anticipation of hearing her voice again. It soothed him…made him want to hear her crying out his name.

Far enough, pal.

"What about you?" he ventured.

"What about me?"

"You grew up in Virginia?"

"Roanoake."

"Sisters? Brothers?"

"One brother. He was killed in Iraq in 2003."

"Damn. Sorry." Rocky didn't recall hearing about that. And it wasn't exactly something a guy forgot.

"It was a bad time for my family."

"I can only imagine." His family hadn't faced that kind of tragedy. They were damned lucky.

"My mother sends me those same vibes you get from yours."

He met her gaze again. "The marriage-grandkids thing?"

She nodded. "My brother was older than me. He'd gotten married six months before he deployed. My parents had high hopes for grandchildren. Now all that pressure is on me."

Rocky didn't hesitate to give her as good as she'd

given him. "So no close encounters of the marriage kind for you, either?" 'Course she wasn't thirty yet. And she was a career woman. No reason there should have been any already.

"Only once."

Aha. He'd known it. "Your *friend* Burton?"

"We talked about it, but never quite reached the doing something about it step."

Man. "Is he the real reason you left D.C.?" Seemed a reasonable hypothesis.

"No. I left D.C. because I couldn't work with Senator Castille any longer."

"You want to tell me about it?" If she didn't want to discuss her falling-out with the senator he understood. They didn't know each other that well beyond the work environment.

"He was into amassing power and wealth rather than representing the best for his constituents. I got to the point where I disagreed with him more than I agreed. Not a good trait in a personal aide."

"Sounds like the usual fare for politicians." The words were no sooner out of his mouth than he regretted them. Kendra's education and career had been in politics until three years ago. "For most of them, I mean."

"Reaching a position that high within the government is about power and wealth to some degree. That's true." She paused a moment. "But when that desire overrides all else, it's wrong. I called him on one particular action he'd been persuaded to take and he blackballed me. At first, I was determined to prove my case…but I realized pretty fast that I was wasting my time. It was time for me to go. I realized I wasn't cut out for that world."

"Good for you. Too many people waste a lot of time and energy butting a brick wall. It's better to turn to something more constructive."

She sat up, pushed the hair out of her eyes. "That's exactly right." She shrugged. "I couldn't change the system but there were other ways I could make a difference. That was what I really wanted to do."

"What about you and Burton? Were you already over at that point?"

Kendra pulled her knees to her chest and rested her chin there. She hadn't talked to anyone—not even her mother—about the break-up with Burton. "I couldn't stay. He couldn't go." Was that really the reason the relationship died? No. "He was too wired in to things here. Too by the book rather than by the heart. I had known for a while that we weren't a good fit."

"Wow."

Yeah. She couldn't believe she'd said the words out loud. "He's a good cop." Was that still true? Maybe, maybe not. "At least he was three years ago." Didn't seem that way now. He was ignoring valid points regarding Yoni's murder. She didn't understand that. Had someone named his price? Did he belong to that exclusive, elusive boys' club now? She hoped not.

"A lady like you shouldn't have any trouble finding someone new. What's the holdup?"

She raised her eyebrows at that one. "A lady like me? What exactly does that mean?"

Rocky closed his arms over his chest and ducked his head toward one shoulder in a half-hearted shrug. "Pretty. Smart. You know what I mean."

If only it were that easy. "I'm afraid those particular skills are vastly underrated by the male species, Mr. Rockford." She adopted a knowing look. "When was the last time you dated a woman because she met the criteria?"

The sheepish look that claimed his expression answered the question without him saying a word. He hadn't.

"I didn't think so."

"It's a defect of the species," he offered with over-the-top humility.

"Yeah. Among others."

"So you've sworn off men," he suggested.

Kendra shook her head. "No, not consciously."

"What's your dating criteria?"

"Good-natured. Considerate of others. Financially stable. Sound judgment." She couldn't be sure but it looked as if his eyes had glazed over. "All that's presuming I'm dating."

His eyes narrowed. "Are you trying to tell me you don't date?"

"Not in three years, two weeks and a couple of days." She shouldn't still remember the exact date, but she did. Down to the hour, in fact, but she wouldn't mention that part.

"Not one single date?" he pressed.

"Sheesh, Rocky, don't go out of your way to depress me."

"Seriously. Not one?"

She moved her head side to side. It was pathetic now that she confessed it out loud to another human being. "No dates. Nothing. I haven't been kissed in three years, two weeks—"

"And a couple of days," he finished for her.

"Right."

"Wow."

He used that word a lot. "I would choose a number of words to describe the condition, but wow isn't one of them."

"Just haven't met a good-natured, considerate-of-others guy who's financially stable and of good judgement, is that it?"

"Guess so." She leaned back against the pillows. "Your mother would say I have issues."

"Join the crowd," he said with a laugh. "I've been

made aware of my many issues my whole life." His lips curved into a smile. "My father would tell you that life is an issue."

Rocky was right. She would hit it off with his mother. His father, too, from the sound of it.

"Thanks," she felt compelled to say.

"For?"

"Taking my mind off exploding glass and panicked screams."

He dropped his feet to the floor and stood.

Before she could guess if he'd decided a pot of coffee was in order or a bathroom break, he walked around to the side of the bed and sat down on the edge of the mattress, careful not to crowd her.

"That was my mistake." He shook his head. "I shouldn't have left you. I feel really bad about that."

This big guy never ceased to surprise her. "You did what I told you. It was my decision." She shrugged. "I lived through it. And we learned something significant."

"Castille's wife and/or an accomplice killed Aleesha Ferguson."

She'd told him what she'd learned from the girl who called herself Delilah. "And that we're on to something. Otherwise no one would care to watch or to interfere with our efforts."

He traced the small bandage on her cheek.

"They're getting nervous and that makes you a target."

"Makes us both targets," she amended.

He nodded. "They don't like that we're getting so close."

Close. Yes. Too close. *This close* she could see the tiny gray specks that gave his deep blue eyes such depth and vividness. She liked his lips…the cut of his jaw and the impact of his high cheekbones. She wondered vaguely if there was Native American blood in his heritage. The blue eyes appeared even more profound framed by that coal-black hair.

"You keep looking at me that way and we're going to have a problem."

She'd made some statement to that effect on the elevator this morning. She didn't let his statement or the idea that she'd given him the same prevent her from continuing to look into his eyes. Really look. The soft admiration and respect for her that she saw there fueled the warmth his nearness had ignited.

"What kind of problem?" she prompted. Did she have to spell it out?

"The kind where I end that long dry spell of no kisses."

She moistened her lips. "I wouldn't categorize that as a problem."

He leaned closer. "In that case" he brushed his lips against hers "let's bring on the rain."

His lips settled on hers…softly…softly…a little more pressure…a little more intensity…until the heat that had been simmering inside her exploded into flames. She wrapped her arms around him and lost herself in his kiss.

His arms went around her and he leaned her into the pillows. She moaned softly. Loved the feel of his weight on her…the strength of his arms.

Her hands found their way beneath his open shirt. The feel of his warm skin lit a frenzy in her veins. Made her want to become one with all that heat searing every place his skin touched hers.

He drew his lips from hers. "Close your eyes," he murmured. "Get some sleep. I'll be right here."

Her heart launched into her throat. She wasn't ready for this incredible feeling to end…

He moved around to the other side of the bed. An argument tightened her throat. The mattress shifted. Relief slid through her as he climbed into the bed next to her. He pulled her close to his chest.

"Sleep." He pressed a kiss to her temple. "We've got a lot to figure out when dawn comes."

She relaxed into the protective heat he offered. Closed her eyes and allowed the worries and tensions of the case to drain away.

For the first time in more than three years she

felt connected—really connected—to something besides work.

To someone.

Chapter Ten

He was a United States senator. This lack of control over the situation was unacceptable.

Completely unacceptable.

His wife had gone to her sister's.

Controlling his own wife had become an impossible task. She refused to cooperate. Instead, she had run away.

At the moment her theatrics were the least of his worries.

Judd stamped to the mirror and checked his reflection. He straightened his tie and squared his shoulders. Generally Sharon picked out his tie. A small thing she'd always handled for him. This would do.

His wife had no idea the pressure of carrying the weight of his office. He'd protected her from the ugliness all these years. What had he gotten in return? She'd run away when he needed her most.

He could rely on no one, could trust no one.

He was in this alone.

At thirty he had risen to the position of state representative. By forty he was governor. He'd spent the past twenty years as a senator. That climb had been the cumulative result of complete dedication and unyielding determination.

This tragedy was not going to put a black mark on his record. The only mark to be left would be the one he accomplished with this history-making bill.

He glared at the newspaper lying on the console. Yoni Sayar's name was splashed across the front page headlines. An anonymous source had provided confirmed evidence that Sayar cavorted with terrorists. The accusation was ludicrous. Worse, Judd's enemies would attempt to tie this nasty business to him.

This had to end.

He pulled the cell phone from his interior jacket pocket that he used for making calls he wanted kept off the record. The phone was quite handy and utterly disposable. Most important, it could not be traced to him.

He entered the number. Waited for the voice on the other end. "This is unraveling at warp speed. I don't want to hear any more about the problems you're encountering. I want to hear the solutions you've *already* put into place."

More excuses! Judd's face tightened with the fury roaring in his chest. "You do whatever necessary to stop this now...today. Are we clear?"

"Yes, sir," resounded hollowly.

Judd closed the phone.

It was true. He could depend on no one!

Except himself.

He surveyed his reflection in the mirror once more. There was one aspect he could handle himself.

Today.

Chapter Eleven

7:50 a.m.

"I can't ask Wayne to run her prints." Kendra considered the sunglasses she had carefully plucked from her battered purse. At the time she'd improvised and gotten Delilah to hold the sunglasses, Kendra had been grasping at straws. Once the woman walked away the chances of locating her again, without a last name, phone number or address, were slim to none.

Latent fingerprints would help identify her—if she had a criminal record. Bearing in mind her profession, that was a logical conclusion.

"Seems he's on the other side," Rocky noted.

Kendra wanted to believe Wayne was the same dedicated professional he'd been when they first met, but last night had indicated otherwise. Castille likely owned him as he did so many others in positions of power.

"I can lift any prints on the glasses," Kendra said, more to herself than to her partner. "But scanning what I find and getting it into the system for a comparison is the problem."

"That's one of the things that impressed me about the Colby Agency." Rocky chuckled. "You carry your own little CSI kits."

She smiled at the man seated next to her in front of the hotel desk. "That's new this year." She bit her bottom lip, considered the difference between the Colby staff and the Equalizers team. "How did the Equalizers take care of a situation like this?" Didn't really matter. They were all on the same team now. If she were completely honest with herself, she just wanted to hear him talk. She liked the sound of his voice. Liked the way he kissed even more. Heat shimmered through her as the memories from the wee hours of the morning whispered in her mind.

A grin lifted his lips, creating enduring little creases at the corners of his eyes. Something else she liked. "Excessive force. What else?"

"Ha-ha."

"You do your *CSI* thing," he offered. "I'll take care of scanning the prints and getting them into IAFIS. Don't sweat it."

"How the hell can you do that?" The Integrated Automated Fingerprint Identification System belonged to the feds. Breaking into that system, assuming anyone could do it with nothing more than a laptop and a hotel Internet server, was a serious crime.

He leaned closer and whispered in her ear, "If I told you that would make you an accessory."

Kendra shivered at the feel of his breath against her ear. That morning had been a little awkward, but waking up in his arms had been more than worth the discomfort. He made her feel like a woman on every level. Something no one else had been able to do.

Not even Wayne.

While she'd slept, Rocky had gone through her bag of damaged clothes and dug out the only pair of jeans she'd packed. One of only two pairs that she owned. The jeans only had one slash, low enough on the leg not to be a problem. He'd laid out another pair of her lacy panties that had survived. Her cheeks warmed at the thought. Sexy lingerie was her one secret vanity.

She liked the way it felt against her skin even if no one but her ever saw it. The T-shirt sporting her alma mater had only a small rip on one shoulder. The getup looked a little odd with the only other pair of shoes she'd packed, high-heeled sandals. But it was better than a shoe with a broken heel and a bloody suit.

The shimmy of her cell phone against the wood

desktop reminded her that she was supposed to be focused on the case, not on Rocky's ability to make her want things she'd thought she might never again want. She picked up the phone, read the display. Her gaze connected with Rocky's. "It's Castille."

Rocky's eyebrows lifted at the news. "I guess the wife ratted us out."

No doubt. Kendra opened the phone. "Kendra Todd."

"Have you seen the paper?"

Kendra turned the phone away from her face and whispered to Rocky. "Check to see if there's a newspaper outside the door."

He nodded and headed that way.

"You do realize," Kendra said to her former boss, "that the press conference related to Yoni's death was rubbish."

"I have complete faith in our law enforcement system, Kendra. Perhaps if you listened to their advice you wouldn't be finding your way into so much trouble. You've lost that professional edge that landed you the position on my staff. I don't understand what happened."

She touched the bandage on her cheek. Last night had been a close call—closer than she wanted to admit even now. "What do you want, Senator?"

Rocky returned to the desk with newspaper in hand.

Respected Lobbyist's Murder Reveals Ties to Terrorism

Yoni's family would be devastated all over again. This was so unfair.

"We need to talk, Kendra. *Now.*"

Frustration and anger twisted painfully in her stomach. "Isn't that what we're doing?" She wanted to shake this fool. What in God's name was he covering up? What had he gotten Yoni into? This was the threat Yoni had feared…smeared across the headlines.

"Meet me at the C & O Park, Fletcher's Boat House. Quarter of nine."

"Senator, we—"

Dead air echoed in her ear. He'd ended the call. She stared at the screen, furious all over again. Pompous fool. He had issued his order and fully expected her to obey.

"Looks like whoever was blackmailing Sayar went through with his threat." Rocky tapped the headline. "If this story has no merit, it's a damned shame to do this to a man no longer here to defend himself."

"It's lies," Kendra snapped before she could regain her cool. "All of it." Yoni was dead, what was the blackmailer's point in this? There was nothing more to gain from Yoni Sayar.

She pushed back her chair and stood. "The senator wants to talk." So did she, she just didn't like him making all the terms. Kendra had a lot of questions. Questions the senator wasn't going to like in the least. Somehow she had to get him cornered and responding on her terms.

"I guess we have his full attention."

"That's the thing about politicians, Rocky," she explained as she grabbed her purse. "Even when you have their full attention, you never know how they're going to spin what you believe you have."

Fletcher's Boat House,
Chesapeake & Ohio Canal Park, 8:43 a.m.

FLETCHER'S, WHICH OFFERED boat rentals and concession services for this area of the park, was closed at this hour of the morning. The parking lot was empty. Rocky had scoped out a slot on the far side of the building to avoid being spotted right away.

He wasn't too keen on meeting Castille in an out-of-the-way location like this. He and Kendra had every reason to believe Castille was behind the drive-by shooting last night, if not the termination of Sayar's life. Who else had anything to gain by forcing Kendra off the search for the truth? So far, Castille was the top name on that too-short list.

This could be a trap. With that in mind, Kendra had notified the Colby Agency as to their planned movements. Unsatisfied with the openness of the location, Rocky had insisted on taking a position in the trees that flanked the parking lot. Once Castille arrived, depending upon where he parked and whether or not he approached Kendra or she approached him, Rocky would adjust his position for the best possible backup scenario.

He tightened his grip on his weapon. This time he intended to make sure Kendra stayed safe.

A black luxury sedan rolled into the parking lot. Rocky scanned the interior of the vehicle. A driver up front and Castille in the back. No other occupants were readily visible.

He'd warned Kendra not to get out of the car. To force Castille to come to her. Rocky hoped she would heed his advice.

The car circled the lot, then parked beside the rental where Kendra waited. Castille got out before the driver could come around and open his door. Looked like the man was in a huff this morning.

"Hold your position until the driver is back in the car," Rocky ordered his partner via the communications link.

"Copy that." Kendra held her position until the driver had gotten back behind the wheel and closed the door.

Rocky watched her movements as she emerged from the rental, while monitoring Castille's, as well.

As Kendra approached the man, Rocky braced for trouble.

"Whatever you think you're doing," Castille said as soon as she'd come to a stop in front of him, "you are making a monumental mistake. One that will only detract from the truth you claim to be seeking."

"What truth is that?" Kendra demanded. "Your version of the truth or the actual truth?"

"My wife has nothing to do with any of this," he roared, his tone literally vibrating with fury. "Stay away from her."

"Were you aware that last month she sustained damage to that very nice *white* car you bought her for Christmas three years ago?"

"What're you talking about?" he demanded, the fury evolving into a low growl.

Rocky watched the senator's body language very carefully. The man kept his arms at his sides. If he made a move toward the interior of his jacket, Rocky was going to make a move of his own...one that would likely land him in prison for the rest of his natural life.

"June 2," Kendra explained. "There was a hit-and-run on L Street. The victim died at the scene. I have an eyewitness who says it was your wife driving that car."

Castille's arm came up.

Rocky braced.

The senator shook his finger at Kendra. "Do not include my wife's name in your ridiculous theories! She spent a week with her sister in Alexandria the first part of last month. She wasn't even here!"

"Perhaps she was jealous of your involvement with Aleesha Ferguson," Kendra suggested, ignoring the alibi he'd tossed out. "Or maybe she just enjoys spending time with her sister rather than you."

Castille took a threatening step toward her.

Rocky leveled his weapon. Cleared his brain of all else save for a clean head shot.

"I will see that you're held responsible for spreading such lies!"

Kendra didn't flinch. "You sound almost as if you really believe that."

Rocky held his breath. She was pushing hard.

Castille suddenly executed a three-sixty, scanning the woods. "Where's your friend? I'm certain you didn't come without him."

"This is between you and me, Senator," she hedged. "A private conversation about the truth."

"Is he filming this meeting?" Castille glanced around again. "Is that your game?"

Kendra fully recognized that Castille wasn't going to let the idea of Rocky's hidden presence go. "He's here for my protection," she admitted. "There's no camera or other documentary source."

"Tell him to come out," Castille demanded. "I want him here where I can see him or I'm not saying another word."

That the senator appeared prepared to continue their conversation suggested that he in fact had something else to say. That was more than she'd hoped for. "All right." Kendra motioned for Rocky to join them. Though he'd heard the senator's demand, the goal was for Castille to believe the conversation thus far had only been between the two of them. Rocky wouldn't give his presence away without Kendra's approval.

Her partner stepped from the dense tree line and strode toward the parking lot where she and Castille faced off.

When he stopped next to her, she said to Castille, "See, no electronic devices."

Castille wasn't entirely convinced. "Put your hands up high so that I can see for myself that there are no recording devices." He glanced at Kendra, his gaze openly accusatory. "Both of you."

Kendra indulged him by raising her hands. Rocky followed suit. She hoped the senator didn't overreact when he found Rocky's weapon. That could complicate matters considerably.

Castille patted down Rocky first, then Kendra.

She schooled her surprise that he didn't find the handgun she knew for a certainty Rocky was carrying.

"Put your purse," Castille said to her, then to Rocky he added, "and your cell phones in the car."

Kendra dropped her cell into her purse and turned to do as the senator had requested.

"He can do it," Castille qualified.

She handed the purse to Rocky who did as the senator insisted.

"Are you satisfied now?" she asked the man she'd once respected and admired.

Castille held his tongue until Rocky returned to her side. "What I'm about to tell you is of an extremely sensitive nature. If you dare to leak a word of this to anyone, I will staunchly deny all of it."

"What about your driver?" Rocky countered with a nod toward the senator's car. "Is he armed? Or using any monitoring devices?"

Castille's gaze narrowed with irritation. He opened his jacket so that they could see when he removed his cell phone. He entered a speed-dial number, then said, "Take a walk." He closed the phone and slid it back into his pocket, once again ensuring his movements were fully visible.

The driver's door of the senator's car opened

and his employee emerged. He closed the door and started walking toward the parking lot entrance.

Whatever Castille had to say, it was clearly startling news. Truth or not. He'd taken the cooperation thing way beyond Kendra's expectations.

"Yoni and I," he began, "have worked long and hard developing the Transparency Bill. You may have heard rumors in the media," he said to Kendra.

"I've heard some rumblings." She elected not to reveal the information Yoni had passed along to her before his death.

"As you can well imagine," Castille continued, "this is not a popular piece of proposed legislation. However, Yoni and I had orchestrated a careful plan for revealing it to the public. We both knew that once the American people were aware of what we were proposing, none of those opposed would be able to actually vote against it and save face with their constituents."

"Or salvage the next election," Kendra offered.

Castille gave an acknowledging nod of her assessment. "Strongly worded advice began around one month ago. Then the threats came."

"What sort of threats?" Rocky asked.

Castille considered Kendra's partner at length. "The ruthless kind that ends careers and damages personal relationships."

"Did you report this activity to the proper authorities?" As she had known with Yoni, she knew full well the senator's answer would be no. A long-established game of merciless tug of war.

"No." The senator's face cleared of emotion.

Renewed fury detonated deep in Kendra's chest. "With all due respect, Senator," she challenged, "how could you be so irresponsible? Your lack of action may very well have cost Yoni his life?"

"May yet," Rocky tagged on, "cost yours."

"I have my reasons."

Kendra felt confident she knew at least two of those reasons. "The story in the paper this morning about Yoni is completely false."

"Indeed."

"What do you plan to do about that?" If he said nothing she might not be able to maintain any sense of professional decorum.

"I have someone working on it as we speak."

"Wayne Burton?"

Surprise flared for the briefest of seconds before Castille banished it. "Are you referring to the homicide detective investigating Yoni's murder?"

Like he didn't know. "You know exactly who I'm talking about. He showed up at the café last night after I was shot at. I can only assume since there were no homicides involved, that he's watching me. On your orders."

Castille's guard visibly fell into place. "I wasn't aware you'd been in an altercation? What in God's name are you talking about?"

"Three men tailed us," Rocky detailed. "One of them shot at Kendra. No one was seriously injured but it wasn't due to a lack of effort."

The senator shook his head. "I was not aware of this. I received the call around two this morning that the article in the newspaper would run despite my efforts to stop it. There were no other calls."

Rocky looked to Kendra. She hated to admit it, but she sensed that the man was telling the truth—at least about that part. Even though he mentioned her getting into trouble, that may have related to when she'd walked away from her work on his staff.

"If Burton isn't representing you," Kendra asked, "then who would he be working for? He's been on top of my every move since I arrived."

"My new enemies. Men I've worked with for two decades. There are at least three who I believe would go to any lengths to stop this piece of legislation from reaching fruition."

"Yet you're still not prepared to go to the authorities," Kendra tossed out a second time.

"You are surely aware of what would happen if I chose that path."

He was correct. She was quite aware. "All-out war."

Her assessment prompted a somber nod from him. "Make no mistake, I have an ongoing effort to catch them at their own game. However," he confessed, "proper evidence is essential to taking the appropriate steps to see that they answer for their actions."

"What about the accusation against your wife?" Kendra wasn't going to let that go until she had a better sense of the senator's involvement. She had seen the pictures. He was at the very least acquainted with Aleesha Ferguson. That was a given.

A frown lined his brow. "Since I'm unaware of any such effort, I have to assume that this is yet another strategy to discredit me."

Yoni had not mentioned the troubles related to Mrs. Castille. And the senator stuck by his story. That left Grant Roper, Kendra's replacement on the senator's staff. He was the only one spouting this other theory. That he had pictures which seemingly backed up his accusations, left Kendra with no choice but to believe that some truth was buried there.

The facts were indisputable. Aleesha Ferguson was dead. Killed by a hit-and-run driver on June 2. And her associate Delilah insisted Sharon Castille was involved, if not driving the automobile used to murder the victim. The latter was ultimately hearsay but when considered in light of the photos Roper had shown off, difficult to dismiss.

Kendra posed to the senator the same question she'd presented to Yoni. "Is there one iota of truth to any of the levied threats? Like this alleged terrorist connection to Yoni? Anything at all upon which your enemies could be building their case?"

The extended hesitation before he responded warned that Kendra and Rocky were about to be given a pivotal piece of the puzzle.

"I understand that you grew disillusioned with *things* here," Castille asserted, the effort obviously painful. "I will be the first to admit that there was a phase through which I failed to live up to the expectation of those who had graciously elected me to office." The senator's gaze grew distant. "I allowed my perspective to grow skewed. The power rather than the privilege became the goal. It was wrong and I must live with those choices for the rest of my life."

Kendra let the pause pass without saying a word. She wanted nothing she said or nothing he saw in her eyes or on her face to stop his momentum.

"But, with Yoni's encouragement and support, I reached a place where I recognized it was time to give back. This bill is my legacy to the American people. I will not allow anyone or anything to taint the effort.

"No one is without a history or mistakes. Except perhaps Yoni." Castille moved his head side to side in disgust or defeat, maybe both. "This so-called connection is related to an event in his father's youth. One that is about to be blown completely out of context and grievously out of proportion."

"And you," Kendra dared to push.

"As I said, no one is without a history." Determination solidified in the senator's gaze once more despite the uncertainty quavering in his voice. "But I will not allow ancient history to destroy my family or to derail what is best for the citizens of this great nation. That I can promise you."

"Is Aleesha Ferguson one of those mistakes?" Rocky asked.

"Yes."

Anticipation whipped through Kendra. "Then it is possible that there could be some truth to the theory that your wife was involved with her death."

"Sharon doesn't have the stomach for harming another human being, much less ending a life. She knows nothing about that tragic mistake of mine."

"Someone knows," Rocky countered. "Otherwise we wouldn't."

Another weighted pause. "I can't see how that's possible when no one knew," Castille insisted. "Absolutely no one."

"What about my replacement? Grant Roper?"

Kendra ventured. "Is he aware of these threats and any basis, however flimsy?"

"Grant fully supports the bill," Castille assured her. "He would not jeopardize this opportunity. What purpose would it serve? With any notoriety I gain, he is sure to gain, as well."

And yet, he had jeopardized that opportunity. Kendra had seen the photos. "Does he know anything about your involvement with Ferguson?"

"That's not possible," Castille vowed. "No one knows. This is frivolous nonsense exhumed and redecorated by those who wish to keep intact the self-serving veil of secrecy. The Transparency Bill would lift that veil once and for all."

"This has gone far beyond frivolous nonsense, Senator," Kendra reminded. "Yoni is dead. Aleesha Ferguson is dead."

"What happens," Rocky interjected, "if you're next on that list?"

Chapter Twelve

9:30 a.m.

"What now?"

Kendra dropped her head against the seat. Castille had driven away with Rocky's warning still echoing in the thick air.

What happens if you're next on that list?

The morning, like the situation, was shaping up to be a hot, muggy one. Whether it was the heat or the tension, Kendra's instincts were humming. *This*—whatever this was—was racing to a climax.

Yoni was dead. Aleesha Ferguson was dead. Mrs. Castille had gone into hiding. Grant Roper had tossed aside his loyalty to the senator. His motives so far from clear that she needed a spotlight and a magnifying glass to even attempt to decipher them.

The senator insisted three of his enemies had spearheaded an effort to kill his bill. Kendra had chosen not to mention her meeting with Roper as a precaution. If the senator was responsible for Yoni's murder—which she highly doubted—Kendra wasn't about to be responsible for anyone else being added to his hit list.

Then there was Wayne. He was up to his neck in this somehow. But how?

"I want to talk to Wayne again." Kendra wasn't sure what she hoped to accomplish, but they had to start somewhere "After that we'll track down Grant Roper again."

"How about," Rocky said as he started the engine, "we get Patsy T. to run down the relevant details about Sharon Castille's car and check with the various vehicle repair shops in the Alexandria area. It'll take some time but if Castille mowed down a pedestrian, there would have been damage to the car."

Absolutely! "That could be why she went out of town last month, assuming she left after the second of June." Sheer conjecture. Damn it. She needed something concrete! All these theories were leading them nowhere.

Rocky pulled out his cell phone and put through the call. Kendra suffered a twinge of jealousy at his easy way of talking to Patsy. He smiled as he listened to her responses. Did he have a thing for Patsy? Then why had he kissed Kendra last night? Held her in his arms the entire night?

She closed her eyes and shook off the ridiculous

thoughts. They were colleagues, partners on this case. She had no right to be jealous or anything other than thankful for his backup on this case.

He closed the phone and dropped it on the console. "Patsy's on it. She'll call us with anything she finds."

"Excellent." Kendra focused front and center. She swallowed back the foolish, foolish adolescent reaction. "I'll check in with Wayne's office. Try to find out where he is this morning."

"Meanwhile," Rocky offered as she entered Wayne's number into her cell, "I'll hit a drivethrough. I don't know about you, but I'm starving."

"That'd be great." Kendra waited through a ring. "I'll have whatever you're having." Finally on the third ring the division operator picked up and recited the practiced greeting.

A half minute later Kendra closed her phone. "He's in a meeting until around ten-thirty. If he comes out before we get there she'll have him call me. We'll figure out a time and place then."

Rocky made an agreeable sound.

He stopped at a fast-food restaurant and they ate inside the car in the parking lot. Not two words passed between them. What was worse, she couldn't meet his eyes.

Once they were back on the road, the silence

continued. Kendra stared at the passing landscape in an attempt to suspend the mounting awkwardness. First thing this morning she'd understood that momentary unease. But now…she hadn't anticipated having to fight it again. Had to be her. She'd never been good at interacting with the opposite sex on an intimate level.

"You want to talk about it?"

Apprehension spread through her limbs, emanating from her chest like spilled coffee. "We have a plan. What's to talk about?" Frustration twisted in her belly. Her voice held that high-pitched anxiety-ridden quality.

"We kissed. Had a moment, so to speak. It was… nice."

She moistened her lips. Nice. Definitely. "But it was out of line." Might as well put that one on the table. They were colleagues working an investigation. Allowing that kind of personal interaction was inappropriate. And, honestly, maybe he would change the subject.

"Yeah, you're right. Definitely out of line," he agreed.

"It was…nice though," she felt compelled to say.

More of that crushing silence.

So…he thought it was it was out of line. She'd said the same, but it felt somehow worse hearing it from him. Could she glean from his statement that the *moment,* as he called it, meant nothing to him? Other than…nice?

Why did she expect a mere kiss would mean anything to a guy like Rocky? Just because she had no sex life didn't mean he had foregone his physical needs. She'd been so busy recreating her career she'd completely ignored any semblance of a social life. Now somehow she was utterly out of practice.

"This is probably going to be out of line, as well," Rocky said, breaking the mini-eternity of silence. "But I'd like to do it again sometime."

Her heart bumped against her sternum as another rush of heat flowed inside her, this one emerging from her belly button and cascading downward.

Confusion abruptly cooled the warmth his words had generated. She kept her attention straight ahead, didn't dare look at him. Was she, in his opinion, just another sexual conquest? Would getting involved with a coworker be a mistake? What if things didn't work out? That could be incredibly awkward.

If she agreed, would he think she was needy?

"We should probably give the idea lengthy consideration before making a decision." She winced. Her explanation hadn't exactly come out the way she'd intended. "I mean, there could be difficulties—"

"Agreed."

She replayed the single word over and over in

her head. Tried to analyze his tone. Curt? Irritated? Matter-of-fact?

More silence.

Her cell phone vibrated. Thank God. "Kendra Todd." She was so relieved for the distraction she didn't bother checking the caller ID on the screen.

"You gave me your card."

Delilah? "Yes." Kendra held her breath, prayed this would be a viable break in the case.

"Kendra Todd? The sister Aleesha never had?"

Kendra closed her eyes and nodded. "That's me. This is Delilah, right?" Her gaze collided with Rocky's.

"I have stuff to tell you…but…"

More of that coughing Kendra had heard last night rattled across the connection. The woman needed to give up the cigarettes.

"I need money to get out of town."

"Just tell me where to meet you and how much money you need and I'll be there."

"The Smithsonian. A thousand bucks."

"Thirty minutes. I can be there in thirty minutes," Kendra assured her, not wanting to spook her or to put the meeting off any longer than absolutely necessary.

"Two thousand bucks," Delilah said quickly. "I'll be at the main entrance."

The connection ended.

"She wants to talk," Kendra said in answer to Rocky's questioning look. "And two thousand dollars." Damn it. One thousand was Kendra's daily ATM withdrawal limit. "We may have to combine our resources." Of course it would all end up on the expense report anyway.

"No problem."

He didn't look at her this time. Kendra wondered if he was ticked off by her noncommittal response to…to more of those hot, wild kisses. Her blood heated as memories bombarded her.

She needed to figure this out. Later…when they'd solved a couple of murders.

10:15 a.m.

"THAT'S HER." KENDRA DIRECTED Rocky's attention to the skinny blonde sprawled on the front steps, a cigarette dangling from her lips.

"She looks ready to hit the road," Rocky commented. A backpack sat at their target's feet. A long, thin strap looped around her neck, holding a small purse against her hip. The T-shirt, ragged jeans and flip-flops allowed her to blend in with the dozens of teens drifting in and out of one of D.C.'s most esteemed tourist attractions. Come to think of it, Kendra looked younger than usual in her jeans and tee. She looked more relaxed than she had a right to under the circumstances.

He liked her in jeans.

"She said she needed to get out of town."

Rocky snapped back to attention.

Kendra considered the woman a moment. "Guess she wasn't exaggerating."

Delilah looked up when they neared. As if suspecting someone might be watching or that they might have sold her out, she immediately surveyed the crowd. When her gaze fixed on Rocky and Kendra again her eyes were wide with worry or fear.

Kendra sat down on one side of her. Rocky leaned against the stair handrail, keeping an eye out for anyone coming too close.

"You okay?" Kendra asked her.

"No way." Delilah looked around, clearly nervous. "After that thing at the café some dude chased me for three blocks. I wouldn't have lost him at all if I hadn't run into a friend who picked me up."

Worry claimed Kendra's face. Rocky understood that she likely felt responsible.

"You have some additional information for me?" Kendra asked, her words careful.

"Aleesha said," Delilah drew in a big breath, "the senator was her ticket to a better life. He promised her big bucks. But I guess his wife didn't want to share. She and that guy killed Aleesha. I saw it.

He ran into her on purpose. I saw it with my own eyes."

"Were you drinking that night?" Rocky asked without looking down. He'd spotted a guy in the crowd that had his instincts moving to a higher state of alert. "Drugs? Anything that might have altered your perception?"

"No way, man. I'm clean. I don't do any of that stuff. Aleesha got me clean."

"Where were you when the accident occurred?" Kendra asked gently.

"We was talking on the sidewalk." Delilah shrugged. "The night was done. When Aleesha crossed the street to go to her place headlights came on and that white car raced toward her like the driver had been waiting for her to show. I screamed…but Aleesha was like paralyzed or something. Then…" She closed her eyes and shook her head. "Her body just kind of flew through the air. I won't never forget that sound when she hit the street."

Rocky's jaw tightened with anger. Did the senator or his wife or both think they could get away with this? Just because Ferguson had been a hooker didn't mean she was any less than human.

"What did you do then?" Kendra prodded softly.

"I ran into the street to help her.…. I was crying so hard I couldn't see. My heart felt like it was gonna explode. She wouldn't wake up. I kept shaking her. Then I got my cell phone to call 911, but the car came back." She looked from Rocky to Kendra. "They would've run over me if I hadn't got out of the way in time."

"Did you call 911?" Rocky asked.

Delilah shook her head. "I shoulda but I was afraid they'd come after me if they got a good look at me. I been keeping a low profile ever since." She dropped her head. "She was dead anyway."

Kendra's eyes met Rocky's. Until they had invaded her street Delilah had stayed under the enemy's radar. Their actions had gotten her noticed again.

"Was Senator Castille having an affair with Aleesha?" Kendra asked.

Rocky was aware Kendra was having trouble accepting that idea, but confirming one way or the other was imperative.

Delilah shrugged. "She wouldn't tell me. Said it was too dangerous. She had to keep it a big secret."

Kendra and Rocky exchanged another look.

"I need that money," Delilah said. "I gotta get outta here or they'll kill me."

Kendra placed a hand on Delilah's. "We're going to make sure you're safe. Don't worry about that."

"I just need the money."

"I know you're afraid," Kendra soothed. "We

have your money. If you read my card you know we work for a private investigations agency in Chicago. We're going to take you to the airport and send you there. One of our associates will meet you at the airport and ensure you're taken care of until this is over."

"I…I don't know…"

Rocky offered his hand to the frightened woman. "Come on. You'll be safe with us."

Delilah's gaze met his, hers filled with terror. "What if they find me?"

"They won't find you," he promised. "You can trust the Colby Agency."

Delilah stood, hauled her backpack up onto her skinny shoulder. Kendra got up, wrapped her arm around Delilah's. "Have you ever been to Chicago?"

"Nope."

"You'll love it," Kendra assured her. "The Colby Agency has an amazing safe house right on the water. Anything you want to eat. Clothes. It'll be like a vacation only you don't have to pay and you get anything you need. You can keep your money for your fresh start later."

Rocky hoped that Kendra would give him a fresh start when this investigation was over. He'd crossed the line last night…scared her off.

He'd thought she had mapped that same route.

Truth was, she'd just survived a harrowing experience. Maybe he'd taken advantage of her vulnerability.

And screwed up his only shot at the real thing. His mother would be all over that.

1:38 p.m.

THEY HAD GOTTEN DELILAH off to Chicago. The two-hour wait for the flight had unsettled her, but Kendra had managed to keep her calm. Delilah had spent most of that time talking about what a great friend Aleesha had been to her.

By the time Delilah had boarded the plane, Kendra felt as if she'd known Aleesha herself.

Ian Michaels, a second-in-command at the Colby Agency, would be meeting Delilah at the airport. He would take her to the safe house and leave her in the care of another staff member.

Kendra's cell phone battery had died. She pulled the car charger from her purse and plugged it into the auxiliary port in the rental. As the phone resurrected the alert that she had two missed calls appeared. Both from Wayne.

This time she wanted some real answers. Depending upon how the conversation progressed, she might or might not tell him about her witness. At this point she would prefer to be armed with some physical evidence, as well. The smart thing to do would be to get her emotions in check before confronting him.

Rocky pulled his cell phone from the pocket of his jeans and glanced at the screen. He sent Kendra a look. "Patsy."

Kendra listened as Rocky conversed with their colleague. Again Kendra noticed that his tone sounded almost playful as he spoke to Patsy.

Why was she obsessing on his interactions with women? He was her coworker. She loved her work, loved the agency. Getting involved with a colleague could prove a potential mistake.

It wasn't like he was the only man in the world who could kiss her that way…though she had admittedly never experienced quite that level of arousal. All these years she'd thought something was wrong with her. Shortchanged in the sex department. Inept when it came to intimacy.

Now she knew that wasn't true. This man—she dared to peek at him from the corner of her eye— had proven she was perfectly capable of raging hot desire.

"Patsy came through," he said as he closed his phone against his thigh and slid it back into his pocket. "She not only got the details on Mrs. Castille's white sedan, she found the repair shop that made some front-end repairs on the fifth of June."

Kendra's pulse skipped. "Was she able to get a copy of the invoice of repairs?"

Rocky shot her a grin. "She not only got it, she also forwarded a copy to my phone." He passed Kendra his phone. "Check it out."

She accepted the phone, catching her breath when her fingers grazed his palm. Since he didn't glance at her she hoped that meant he hadn't heard the little gasp.

Shaking off the silly thoughts, she opened the document Patsy had forwarded. "Front-end damage," she read. "Bumper and hood mostly. New paint on both. She paid in cash. No insurance claim was filed."

Would this be enough evidence to prompt the truth from Senator Castille or his wife? Wouldn't be admissible in a court of law, but it might work as a point of coercion.

Something else tugging at her investigator's instincts was how had Grant Roper gotten those photos of Senator Castille with Aleesha Ferguson?

Was Grant Roper the man who'd run Aleesha down?

Kendra blinked. Roper could be the one leaking information from the senator's office. Was he also the one responsible for the threat to and ultimate murder of Yoni? Anger began to crackle deep inside

Kendra. If she learned that weasel had done this… she would ensure he paid.

Her cell vibrated. She checked the caller ID, then turned to Rocky. "It's Wayne."

She had a voice mail from him but she hadn't listened to it yet. Oh, well. "Kendra Todd."

"Hey, where've you been? I've called three times."

Two actually. "My phone died. I just got to my charger." That was true. The rest he didn't need to know…yet.

"I was surprised to hear that you're still in D.C."

Did he really think she would run back to Chicago just because he suggested it? Please. "I'll be here until my investigation is complete." He might as well get used to the idea.

He made a skeptical sound. "We don't have anything new on the shooting," he said, disappointment in his voice. "But I guarantee I'll find those responsible."

She wasn't holding her breath. "Thank you." Just go for it. "I was hoping we could talk soon…today if possible. There are some things I want to hash out."

"I've been thinking we need to do that. Let me check my schedule." Rustling of papers. "How about two-thirty? Is that too soon for you?"

"That'll work." She held up two fingers, then three, and finally a zero using her thumb and fore-finger for Rocky's benefit. He nodded his agreement to the time. "Your office?"

"How about I call you since I may be out of the office? You never know around here."

"I understand. So, I'll see you then."

"Is your friend coming?"

Was that jealousy she heard in his voice? No way. "I'm not sure about whether he's coming or not." Rocky sent her a look. "I'll be waiting for your call."

"Oh, one other thing."

Anticipation zinged inside of her. Was she finally going to learn something real from this guy? "What's that?"

"The paper will be retracting the story about Yoni Sayar."

Kendra waited for more. She restrained the relief that burgeoned in her throat until she'd heard the whole story.

"Apparently the reporter's source had faked the confirmation. A full retraction and apology to the family will run in tomorrow's paper."

The relief she'd been holding back rushed through her. "Thank you for telling me."

Wayne said something else but Kendra didn't catch it, the connection faltered. She reminded him she would be waiting for his call and closed her phone. Still in a bit of shock, she passed the news on to Rocky.

"That's good," he said, apparently noticing her uncertainty. "Isn't it?"

"It is…but what was the point?" Kendra knew many of the D.C. reporters. She also knew the rigid rules at the city papers. No way a story would have been allowed to run without credible confirmation unless someone very powerful had a major motive. One worth the risk of a lawsuit.

"Doubt," Rocky offered.

She turned to him. He was right. A shadow had been cast on Yoni's reputation. And no amount of retractions could undo all the damage.

But…since he was dead why bother damaging his reputation?

Back to the same question: What was the point?

Chapter Thirteen

2:20 p.m.

Rocky checked the time on his cell again. Still no call from Burton.

So they would wait.

Operating under the assumption the meeting would be held at Burton's office Kendra had directed Rocky to a parking garage close by.

He studied her profile as she spoke with Sayar's mother. A memorial service was planned for Sunday afternoon. Kendra had promised to attend.

If the investigation remained ongoing, Rocky supposed he would be attending alongside her. Beyond this case and their continued employment at the agency he wasn't sure he would be seeing her again.

Since this morning she'd taken care to avoid direct eye contact unless unavoidable. He wanted to bring up the subject again and clear the air, but the opportunity hadn't presented itself.

She dropped her cell phone into her lap and closed her eyes a moment. A smile tugged at one corner of his mouth as he visually played dot to dot with that tiny sprinkling of freckles on her nose.

Her passion for her work and her compassion for others pulled at something deep in his chest. His mother would say he'd finally taken notice of a woman who didn't fit his usual profile. And now he was captivated by all the little things he'd never before paid attention to.

Just his luck.

She opened her eyes and he asked, "The Sayars holding up okay?"

"They're hanging in there."

"How 'bout you?"

She turned her face to him but quickly shifted her attention away, as if she'd abruptly realized that looking at him wasn't something she really wanted to do. "I'm disgusted with all the misleading information. Castille is either flat-out lying or innocent. Grant Roper isn't returning my calls."

Kendra had attempted to reach Roper twice today. Jean, Castille's secretary, hadn't seen him. He'd missed two appointments that morning and hadn't called in. Castille was in meetings and couldn't take any calls. There was no answer at the residence of Sharon Castille's sister in Alexandria.

And Burton hadn't called yet.

Meanwhile they sat in the car in a parking garage that was moderately cooler than the ninety-four degrees outside.

Waiting.

For the other shoe to drop.

When Kendra's cell phone rattled, she blew out a breath and checked the screen. "It's Roper."

"Put it on speaker," Rocky suggested. He had a bad feeling about this dirtbag.

Kendra tapped the necessary button. "Kendra Todd."

"I have new evidence."

This time Kendra met Rocky's gaze. "Really? I thought maybe you'd skipped town since you hadn't returned my calls."

"That's exactly what I'm planning to do." He sounded panicked. "I have to get out of here. Castille knows I have the photos. Other than sharing this evidence with you, there's nothing else I can do."

"You could go to the police," Kendra said flatly. "That's what people generally do when they have evidence of some crime."

"Don't pretend you don't know how this works,"

he growled. "There are times when you can't go to the police. This is one of those times."

"Why are you calling me, Roper?" Kendra's patience had frayed.

"I told you," he barked right back, "I have evidence. Do you want it or not? If not, I'm out of here. You can figure this mess out on your own. I can't take it anymore."

"What kind of evidence?" Kendra asked calmly this time.

"Proof that Castille is working with Lieutenant Burton to blame everything on Yoni. And you."

"Me?" Kendra laughed, the sound dry and filled with disdain. "What could Castille possibly hope to pin on me? I haven't worked for him in three years."

"A paper trail," Roper explained, "that's all I've been privy to. They've trumped up evidence that Yoni wanted to bring down Castille. And they can tie that evidence to you. You wanted vengeance."

"Since I know no such paper trail exists," Kendra countered, "I'm not the least bit concerned about what the senator is orchestrating in regards to me."

"Burton is working with Castille, Kendra. He's manipulating e-mails you apparently sent to him since you left D.C. to make it appear as if they were sent to Yoni. Think about that. Did you ever say anything negative about the senator? Or about how angry you were?"

Kendra's face gave away her astonishment. "Where are you?"

Roper gave her the name of some park Rocky had never heard of. Kendra agreed to meet him there within half an hour.

She ended the call and recited the driving directions without looking at Rocky.

He didn't ask.

She didn't clarify Roper's statement regarding the e-mails she had sent to Burton.

Since leaving D.C.

Not that it was any of Rocky's business. It wasn't. But he'd gotten the impression that she'd walked away from her relationship with Burton without looking back.

Evidently he'd been wrong.

The twenty minutes of maneuvering in traffic and executing the necessary turns were spent in near silence. She spoke only when necessary to give him a direction. He didn't speak at all.

He was resentful of a past relationship. Ridiculous.

Mostly he was mad at himself for not handling last night better than he had.

The final few miles of road were curvy as hell. Seemed seriously out of the way for a meeting.

Roper was either scared to death or planning something Rocky wasn't going to like.

The black sedan Roper had driven the night before last sat on the side of the deserted stretch of road that led deeper into the wooded park. The area was secluded and deserted. After the drive to get here, Rocky could see why the park wasn't crowded with nature lovers.

He pulled up behind the sedan. Roper appeared to be in the driver's seat.

"Stay here." Rocky removed his weapon from the console. "Let me check it out first."

Kendra arrowed him a you-must-be-kidding look. "I appreciate the offer, but no thanks." She pulled her weapon from her purse and opened her door.

"Whatever you think. You're in charge."

Her look this time warned she didn't find his remark humorous.

This was actually the first time he'd thought about the idea that she was in charge. They'd worked together so well…no power struggle.

Too bad he'd made the mistake of trying to connect outside the realm of work.

Rocky moved ahead of Kendra and approached the driver's side of the car. She headed for the passenger side. If she took that as a power play that was just too bad. He'd already failed once to protect her—wasn't happening again.

The instant he was adjacent to the driver's door, he held up a hand for Kendra not to move any closer.

Grant Roper was dead.

Rocky opened the car door and reached in to check the guy's carotid pulse, being careful of the blood. Skin was still warm but no pulse.

"Oh, my God!" Kendra yanked the passenger door open and ducked inside.

"Watch the blood," Rocky warned as he leaned forward enough to survey the interior of the vehicle. A nine millimeter lay in Roper's lap.

Whoever had killed Roper apparently wanted it to look like a suicide. But this was no suicide. "Roper was left-handed, right?"

The bullet had exited on the right side of his head and plowed into the passenger seat. Blood and tissue had left a nasty pattern over the interior of the car.

Kendra groaned. "It's not coagulated."

Rocky looked at the hand she held up. Blood covered her fingertips. Her hand shook. Rocky's gaze bumped into hers.

She moved her head side to side, her brown eyes wide with a whirlwind of emotions. "He hasn't been dead long." She nodded jerkily. "Yes, Grant was left-handed."

"Get back in the rental car," Rocky ordered. Whoever had set this up had carefully covered all the bases.

He drew back, straightened to survey the tree line on the opposite side of the narrow road.

Roper had spoken to Kendra less than one hour ago. Claimed to have additional evidence. He didn't drive out here to kill himself. No way. This was a murder scene. Judging by how recently the bullet had plowed through the victim's brain, his killer could still be close by.

Who else had he invited to this little get-together? Or had someone watching his movements followed him here?

Rocky's pulse rate sped up.

None of the above, he realized.

This was a setup.

He moved toward the rental car, constantly scanning for trouble. He had to get Kendra out of here.

"Rocky."

She was walking toward him. Confusion nagged at his forehead. "Get in the car," he ordered again.

She held her open cell phone up so that he could see. "He said to put down your weapon."

What the hell was she talking about?

She moistened her lips, swallowed with visible difficulty, then bent at the waist and placed her weapon on the pavement. When she straightened, she peered at him, her eyes pleading. "Put your weapon down."

"No way."

Glass cracked.

His attention swung to the car—Roper's car. The rear window was shattered.

"Please," Kendra urged, "put it down. They'll kill us both if you don't."

He bent at the knees, lowered far enough to place his weapon down as Kendra had directed. Before he straightened fully, two men, weapons drawn, stepped from the tree line. From the corner of his eye, Rocky saw a third man moving from the trees on the opposite side of the road.

Kendra's cell phone clattered to the pavement and her hands went up.

Rocky held his arms away from his side, his hands up. One man's eyes were swollen, the skin around them discolored, and his nose was taped as if he'd recently survived a brawl.

The injured guy walked up to Rocky, glowered at him then punched him in the face.

The pain shattered up the bridge of Rocky's nose. He flinched, but refused to reach up and protect his face.

"That's for breaking my nose," the guy roared.

Rocky resisted the impulse to swipe his hand across his face. He forced his lips into a smile. "You must've been the driver. You should wear your seat belt." When Rocky had rammed that silver car, the driver's face had apparently had an up-close encounter with the steering wheel.

The guy drew back his fist. Rocky braced.

"Burton's coming. Let's go."

Kendra turned her head to stare at the approaching SUV. Two seconds later her eyes confirmed what the scumbag had announced.

The vehicle rolling toward them stopped, engine still running, and Wayne Burton emerged from the driver's side. "Get them in the car."

A weapon rammed into the back of her skull, Kendra started walking toward the vehicle. As she passed Wayne she glared at him. "You bastard."

He said nothing.

A jab of the muzzle propelled her forward a little faster. When she stopped at the rear passenger side door, the man with the gun rammed it into the back of her head a little harder and said, "Get in."

She opened the door and dropped into the seat. The door slammed, bumping her shoulders. Fury blasted in her chest. With every fiber of her being she wanted to kill Wayne Burton…to tear him apart with her own hands. For what he had obviously done to Yoni…to Aleesha Ferguson.

Rocky settled into the seat next to her. As soon as his door was shoved closed, he searched her face. "You okay?"

"No, I'm not okay." She shifted her attention

to the bastards gathered in the street in front of the car.

Wayne said something to one of the men. The man strode over to Roper's open car door, pulled something from his jacket pocket and tossed whatever it was, one at a time, into the car. Photos, Kendra decided. The photos of Castille and Ferguson flashed in Kendra's head. Was this an elaborate setup to bring down Castille?

The driver's side door of the car Kendra and Rocky were in opened and the vehicle shifted as one of the men slid behind the steering wheel. Wayne called out an order to the other two, then settled into the passenger seat. "Let's go," he said to the driver, then he turned his attention to the backseat. "Well, the gang's all here now."

"What're you doing, Wayne?" Kendra demanded, disgust and rage blasting against her brain.

"Taking care of business, Kendra." He flashed her a tolerant smile. "I warned you. Gave you the opportunity to go back to Chicago. But you didn't listen." He shook his head. "You should have run away this time like you did last time."

"Do you really think you can get away with this?" She laughed at the ridiculous idea. "When did you get so stupid?"

His gaze turned lethal. "I've already gotten away with it. Or hadn't you noticed."

That confirmed her conclusions. "You killed Yoni."

Wayne didn't have to say the words, she saw the truth glittering triumphantly in his eyes.

"What about Aleesha Ferguson?" How could Kendra have not seen Wayne Burton for what he was? How had she been so blind?

"I can't take credit for that one." He laughed. "Mrs. Castille got all fired up about her husband's involvement with the woman and started harassing her. When Ferguson wouldn't back off, the old bag threatened her. Sharon Castille enlisted the help of Roper to attempt scaring off the gold digger. Things got out of control and Ferguson ended up dead. The two called me for help." Wayne's smile broadened into a grin. "It's always useful to have a senator's wife in your pocket."

"What did any of that have to do with Yoni?" Kendra demanded.

"Nothing at the time." Wayne looked beyond Kendra to the street. Likely checking to ensure his other two minions were following.

"But an opportunity presented itself," Wayne continued, shifting his attention back to her. "If the senator wants to keep his wife out of trouble, he'll do as he's been told. Sayar was only a warning. I think the senator will pay a little more attention now."

"You didn't have to kill Yoni," Kendra said, her voice shaking with anger.

"But Yoni was trouble," Wayne countered. "He wasn't going to just shut up and move on. And Roper was getting nervous, running off his mouth about Ferguson and the senator. His suicide ties up all the loose ends. You see," Wayne shook his head, "Roper had a thing for Sayar. But Sayar wasn't interested. Roper was scorned, killed the object of his desires and then couldn't live with it so he killed himself. Pictures of his dead idol and notes he'd written to him are scattered inside his car. Too bad."

"You're insane," Kendra said.

Wayne laughed. "I'm a genius, that's what I am. Neither of the two can cause any trouble. I'll be assigned the case and all the evidence will fall into place just the way I want it to."

"The bill," Kendra muttered. Yoni was dead because of the bill. Roper, too. Yoni's integrity wouldn't be bought. Not when threatened with lies, not for anything. Wayne had known that. She stared at her former lover in abject disgust. "Who hired you to do this? How much did you decide your integrity was worth?"

"Better to walk away a rich man," Wayne offered, "than to run with nothing."

"I ran," Kendra tossed back at him, "with my integrity intact."

Wayne stared at her for too long, making Kendra shudder in disgust. "I guess now you're going to die with your integrity untarnished." He nodded toward Rocky. "So's your friend."

Rocky chuckled. "Make the first shot count, friend. Because, trust me, you won't get the opportunity to take another one."

The air evacuated Kendra's chest as the two men stared off, the weapon in Wayne's hand aimed directly at Rocky's face.

"Trust *me*," Wayne said, "even if you weren't going to die very shortly, she would never be yours. She doesn't trust herself enough to trust anyone else on that level." He glanced at Kendra. "She likes being alone."

Kendra wanted to slap his arrogant face but his words hit too close to home. Maybe he was right. Maybe she hadn't given herself fully to anyone. Maybe she couldn't. She stared at the gun in his hand. If Wayne had his way, it wouldn't matter anyway.

THEY DIDN'T GO FAR before the driver came to a stop. Burton got out, opened Kendra's door and ordered her out. The driver did the same, shoving his weapon in Rocky's face to ensure his cooperation.

Parked behind them at an angle just past the guardrail, half on and half off the pavement, was the rental car Rocky and Kendra had been driving, the front tires scarcely clinging to the edge of the road's shoulder. The other two thugs climbed out. The vehicle shifted precariously. Two of the men, one on either side of Rocky, pushed him toward the rental. Rocky got a good view of what lay beyond the shoulder of the road. Air...with a steep drop that ended in the trees below.

Burton ushered Kendra to the driver's side of the rental. "You must have been pretty upset when you found Roper dead," he explained. "You missed the curve and crashed into the trees below."

Rocky's escorts ushered him to the passenger side of the car, allowing an unobstructed view of the ravine below. Considering the distance, surviving the plunge wasn't impossible, but highly unlikely.

It was four against two. Sorry odds any way you looked at it. Not to mention he and Kendra were no longer armed.

"Open the door and get behind the wheel," Burton ordered Kendra.

She hesitated, stared across the car's roof at Rocky.

Rocky needed a plan, damn it!

"Maybe if you'd been able to call for help," Burton taunted, "you might have survived. But no one's going to find you until tomorrow morning. Neither of you will survive." He looked across the top of the car at Rocky. "By the way, we'll need your cell phone."

The man who had stood at Rocky's right but now stood behind him considering their proximity to the shoulder's edge jammed his weapon into Rocky's spleen. "Give me the cell phone, then open the door and get in," he growled.

Rocky glanced over his shoulder at the shorter man. "Make me."

"Putting a bullet into your head," Burton warned, "isn't part of the plan, but I'm flexible." Burton sent a lethal stare in Rocky's direction. "Now, give up the cell phone."

There was only one thing to do.

Rocky's gaze locked with Kendra's. He silently mouthed a single word.

Jump.

Chapter Fourteen

Nothing but air…falling…falling…

Bullets whizzed past her.

Something hot pierced her left shoulder.

Leaves crushed into her face.

Something hard hit her in the stomach, stopped her forward momentum, sending her into a cartwheel-like spin.

Then she was falling again.

Limbs lashed at her, slapped her face.

Reach out, she told herself, *grab on!*

The voice in her brain prompted her hands to reach…her fingers to clutch.

The too small branch slowed her fall for a split second then slipped through her fingers.

Her hip jarred against a larger branch. Pain shattered in her pelvis.

Adrenaline detonated in her brain.

Grab something!

She clutched with her hands, her arms.

Bark scraped at her forearms.

She blinked. Shook her head to clear the spinning.

Her arms tightened around the tree branch.

She wasn't falling anymore.

Voices on the road above…she couldn't see through all the branches and leaves.

Where was Rocky?

She twisted her neck, looked to the right and then the left. All she could see in any direction was leaves and branches and more leaves.

Her heart pounded. Her shoulder burned. Her body ached.

A sudden shift in the air pressure made her heart stutter.

A crash sent her flying loose from the limb she'd been hugging.

Glass exploded…metal whined.

She slammed into something hard. Flung her arms and legs frantically…scrambling for some kind of purchase.

Her face rubbed against something rough as she slid down…down…down.

She bounced on something softer.

The air whooshed out of her lungs.

The ground.

She was on the ground. Alive. And conscious.

She blinked. Where was Rocky?

She wanted to shout his name but a sound stopped her.

Voice…male.

"Get down there and find them! Make sure they're dead."

They were coming. She had to move.

Something above her snagged her attention.

Black…or dark. Metal.

Kendra tried to focus.

Tires.

The car.

The car was lodged in the trees directly above her.

She had to move.

To run!

A hand latched onto her arm.

Her head came up. A scream lodged in her throat.

"We gotta get out of here."

Rocky!

He helped her to her feet.

Pain radiated through her shoulders…her back. Her entire body.

He dragged her forward.

Her right ankle burned like fire.

Ignore the pain.

Run!

The sound of wood groaning and splitting rent the air.

A crash echoed through the trees as the car impacted the ground behind them.

Rocky darted around trees, dragging her behind him.

She tried to focus on putting one foot in front of the other. On keeping up with him.

The pain subsided, allowing her brain to concentrate on escape.

Rocky suddenly stopped. She butted into his back.

A new sound reached her ears.

Water. They'd run into the river.

What did they do now?

He ripped open the buttons of his shirt and tore it off his shoulders.

"What…" she moistened her dry lips "…what're you doing?"

He flung the shirt on the bank near the edge of the water and grabbed her hand once more. "Now we double back, going wide and keeping very, very quiet."

His left eye was swollen. His nose had been bleeding and, like her, his face and neck were scratched.

She nodded. "Okay."

He moved through the woods, going wide to the right and slowly forward.

Her heart pounded hard enough to burst out of her chest. She ducked, following his movements, beneath low lying limbs. He avoided the thickest underbrush to prevent unnecessary noise.

Voices and the sound of slogging through the brush reverberated from their left. The enemy was a ways off but not far enough to suit Kendra.

Rocky pulled her to the far right and into a tall thicket of undergrowth. He parted the foliage and weaved his way inside, towing her along behind him.

Once they were deep into the thicket, he settled on the ground and pulled her into his lap. "Don't make a sound," he whispered in her ear.

She nodded her understanding.

His arms went around her and he opened his cell in front of her. She stared at the screen where a text message from Patsy read: help is en route.

Relief shook Kendra. He hadn't given up his cell and somehow during all this he'd summoned help. She leaned into his chest, fighting the tears.

She was stronger than this…she knew she was. But he was far stronger than her. If they survived… it would be because of him.

KENDRA COULDN'T GUESS HOW much time had passed. Rocky held her in his arms like a child.

The pain radiated along every muscle in her body. She also couldn't assess her injuries. Her shoulder was still leaking blood. Rocky had checked it out. Bullet wound, but it had only cut through the skin and muscle. Nothing she wouldn't survive. Her ankle was swollen…her face burned like fire. But she wasn't having any trouble breathing.

Rocky appeared to be in better shape. No gunshot wounds. Nothing broken, he'd assured her.

The crunch of underbrush snapped her from the worries.

Someone was close.

She felt the tension in Rocky's muscles.

The whisper of leaves against fabric came nearer still. Heavy footfalls. Whoever was coming wasn't afraid of being overheard.

More voices in the distance…maybe in the direction of the river.

Didn't stop the approaching threat.

Someone was right on top of their position.

A familiar whop-whop-whop grew louder and louder.

Helicopter.

Hope swelled inside Kendra.

Had to be the help Patsy said was en route.

Thank God!

The bushes suddenly parted.

The business end of a handgun rammed into the opening.

"Too bad someone had to leave a swipe of blood on these leaves."

Wayne. He shook the bush.

Kendra's hopes withered.

"Get up!" Wayne roared.

Rocky pushed Kendra off his lap and scrambled up. "Hear that helicopter, Burton," he warned. "That's one of the last sounds you'll hear before spending the rest of your life in prison."

Kendra had to do something.

She couldn't see through the bushes. Tried to part the limbs so she could assess the situation.

"Come out, Kendra," Wayne snarled. "I want you to watch your partner die before I kill you."

She parted the foliage and scrambled out but didn't stand. She stared up at the man she'd once cared enough about to share her body with him. His weapon was leveled at Rocky's bare chest.

Wayne laughed as he stared down at her. "You don't look so self-righteous now."

Rocky moved. Pushed the weapon upward. A shot exploded from the muzzle.

Wayne struggled to pull the weapon down low enough to get a bullet into Rocky's face.

Kendra stopped looking…stopped thinking.

She lunged at Wayne's legs. Clamped down on his shin with her teeth. Bit him as hard as she could.

He let out a howl. Tried to kick her off.

Her teeth tore into the fabric of his trousers.

He stumbled back.

She reached up, grabbed his crotch, squeezed then twisted.

He went down.

Wayne's shoe heel connected with her jaw.

Kendra let go. Rolled away from him.

Wayne was suddenly on his feet, swaying with pain. Rocky had the weapon pressed to his temple. "Maybe you won't make it to prison," Rocky snarled.

Kendra scrambled to her feet.

"Get behind me," Rocky ordered.

She didn't question his command. Obeyed without hesitation.

"Stop right there," Rocky roared.

Kendra didn't dare peek around him, but his warning told her Wayne's friends had joined the party.

"Release him and we'll all just go our separate ways," one of the goons suggested.

The helicopter was right on top of them now. Not visible through the trees but there.

Sirens wailed in the distance.

"Put your weapons down," Rocky countered. "I

want you facedown on the ground, arms and legs spread."

Rocky held Wayne in front of him like a shield. His quick thinking might very well be the sole reason they survived.

"Now!" he commanded.

"Shoot him!" Wayne screamed.

Fear burst in Kendra's chest.

If she made a run for it, the other men would be distracted.

The sound of rustling foliage caused her to hesitate.

"Good friends are hard to find, Burton," Rocky taunted. "Looks like yours fall into a different category."

Kendra dared to look beyond Rocky. The three men were barreling through the woods.

The sirens were on the road just above them now.

And she and Rocky were alive.

By the grace of God, his quick thinking and all those lovely trees.

Chapter Fifteen

9:15 p.m.

Kendra leaned her head against the wall of the small office she'd been sequestered to after she'd given her statement. She hadn't been allowed to see Rocky since they'd been treated at the ER.

Statements had been taken at the scene, but then after the doctor had released them from the ER, they had been brought to police headquarters in separate vehicles.

She had been questioned for nearly an hour.

Since then, she'd been sitting in this damned office for half an hour.

Ian Michaels from the Colby Agency had arrived. Kendra had barely gotten to speak to him when she'd been ushered away.

Ian had assured her that Rocky was fine and being questioned in another interview room.

Kendra just wanted this over.

She hadn't been allowed to contact Yoni's parents. She wanted them to know that he had been completely innocent of this entire travesty.

The door opened and she sat up straighter.

Senator Castille entered the room and closed the door behind him.

Anger and disappointment roiled inside her. He was the last person she wanted to see right now.

"Kendra." He sat down in the only other available chair besides the one behind the desk.

"What do you want?" She blinked back the tears of grief that had been building for days...since she'd heard about Yoni's murder.

Castille stared at the floor a moment as if the generic carpet held some secret.

Secrets...lies...she'd escaped this world once.

As soon as this part was over she intended to return to Chicago and never look back. Again.

"I'm sorry you were hurt by all this."

Her gaze flew to his. "All of *this* is your fault!"

He nodded. "To some degree, yes. It is."

The only good she could see coming of this was if he stepped down from the office to which he'd been entrusted.

"I want to explain how this happened."

Like she wanted to hear anything he had to say. "I'll hear it all in court." She had no choice but to return for that. Damn it!

"Sharon found out about Aleesha and she went a little crazy."

Kendra glared at him, wishing desperately that looks could kill. "You should have thought of that when you were chasing that poor girl." She shook her head with the disgust writhing inside her. "I thought you were better than that."

He held up both hands as if to protect himself from her poisonous words. "It's not what you think."

Yeah, right. Every cheater said that.

"Aleesha was my daughter."

Shock quaked through Kendra. "What?"

Castille heaved a forlorn breath. "She sought me out a few months ago. Her mother had passed away and left a note explaining who her father was. I had a one-night stand with her mother more than two decades ago." He dropped his head. "It was foolish. Sharon had lapsed into another one of her depressions." He shrugged. "She wanted children, but cancer had taken that opportunity away from her. I told her it didn't matter, but as the years went by it just ate at her…taking up where the cancer had left off."

Kendra tamped back the sympathy that attempted to rise. "Why didn't you adopt?"

He smiled sadly. "We considered it, but Sharon just wouldn't be suited with any of the options presented. She turned away from me and to the bottle."

His wife had a drinking problem? "I never heard any rumors about a drinking problem." Didn't seem possible. Nothing about a person's life was sacred here. How had Kendra not known this?

"She was careful. Always. She reserved her disgrace for late at night at home where no one could see. Including me.

"Eventually I gave in to the loneliness." He shook his head again. "It was wrong. I know. But I am human and I had needs. But it only happened once."

"She never told you—Aleesha's mother, I mean— that she was pregnant."

"That's the strangest part. She knew I had money. But she never contacted me. I didn't know until Aleesha showed up."

"How can you be sure she was your daughter?" Kendra hated to think the worst, but desperation and greed were strong motivators.

"Anonymous DNA test. Grant took care of the details for me. There was no denying. And, there were other indications." A sad smile trembled on his lips. "She looked exactly like my mother did as a young girl. And the birthmark." He patted his chest. "Over the heart. My mother had it. Aleesha had it."

Kendra couldn't pretend the man wasn't grieving, too. Still. Grant had said...*Grant*. God, he was dead, too. "Grant told me that you'd killed Yoni. That you were having an affair with Aleesha." None of this made sense.

"Grant realized the power he had," Castille explained, "when I trusted him with the task of seeing to the DNA test. He used it to push Sharon over the edge, to extort money from her and then from me."

"Sharon wasn't the one who killed Aleesha." Kendra wasn't ready to let the senator off the hook entirely but he needed to know that.

"Your colleague, Mr. Michaels, showed me the video statement from Delilah Brewer that your agency prepared. You don't know..." his voice cracked "...how much that means to me. Grant had Sharon convinced she had been driving the car when in fact she had been so inebriated that she barely recalls the incident."

"I don't understand why he killed Aleesha. She was a meal ticket for him."

"Aleesha threatened to go public with the whole thing. Grant wanted to continue holding it over

Sharon and I, so he neutralized an unnecessary threat. He had the photos and the DNA results."

Kendra had known the guy was a sleaze. "But why Yoni? Did he find out what Grant was up to?"

"That was my fault."

"How so?" Kendra braced for more shocking revelations.

"I saw Grant and the whole situation with my wife and Aleesha's death spiraling out of control so I contacted Wayne Burton. I asked him to see what he could do to quietly put the brakes on."

She supposed that made sense.

"At first, it appeared he would be successful. He claimed he might be able to prove Grant was driving the car that struck Aleesha. If so, Grant would likely be easy to pay off. Get him out of our lives. But then things changed. About two weeks ago Burton started insisting he'd hit a stumbling block. Yoni came to me with the threats he had received. At first it didn't make sense."

Kendra's stomach knotted. "He believed the threats were connected to the Transparency Bill."

"He was right. Burton had gotten a better offer. He has given up the names of the two lobbyists in hopes of getting a lighter sentence. Bernard Capshaw is the ring leader. He's being brought in as we speak."

"Wayne killed Yoni." Kendra could scarcely believe Wayne would be that heartless.

"He killed Yoni and Grant and attempted to frighten you into leaving. When that didn't work, he was prepared to kill you and your partner. He wanted nothing to get in the way of his big payoff."

Kendra couldn't believe she'd once cared about the man. It was…astonishing to learn that he was capable of such evil.

Castille stood. "I'm going to resign my office before this turns into yet another sideshow."

Kendra looked up at him, saw the defeat and the sadness. She'd thought the worst of him and he hadn't deserved it…at least not all of it.

"But," he qualified, "not until I see that this bill is passed. I owe that to Yoni."

A traitorous tear escaped Kendra's firm hold. "He would be proud."

The senator nodded, then started for the door. "One piece of advice, Kendra."

Until a few moments ago she wouldn't have wanted to hear any advice this man had to give. But, like he said, he was only human. Circumstances had prompted wrong decisions from him, as it did from all mere humans.

"Don't devote all you have to your career. If you do, you'll end up old, tired and alone." He heaved a sigh. "Like me."

The door closed, leaving Kendra alone once more.

The memory of how it felt to have Rocky's arms around her, of his hot kisses made her tremble... made more of those damned tears slide down her cheeks.

Castille was right.

Maybe even Wayne had been a little bit right about her.

But she wasn't too stubborn to acknowledge her weaknesses and to institute change.

"ALL RIGHT, MR. ROCKFORD," the police captain announced, "you're free to go."

Rocky nodded and turned to the door. Lucky for him one of the rescue personnel had given him a T-shirt since he'd tossed his shirt into the river in an attempt to throw off the bastards chasing them. Right now, he was tired as hell and he ached all over. Bruised ribs and lots of abrasions were about all he'd gotten in the fall, except for the sore muscles. Of course that didn't take into account the black eye and split lip that he'd gotten from one of Burton's dirtbags.

He would live.

More important, Kendra was okay.

He stepped out into the corridor fully expecting to see Ian Michaels waiting for him, but Michaels appeared to be in deep conversation with the chief of police at the other end of the hall.

Right now, Rocky just wanted to find Kendra.

As if luck was on his side for once, a door opened and she stepped out into the long gray corridor.

She smiled.

He smiled back, then winced at the burn in his lip.

"You were wrong about Yoni, you know," she said. "You have to wear a suit to work every day for a week."

"I've always been a man of my word," he relented. At the moment he would have done anything she asked. He was just glad she was okay.

She walked straight up to him then. Despite all the scratches and bruises she looked amazing. "I gave lengthy consideration to your offer."

Confusion furrowed his brow making his head hurt. What the hell was she talking about?

"I decided that I don't want to wait or to weigh the consequences or anything else." She threw her arms around his neck, went up on tiptoe and kissed him.

Then he understood.

Kendra was ready to give them a chance. To take the risk.

He drew back, smiled at her even though it hurt like hell. "You won't regret it."

She kissed his bruised jaw. "I know. You're my partner, you would never let me down."

The Colby Agency, Monday, July 10, 5:15 p.m.

"DO YOU HAVE A MINUTE?"

Victoria Colby-Camp looked up from her desk and smiled at her son. "Absolutely."

He swaggered into the room. Such self-confidence. Incredibly handsome just like his father. And full of compassion for others. There wasn't a day that went by that she didn't feel immensely grateful for having him here...where he belonged.

"I was thinking," he said as he settled into a chair, "that we should celebrate."

"What's the occasion?" Tasha, Jim's wife, was due any day, but she felt relatively certain that if he'd gotten a call about that he would already be en route to the hospital. A man didn't get the chance to welcome his son into the world every day. Last week's false alarm had heightened the already merciless tension.

"Considering this latest case and the amazing way our teams have merged, I think it's time to celebrate that success. The Colby Agency and the Equalizers are now one. We have full velocity."

Victoria agreed. Kendra and Rocky were back home, but taking a few badly needed days off. A smile tickled her lips. Rumor was that the two had formed more than a professional bond in the past week.

"I think that's an amazing idea," Victoria agreed. "You call Tasha and I'll call Lucas."

Jim braced to stand. "Excellent."

The phone on Victoria's desk rang. Mildred, her assistant, had already gone for the day so Victoria took the call herself.

"Victoria, is my husband in your office?"

Tasha. She sounded a little out of breath. Victoria bit her lips together…this could be the call. "Certainly, he's right here." Victoria reached the phone across the desk. "It's Tasha."

"Put it on speaker," he said, grinning, "and we'll tell her about tonight's celebration."

Victoria did as Jim requested though she had a feeling there would be a different kind of celebration tonight. "Tasha, you're on speaker. Jim is right here."

"You'd better come home. Now," Tasha said, her voice rising as she spoke. "This boy is ready! For real this time!"

Jim jumped to his feet, his eyes wide with anticipation and maybe a little uneasiness. "On the way!" Jim backed toward the door. "Sorry…about tonight."

Victoria grinned. "Go! Lucas and I will pick up Jamie and be right behind you."

Jim Colby bounded out of the office. Victoria blinked back the tears building in her eyes. She had already been blessed with a beautiful granddaughter, Jamie, now she would have a grandson.

She stood, grabbed her cell phone to put through a call to Lucas.

A new Colby was about to be born.

The name would live on...and so would the agency.

* * * * *

are proud to present our...

Book of the Month

Sins of the Flesh
by Eve Silver

from Mills & Boon® Nocturne™

Calliope and soul reaper Mal are enemies, but as
they unravel a tangle of clues, their attraction grows.
Now they must choose between loyalty to those
they love, or loyalty to each other—to the one
they each call enemy.

Available 4th March

Something to say about our Book of the Month?
Tell us what you think!

millsandboon.co.uk/community
facebook.com/romancehq
twitter.com/millsandboonuk

2 FREE BOOKS
AND A SURPRISE GIFT

We would like to take this opportunity to thank you for reading this Mills & Boon® book by offering you the chance to take TWO more specially selected books from the Intrigue series absolutely FREE! We're also making this offer to introduce you to the benefits of the Mills & Boon® Book Club™—

- **FREE home delivery**
- **FREE gifts and competitions**
- **FREE monthly Newsletter**
- **Exclusive Mills & Boon Book Club offers**
- **Books available before they're in the shops**

Accepting these FREE books and gift places you under no obligation to buy, you may cancel at any time, even after receiving your free books. Simply complete your details below and return the entire page to the address below. You don't even need a stamp!

YES Please send me 2 free Intrigue books and a surprise gift. I understand that unless you hear from me, I will receive 5 superb new stories every month, including two 2-in-1 books priced at £5.30 each and a single book priced at £3.30, postage and packing free. I am under no obligation to purchase any books and may cancel my subscription at any time. The free books and gift will be mine to keep in any case.

Ms/Mrs/Miss/Mr _____ Initials _____

Surname _____

Address _____

_____

_____ Postcode _____

E-mail _____

Send this whole page to: Mills & Boon Book Club, Free Book Offer, FREEPOST NAT 10298, Richmond, TW9 1BR